THE FOURTH LEVEL

EVOLUTION

BOOK FOURTEEN

I0556873

NICHOLAS HUNTLEY

First Edition, August 2020

nichhuntley.ca

WHITEWOLF PUBLISHING

Paperback ISBN 978-1-988765-38-9

Digital ISBN 978-1-988765-39-6

The text of this book is set in Times New Roman.

THE CITY OF HARLECH (c. 2020)

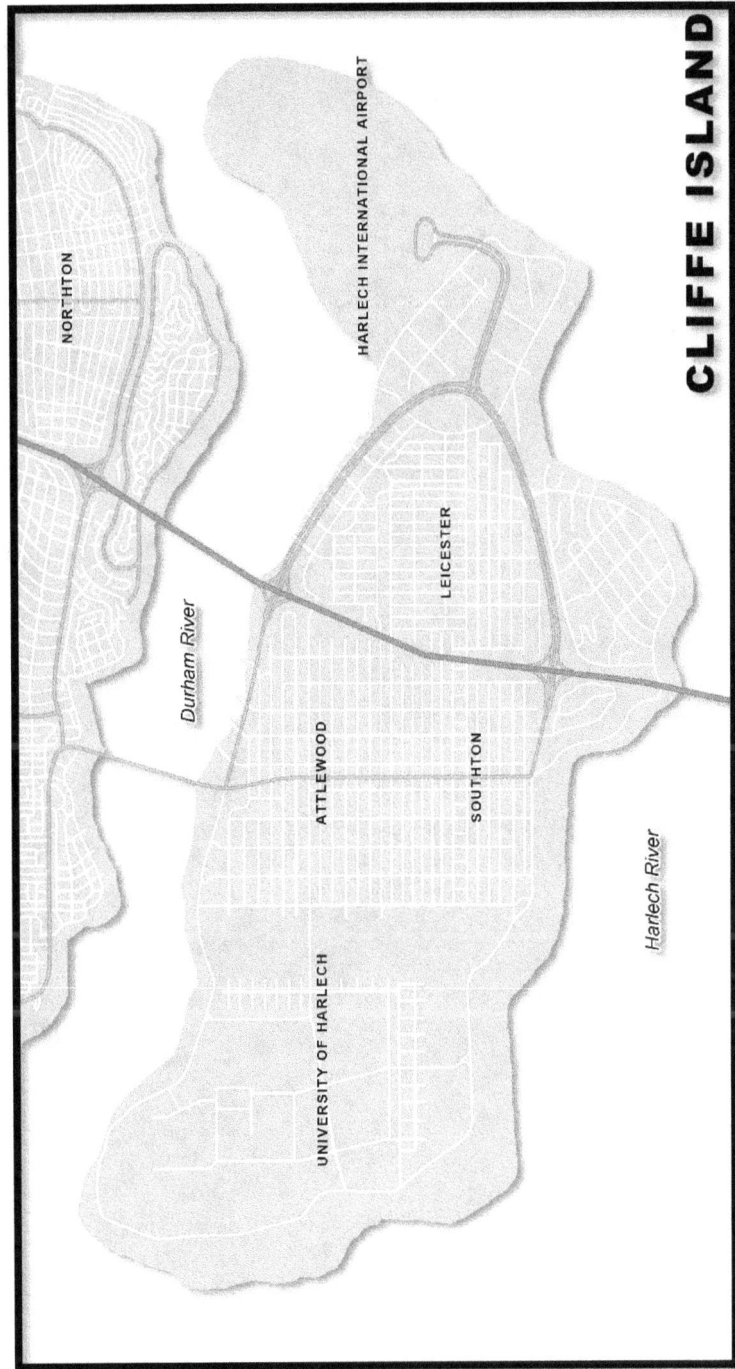

CLIFFE ISLAND

NORTHTON

HARLECH INTERNATIONAL AIRPORT

LEICESTER

Durham River

ATTLEWOOD

SOUTHTON

UNIVERSITY OF HARLECH

Harlech River

JARSDEL ISLAND

Henley River

Walham River

STONERIDGE

SAFFRON

LINCOLN

PORT BURNES

HARTHDAM

NORTHTON

Durham River

ATTLEWOOD

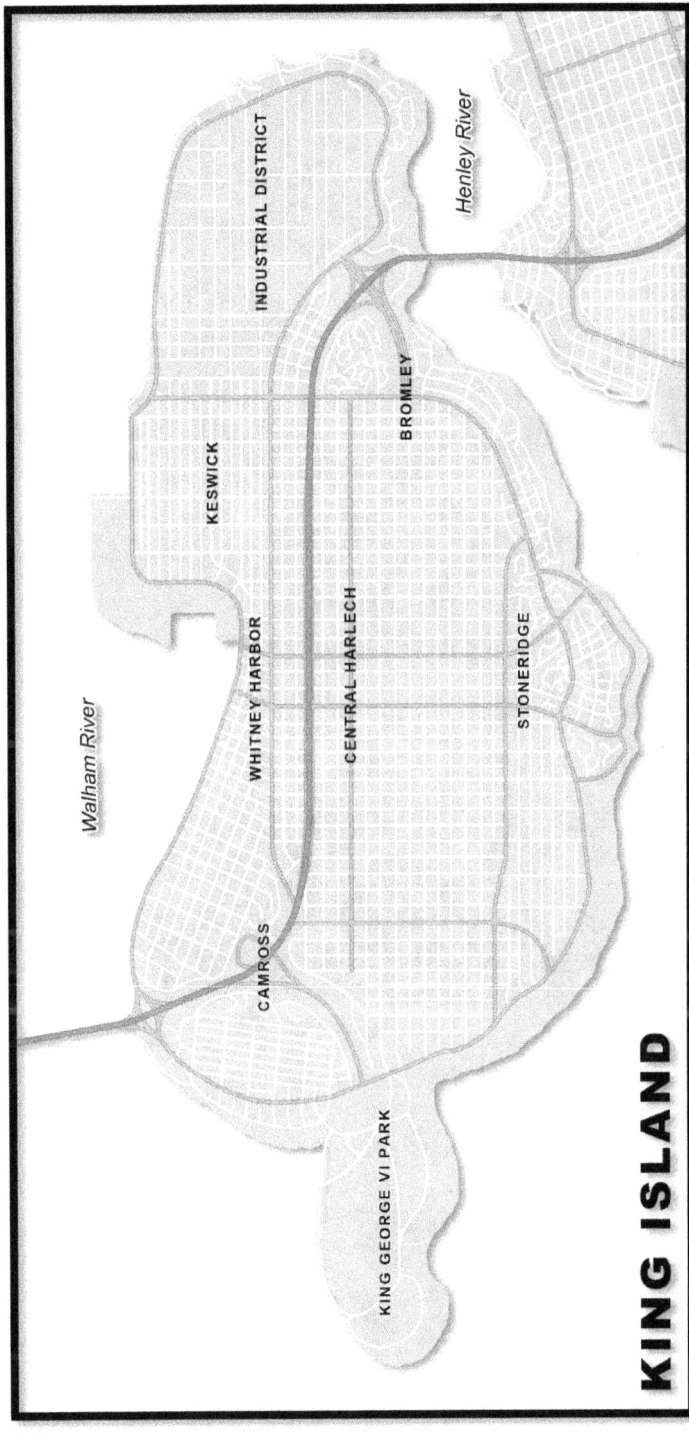

KING ISLAND

INDUSTRIAL DISTRICT

KESWICK

WHITNEY HARBOR

CENTRAL HARLECH

BROMLEY

STONERIDGE

CAMROSS

KING GEORGE VI PARK

Walham River

Henley River

"Do not look forward in fear to the changes in life; rather, look to them with full hope that as they arise, God, whose very own you are, will lead you safely through all things; and when you cannot stand it, God will carry you in His arms."

– St. Francis of Sales

Act 1, Scene 1

The church bells tolled across the Villa Paraiso where thick and dark grey clouds lingered over the tropical town and blocked off the open skies. The main cathedral of the town, with its two towers as the tallest peaks in all of the village, was constructed of a dark beige stone. From the top of the tower, archways at all faces exposed the inside and a second, smaller layer in the exact same fashion sat atop. The very top was crowned with a golden-colored dome, which then consisted of a cylindrical base where a thick crucifix hung from. The roof of the main sanctuary of the church consisted of a deep terracotta red. At the sides of the church were small pens of tall shrubs, palm shrubs, and thick trees. The church bells continued to ring with the strong gust.

Suddenly a crack of lightning lit up the skies and struck the ocean. The thunder boomed across the land. The wind picked up. The boats in the pier bounced upwards and downwards. The waves that crashed against Icaria Beach were harsher than typically present and although the sun could not be seen, its immense strength and warmth permeated through and radiated across the humid land. The leaves of the palm trees on the beach waved and the trunks bent in the opposite direction from the wind. The curtains and canopies of local homes and businesses fluttered as the gust became stronger. The ring of chimes from the patios of local homes could be heard. Crumples of newspapers and litter bounced over the streets. The deep grey clouds, which refused to weep, but instead built in their size, hovered over and brought with them the harsh wind of a storm that was coming.

In contrast, at the opposite side of the island, no bells could be heard, but instead the gentle brush of water against the shores of the southeast beaches and chatter of tropical birds. There, the finest, purest of sand could be found of the beaches of Isla Paraiso, which complimented the shallow, calm turquoise waters that surrounded the southeast coast of the island. The skies above were clear and as light a blue as they could be. A flock of seagulls cried out at each other from above and a mild wind gently rustled the palms of the tall trees with their fresh produce of coconut. The heat from the sun hit hardest as the sun, larger and closer to the Earth than ever to the tropics of the equator.

The visible and tangible blessings of nature would have been in perfect harmony with the natural orchestra of the beach and its gentle patter of waves onto the shore had it not been for the clanking of metal from nearby. At the small camp on the southeast of the coast where there were few tents pitched and many items packed up in crates, the heat radiated not too far at either side. A burnt out bonfire could be seen in the center of the camp with crumbling pieces of charcoal as all that remained. Towards the right of the camp where vehicles were parked, the rude noise that disrupted the peace was loudest as a man threw equipment into the back of a jeep.

Charlemagne de la Cabernet was dressed for the day in khaki shorts, a white t-shirt and vest, and a panama hat that covered his hair. He wore hiking boots at his feet, a backpack around his shoulder, and a clean bandage around both the palms of his hands and to his wrists. He carried with him a dead appearance, solemn and grim, which he carried with him since earlier last month when the woman that gave him life had died. Charlemagne raised himself up onto the side of the jeep and threw a shovel into the back and his backpack into the passenger seat in the front.

The jeep sprang to life once he sat down. Charlemagne leaned to the side and opened his backpack, rummaging through it to produce a journal and a map. He opened the map, which showed the entirely of the island, hand drawn and with notes in a neat cursive handwriting. Charlemagne looked closely at the map and then set both it and the journal aside to drive off from where he was parked to head into the jungle once more. He looked with intent before him with his steel blue eyes, a same steel-color that his moustache carried, less the blue, although it and his hair were appearing whiter. He drove along the dirt road that led to the village, but did not continue straight. Instead, he stopped at a fork in the road and continued leftwards. The jeep drove handsomely over the roads until it reached an open field, which Charlemagne diverted into.

Charlemagne drove across the small hills that went for a mile before turning up to another dirt road on the other side, which led back into the dense tropical rainforest. He continued to drive through under the gentle shade of the jungle which only took one out of the face of the sun, but not the presence of the almost unbearable humidity. Charlemagne drove for five or six miles before exiting and finding himself in a small grassland valley between two cliffs with hillocks covered in white flowers colored like the moon at its brightest, dancing proudly in the wind and glowing elegantly under the sunlight. Charlemagne parked the jeep at the base of one of the hills and then packed the map and journal back into his bag.

Afterwards, Charlemagne stood up and picked up some tools from the back of the car that he had loaded, including the shovel. He then picked up his backpack and brought the strap around his shoulder. Charlemagne hopped off the vehicle and went around to the base of a hill that he began to climb. The flowers brushed against his ankles and busy bees that were attempting to pollinate the flowers buzzed off in a panic as the flowers swayed.

Charlemagne reached up the side of the tall hill and the looked down at the area he had discovered.

Thousands upon thousands of these small white flowers covered the entirety of the area that was surrounded by jungle behind Charlemagne and tall cliffs before him. A cascade fell down from ahead and into a pond before the cliffs. The water of the pond was so clear that one could see the fish that swam around. Charlemagne looked around the area and its thousand upon thousand flowers, eyeing a section beneath the cliffs where the rocks perched over and cast an almost perpetual shadow, which gave the flowers a darker tone. However, among these flowers that were made to be darker by the lack of light, there were flowers that were true in the lack of color as they were a deep black. Less than a thousand of these flowers – more than a hundred, sat in the furthest reaches below the perch where they were safe in the never-ending shade that covered them.

Charlemagne approached the flowers and knelt down to take a closer look at them. He brought a hand to the petals and looked down at its dark yellow core, which contrasted the wild-type around that was a deep red with white petals.

"Every species has its mutants," Charlemagne said, sitting down with his feet apart as he continued to observe the flowers. "I shall name this one, 'Sycorax' for its bewitching qualities in hopes that it may just deliver me a cure."

Charlemagne unlatched his backpack and took out his journal. He also took out a pen. He proceeded to write down some observations of the plant, of its surroundings, and then began to draw it. He also noted some more finer details of its surroundings, including the humidity level, air pressure, altitude, and its geographical position. Charlemagne made several other notes before finally plucking one out from the ground and pressing it down into his journal, wrapping the book with the elastic ribbon that tightened the contents together.

Once Charlemagne had finished with his journal, he returned it to his backpack and took out a small plastic pot. He then picked up the shovel and inserted the spade into the dirt to begin uprooting a flower from the dirt and transplanting it into the pot. He took some dirt from nearby and filled it into the pot before patting it down. He then picked up the pot and looked at the plant, standing up and then taking it into the sunlight so that he could have a better look. Charlemagne examined the flower and saw that its petals had a slight glittering shine to them like the pure night sky.

Charlemagne didn't keep the flower in the sun for too long as he returned back to the dig site and sat down the pot next to his backpack. He then picked up his shovel and re-approached the bunch of dark flowers. Charlemagne jabbed into the earth once more and began to uproot another flower. He pulled it out and then took it over to his backpack where he took out a large clear plastic bag. Charlemagne shook the flower to get pieces of dirt to fall back down. He then stroked at the roots to remove any pieces that refused to fall until for the most part, there was little dirt left behind and he could bag the flower in. Charlemagne sealed the bag slightly and flattened out the sides to push out the air within. He then completely sealed the bag and entrapped the specimen inside for him to take with him. Charlemagne placed the specimen into his backpack and then returned to the flowers. He looked at them for a moment more before he started to cover the small holes that he had made. Charlemagne then walked back to his backpack and picked it up. He inserted the shovel into a holder on the side and then picked up the pot. Charlemagne brushed some dirt off the side of the pot before he stepped forward.

Once all was set, Charlemagne stepped out of the shade and back into the center of the beautiful field only to look upwards at the former clear blue sky as a dark cloud began to encroach from the north. A mild wind picked up too. Charlemagne looked at it with slightly worried eyes and then carried his pot back to the jeep so that he could return to the base camp.

Act 1, Scene 2

Tristan awoke with a grumble at the extensive heat that he felt entrapped from outside and from the woman he loved next to him. His tanned skin was wet with his own sweat, which he more or less had become used to by now. His eyes appeared to be tired as if he had not slept. His reddish-blonde hair was cut short so that he could cope with the climate. His shoulders were exposed with the burn scar at the center of his right shoulder, like a curled in beast. His bare chest and abdomen stuck to the breast and abdomen of the mature woman he had slept with by their sweat, hiding his other scars. The closeness of his chest to her breasts was so intimate that he could feel the vibration of the pitter-patter of her rhythmic and relaxed heart. Her legs were entwined with his, under the thin blanket knitted from a local weave, and her right arm wrapped around his torso. Her head lay gently on the surface of the cot as she slept peacefully. Tristan carefully pulled himself away from her on her cot within her tent.

Diana gave a faint moan, rolling to the other side from where Tristan brought his feet out to sit. The blanket continued to cover Tristan as he let out a big stretch, extending his arms out to let his bones and muscles extend outwards before he brought them in for a flex. Once Tristan had stretched, he leaned over and brought a hand to his face, resting his elbows on his knees. He then turned around to face her. Diana slept with absolute ignorance of her surroundings, closed eyes and gentle breaths that escaped from her petit nose.

Even in the heat and exposure of the sun, her fair skin remained the same in its light tone. Tristan looked at her closely. The skin of her back was smooth. Her dark brown hair was clean, long and slightly wavy. The cheeks of her face were slightly rosy and tender. The sides of her breasts were plump and firm. Her waist was curved inwards. Tristan turned away from her and began to lightly bang his head with a fist with a pensive look on his face. He then began to look around the room and then tilt his head down before him as he lowered his hand to his eyes. Tristan then removed his hand from his eyes and began to squeeze his eyes shut and then open again. The heat in the tent forced Tristan to blow some air out and finally stand up.

Tristan grabbed some of his clothes from nearby to cover himself, bringing his underwear up and then finding his shorts. Finally, he brought a t-shirt down over his body and then turned to the empty crate that Diana had converted to be a makeshift end table for her. A gas lamp sat atop of the crate alongside various effects that belonged to both of them. Tristan picked up his watch and brought it around his wrist. He then checked the time to be almost one o'clock in the afternoon. He also took his cellphone, which lay next to Diana's and sat down on the cot again as he swiped to unlock his phone. Tristan began to look through his photos of him and Diana.

Diana's deep blue eyes looked back at him through the photos of them together and some of her alone. Tristan focused on her smiles in the pictures. He then came to one of them together in which Tristan only held a mild smile. His skin was tanner than it usually gets at almost a pure orange sheen from an entire summer of being outdoors, especially on the beaches surfing. Tristan's eyes carried their jade color. He soon turned off his phone and let out a sigh. Tristan twisted his body and leaned over to kiss Diana on the head. Diana tightened her body as Tristan kissed her.

Tristan gently moved his lips away from her and then stood up. He fetched his sandals at the other side of the tent and put them on. He then looked at Diana one last time with loving eyes before he left out the tent. From the tent, Tristan looked around the campground and gave a sort of saddened expression as his eyes bounced from where tents used to be and where crates now sat. The camp was quiet and there was nobody to be seen. Tristan's eyes then shot towards a cloud of steam that floated above the kitchen tent. Tristan proceeded in that direction and as he got closer, he began to catch a waft of cooking.

Allodia turned to Tristan as he entered the tent.

"Well, good morning!" Allodia greeted, "or should I say afternoon?"

"Afternoon, I think," Tristan replied in a calm tone.

Allodia looked similar in appearance as she was last month. Her silver-blonde hair was tied back in a ponytail. She wore a bright green tank top and white shorts with sandals. Allodia brought the sandwich she was grilling onto a plastic plate and then looked to Tristan.

"Here, let me offer you a fried egg sandwich," Allodia said. "You must be hungry."

"It's okay," Tristan replied with a kind expression. "I can cook my own."

"I don't mind," Allodia insisted. "There's some fresh water in the kettle if you want to make some coffee or tea. We don't have any milk, but there's plenty of sugar left…"

"Thanks," Tristan responded, going over to the stove to take over.

Allodia stepped back as Tristan took the pan from her.

"You know, after the time we've spent together here, I have to admit that Charles was right," Allodia expressed. "You and Diana really are mature – more mature than the kids I've seen your age. When I look back on the two kids that I had met in Russia, I'm astonished at the change in such short time."

"It's been three years," Tristan remarked with a mild laugh, "not a short time…"

Allodia returned a laugh and replied, "For a woman my age, it is a short time."

Allodia went and sat down at a nearby table to eat. Tristan proceeded to cook his own sandwich before turning off the grill. He then made a cup of coffee with some sugar before he joined Allodia at the table.

"We still have lots of packing to do before we leave," Allodia remarked. "Charles told me that there's a storm coming, which means we'll have to leave before it gets anymore rough. Luckily, the plane is already here, so we'll just have to do the tedious task of taking the supplies to the airport, returning the trucks, and then leaving before nightfall."

In comparison to Tristan, Allodia was perkier and more alive than him who was groggy and drowsy.

"Is Charles or Everest up yet?" Tristan questioned, sipping the coffee.

"Charles is in his tent," Allodia answered, "and my dad left early this morning."

"Oh, right... I forgot last night was his farewell party..." Tristan replied. "I remember now..."

"You seem out of it," Allodia noted. "You're not suffering a hangover from the little bit that we let you drink, are you?"

Tristan paused for a moment to recollect. He then looked down to his food and shook his head.

"I didn't drink," Tristan corrected. "Diana didn't let me. Instead, we went back to her tent."

"Really?"

Tristan nodded.

"I'm sure of it," Tristan responded. "I'm usually worse than this when I wake up with a hangover. I'm also incredibly dehydrated..."

Tristan paused for a moment. Allodia looked at him.

"Sorry, ignore me," Tristan deflected.

"Relax," Allodia assured him. "I was a teenager once before. I understand... I was worse... Just be careful and responsible..."

"Diana doesn't like alcohol or alcoholics... I'm certain to be careful. I don't want to upset her."

"That's good of you..."

Tristan didn't respond. Instead, he ate some of his food.

"So anyways," Tristan said. "Where did Everest go?"

"Kenya," Allodia quickly replied. "He wanted to get a head start on the project that he and my mother had planned on the Kenyan-Ugandan border. The Foundation is taking over and I'll be joining him. We have to clean up here so that I can quickly get ready to join him there."

Allodia finished her sandwich and began to sip at her own coffee.

"I want to take a week off to recover from this trip before I head off to the Africa though. I have some paperwork to review and a bit of administration to catch up on. Technically, I've been on vacation for the last two months, but I'm not complaining. Aside from the hiccup at the start of July, it's been a peaceful experience being here with you, Diana, my brother and Everest. The only shame and regret is in what happened to my mother and those children..."

"I'm glad we could do all that we could for Everest," Tristan remarked.

"You should be very happy with yourself, Tristan," Allodia said to him. "You put in 150% percent this summer between what I heard you and Diana did to help those kids, and the fact that you helped build the houses. Honestly, that's not a feat you should simply brush under a rug. It'll look good on a resume when the time comes."

"Thanks," Tristan simply responded, looking aside. "I was happy to help... it was a... meditative task for me, and I suppose therapeutic."

"That's good to hear," Allodia replied. "I hope you're nice and recharged for what come next with university. You have a long path ahead of you."

"Yeah, I know," Tristan agreed.

"Are you in Diana ready to live apart from each other? In two different dorms? In two different campuses on two different islands? I suppose you'll have weekends to see each other... when you're not studying for midterms and finals."

Tristan looked back at her.

"Oh, what an exciting moment. Big changes are coming for you two" Allodia expressed, bringing her hands together. "I remember when I did my first year of university in science. Charles pressured me into the science program – it was between zoology and ecological sciences, and I went with zoology of course."

"I'm expecting the worst," Tristan stated, "but it'll be the last four years before medical school."

"Oh, you'll do fine," Allodia encouraged. "It'll be a lot of work, sure, but nothing I'm sure you can't handle. You've had my brother as your personal mentor, and there's nobody I'd have more confidence in than him to prepare and tutor someone. Even then, relax. A ton of different opportunities and experiences will compensate for the misery that education is about to become. What I'm certain of though is the different style in which that education takes place. You'll be dealing with professors and their knowledge, and not merely just curriculums. Be sure to befriend these people... I know that I had to do that – they appreciate the company and between you and me... it encourages bias in your favor. That aside, remember to care for yourself and not burn out. I can't stress how important it is to stay social and avoid loneliness. Does your dorm have a roommate?"

"Yeah, but I haven't met him," Tristan replied. "In fact, I'm not even sure who he is since I haven't been on a computer since June, but I just hope they're not... weird. We did a personality survey so they could hopefully match like-minded people, and there was also an option to request people you know."

"Anyone you know going to UH?" Allodia asked.

Tristan shook his head.

"Well, you'll have opportunity to make new friends, I'm sure," Allodia remarked. "Trust me, in comparison to high school, university is a different atmosphere. You'll prefer it more..."

"Do you think I'll have time for extracurriculars? I want to keep busy... Diana scolds me for it, but I like to keep busy."

"Well, if you're ambitious, then I don't see why not," Allodia replied. "What extracurriculars did you have in mind?"

"Sports," Tristan clarified. "Perhaps lacrosse."

Tristan let out a sigh.

"You seem anxious," Allodia remarked.

"I am anxious," Tristan confessed. "Diana is too, but not because of school. She's jittery because she's returning to her hometown. She hasn't been to Harlech properly since she left and only been there for the airport and such. This'll be the first time we're really in Harlech, you know?"

"Hm," Allodia agreed. "I suppose this'll be the first time you're really in Harlech too. To move to the big city is a milestone moment for the both of you... especially given where you're both coming from, Allabrese."

"Yeah..."

"Well, luckily for you, Diana should know the place well and be happy to show you around," Allodia remarked. "It's certainly a big place and not much has changed in the last four to three years…"

Tristan nodded and then stood up.

"Please, Tristan, leave your plate and let me wash up. If you feel too guilty about that, then do me a favor and take a cup of coffee to my brother please. I forgot he asked me to send him one and he'll kill me if I show up thirty minutes later."

Tristan nodded again and left his plate. Instead, he went to fetch a mug and mix some instant coffee. He also took his own mug and made a second cup in the cup that he used. Tristan then took both cups and left the kitchen tent.

"Don't forget that we have lots of packing left to do!" Allodia yelled. "We're going to need our fittest boy, or man, to help us out."

"Yup," Tristan responded before he set off to Charlemagne's tent.

Tristan looked to the east and noticed the sudden appearance of some grey clouds inching from ahead. He then continued towards Charlemagne's tent, which had moved and expanded since the start of their vacation on the island. Tristan had moved out and pitched his own tent next to Diana's in lieu of this expansion and the availability of more tents. Tristan went to Charlemagne's tent and then entered.

Charlemagne sat at a workbench with his arm stretched overtop. An intravenous needle was stuck in the medial cubital vein as he extracted blood from himself. Tristan slightly cringed at the sight and placed the cup of coffee onto the workbench. He then looked around at the mess in the tent. Charlemagne had yet to pack up as Allodia had told him to a week ago.

"Morning," Tristan greeted Charlemagne in a neutral tone.

Charlemagne didn't turn to face him and instead continued to focus on the blood extraction. Once he had taken a vial of blood from himself, he gently removed the needle and then placed a cotton swab over the hole and some tape overtop. Charlemagne then took the vials into a tray and then went to a workbench in the center, which was simply another foldable table.

"Better your blood than mine for whatever it is that you're doing," Tristan remarked as he glanced at the needle with a strong discomfort in his face. "What are you doing?"

"I'm simply drawing some blood, my dear boy," Charlemagne said in a quiet voice. "What's more to say? How can I help you?"

"I just came to bring you your coffee," Tristan replied with a sigh.

"Thank you," Charlemagne half-heartedly thanked, taking another needle to the plant that lay on a dissection mat.

Tristan took notice of the pot next to the mat which contained a similar dark flower, Sycorax. His eyes then went to the picture frame next to it, which contained a photo of his mother, Vienna Cabernet. He watched as Charlemagne began to cut into the plant before him. He examined the roots carefully where there were small seeds. Tristan continued to watch before looking up to Charlemagne.

"We're leaving before sunset," Tristan said to break the silence one last time. "I just thought I should remind you about that."

Charlemagne stopped what he was doing and turned to face Tristan. He gave a simple nod to him before he went back to focusing on his project. With the needle in his hand, he inserted it into the largest root of the flower and extracted a viscous lime-green liquid. Tristan watched for another second and then left. Charlemagne carried on.

Tristan walked out of Charlemagne's tent and then went to Diana's with his cup of coffee in hand. He bent over as he pushed through the flaps and then stepped towards the crate to place the cup there. He then sat down at the side of the cot and brought a hand to Diana's arm. Her skin was slightly wet from her own sweat. Tristan began to gently awaken her, which caused her eyes to slowly open.

Diana let out a moan.

"A few more minutes..." Diana requested.

Tristan gave a little smile and then shook her harder.

"Come on," Tristan said. "We've got to get up and finish packing. We're leaving the island today before a storm comes."

"Why do we have to leave already?" Diana questioned in a soft voice. "The last days here have been magical... I don't want to return to any of it... The studying, the learning..."

Tristan rolled his eyes. Diana rolled onto her back and stretched her body out. Tristan looked at her with the blanket covering her torso. He brought a hand to her cheek and looked down to her. He then lowered that hand to her neck. The two looked at each other lovingly.

"I don't think we've shared a night like last night since the day you said, 'I love you,'" Diana said. "If I could be in that state for eternity... I suppose that's what Paradise really is."

"It's one thing to say I love you, and it's another to show it," Tristan said.

"You showed it alright," Diana remarked with a pleasant smile on her face. "You've never stopped showing it, Tristan. You've listened to me, and we've become better at communicating with each other. We overcame the strife that struck between us when Finn disappeared, and as a result, we've become closer… I got you to open up to me not once, but twice."

Tristan looked into Diana's eyes and nodded.

"What's wrong?" Diana questioned.

"I'm worried, that's all," Tristan expressed, "about next month. We won't be living so close to each other anymore, and…"

"We're not going to drift apart, Tristan," Diana replied. "After the three years we've spent together, it'd take a great evil to tear us apart, and I believe our love is stronger than most evils in the world."

Tristan nodded to her. Diana sat up, keeping herself covered. The couple then kissed.

Act 1, Scene 3

"Careful!" Allodia shouted as the last of the tents collapsed at her and Diana's feet.

Diana collected the poles that supported the wide tent canvas before giving Allodia a hand in rolling the tarp up. The two of them compressed it tightly before wrapping it up with some heavy-duty twine. Several hours had passed and it was nearly sunset. A thickness of the same dark clouds that lingered over Villa Paraiso had reached the beach and brought a minor wind. Allodia looked to the east horizon of the beach as she finished tying the knot and noticed a convoy of all-terrain SUVs approaching them from over the sandy dunes. Diana turned her neck and saw the SUVs too.

"Oh jeez…" Allodia muttered as she stood up, looking around for her brother. "Charlie!"

Charlemagne poked his head up from the back of the truck where he was helping Tristan load some freight up a ramp and into it. He turned his sights to his sister who was pointing to the east where he refocused his gaze to what appeared to be three armored SUVs similar to the ones that gave chase to the children last July. The SUVs skidded at the brake as they arrived, producing a large dust of sand that blew towards the family and the remnants of the camp. It caused all four of them to squint their eyes as some men in white suits and fedoras stepped out of their vehicle.

Each character had wrinkled dark crimson skin and strict black sunglasses over their eyes. They made their way towards the camp where one of the older characters removed his hat, revealing his greying, long black hair tied in a bun as he waved to the family. He had a sort of characteristic friendly grandfather appearance to him in his smile that squinted his eyes. Around his neck he had a leather rope bola collar, which gave him rustic appearance. The man stepped forward while the others stood by the side of the SUVs.

Allodia and Charlemagne made their way over to the man where they stopped to face each, while Diana and Tristan looked from where they were.

"Mr. and Ms. Cabernet," the elderly man said. "I do not believe that we have met yet, but I am Chief Lule Arari of the local tribe here on behalf of my people. I am here to thank you for all of the help you've passed on this summer and the reconstruction of our village to accommodate our displaced brothers and sisters as well as the buildings that were destroyed in the tragic fires earlier last month. We cannot thank you enough for your assistance, especially when it came to vanquishing the malice within led by own brother and his cult."

Allodia and Charlemagne looked at each other as they exchanged a sigh of relief.

"Chief Arari," Allodia greeted, "it was our pleasure to lend a hand."

"Please, Ms. Cabernet," the chief smiled. "The pleasure was ours to have you come to our small, but beautiful island to do so much for my people. Please, if it could be appropriate, we can only extend ourselves with a symbol of our gratitude – a small token – an artefact of our people to seal the bond that has been a tense relationship between us and Europeans."

One of the men behind Chief Arari walked forward with a small handcrafted box made from the local hardwood of the island. The sides of the box were carved with local drawings. The man brought the box to the chief who took it into his hands to show to Allodia and Charlemagne. The chief then opened the box up, revealing a dark pinkish-red stone that almost resembled a meteorite. The rock was long and rough, but heavily metallic in its texture and it glittered in the sunlight. The material was unlike the alien alloy that Charlemagne was familiar with.

"The story behind this piece of our people's history fits well with the work you have done," Chief Arari explained. "Let me tell you a story that must never be forgotten."

Diana and Tristan approached the adults as the chief was about to start the tale.

"Nearly a thousand years ago, before the Portuguese came, our people lived on this island as we were – a united people, until a storm approached us and brought castaways to our island, shipwrecked on the shores. In our language, we came to call these people Yed'yu. When a group of our soldiers went to investigate the shipwreck, they knew there was something more than different about these people. They looked nothing like us, spoke a different language, and wore funny clothes. We permitted them to live on the shore they had arrived on, which back in this day, was a shore that was part of the island, but has since split off. You will know this island to be the one where my brother's home was. To this day, the beaches on the north face of that island are still known as Yed'yu Beach. There, they made their own community and built their own community with some of our women, which made them one with us, or so we thought…

Many of the wise elders of our tribe attempted to warn us of the catastrophe that these people could bring to the island, but the chief at the time did not listen. Chief Te'te was not a smart man and even his own daughter had gone to marry the chief of the Yed'yu, and from her, the chief learned that the Yed'yu were rich in luxuries that they brought from their own world. This brought to our island a system of trade that changed our livelihoods. Finally, the restrictions that prohibited foreigners from stepping foot into our cities came and the Yed'yu were permitted to live with us. Time went by, and within a few decades, the Yed'yu people were no longer called as such as they had more or less become one with the local people. Instead, they took on a new name, Ma'ta, which came from the mercantile behavior. The Ma'ta quickly became a rich nobility that the chief surrounded himself with. However, with all this trade, the chief had no means to pay for a debt that he had accumulated to these people. The Ma'ta deferred payment until the time came in which the debt was twice the worth of the entire chiefdom. In an effort to pay off this debt, the Ma'ta were given control over the economy, and so they began to tax the peasants and artisans. However, this took out a toll of the chief's greed onto the hardworking people and gradual decline in quality of life for the commoners until war broke out. A strong division had broken out not between the people and the Ma'ta, but instead, two factions, one loyal to the king and other rebel faction who took their residence on an island that no longer exists."

"The Ha'huo," Charlemagne surmised.

"Yes, Mr. Cabernet," the chief responded. "The Ha'huo. The result of the war was the establishment of their own chiefdom, and the reunion that has brought us together again should be hailed as a fantastic turn of events where our people can return as one. However, that is not the end of my story. After the war had been fought, many more people began to leave to establish their own tribes, and from here we have the seven other tribes of Kathuoaco Island. The wars only brought further strife to our people as well as a plot against the chief. The Ma'ta ordered the arrest of many conspirators who plotted to overthrow the chief, and one of them was the fiancé of a young girl who was the daughter of the chief, now a king. This young girl then went to the leader of the Ma'ta, who she had known because they had been made acquaintances by his own lust towards her. She begged that her fiancé be let go, but the leader of the Ma'ta refused unless she became his. When the young girl refused, the leader of the Ma'ta forced himself upon her, and this led to her throwing herself off a set of cliffs near the town. The news spread throughout the town and the people had enough of the Ma'ta. The soldiers released the prisoners that had been arrested and a mob stormed their home of the king, who soon died out of grief over his daughter. The leader of the rebels, the fiancé of this girl that had died, pointed to the merchant to be a cruel, heartless beast of a man, and this was all true. A bloody violence then swept between the people and the Ma'ta, and in this struggle, the Ma'ta revealed themselves to be not men, but bloodthirsty monsters – shapeshifters.

The people went to war against these beasts who had plundered and hoarded our wealth, manipulated our leader, and had their way with our women. And then from the skies above, a gift came down. A rock that consisted of this metal you hold in your hands. Our people refer to this metal as Vi'ko because of its red color and strength. From this metal, we fashioned weapons strong enough to penetrate the thick skin of these shapeshifters until they were all dead. Even those that did not morph into these creatures were led to the slaughter until there were no more of them, and the Ma'ta were gone.

However, that was not the end of them. Rumors from my people state that some survivors fled to live with the Ha'huo and other tribes, and from there, they slowly returned. Even then, the lessons were learned from both sides and such a tragedy never struck us again. The damage was done though. Our island had become divided and there was no more peace… this was the way of the island before the Portuguese arrived. When they arrived, our people were naturally suspicious out of the trauma our ancestors had experienced, but they were not like the Ma'ta or the Yed'yu. They had no intentions of subverting our already fragmented society, but they did like to trade with us and by then, our societies had been built on trade, so we did so gladly with them. The point of this story though is in this rock, its importance, the existence of villainy and the precaution towards change…"

Allodia looked to Charlemagne before looking back down at the rock.

"My father told me this tale when I was a young boy. He said that this story was to remind me that monsters do exist and that you must always be cautious. To me though, it's a lesson to never use a credit card," the chief said with a hearted laugh. "I apologize if the emotion of that tale was unsettling. It is a simple legend passed down to us and it is always nice to share a piece of my people's culture to one another, am I right?"

"Of course," Allodia agreed.

The chief handed the box to Allodia who took it into her hands, bowed, and then took a step back. He put on his hat and smiled to the four of them.

"Thank you very much for blessing us with that tale," Allodia said, "and especially with piece of history and culture."

Allodia gave the box to Charlemagne before turning back to the chief.

"Let this not be the last time that we meet, Cabernets," Chief Arari remarked, waving to them. "May you have a safe journey back to your home."

"Thank you," Charlemagne replied as the chief stepped back to go to his SUV, "and I'm sorry about your brother."

Chief Arari looked to Charlemagne and lowered his smile.

"Kau's mistakes are his own," the chief stated. "His suicide certainly broke my heart, but no man can escape their sins in the eyes of the Lord."

Charlemagne nodded. With the chief's last words, he opened the door into the back of the SUV and then sat down. The guards with him then scattered amongst the other jeeps and then they drove off. Allodia and Charlemagne waved goodbye to them and then looked at each other.

"Well, Charlie," Allodia said, looking at the rock with confusion. "You can keep this one."

"How considerate of you," Charlemagne replied, closing the lid.

"You can add it to your personal collection or give it to a museum. I know you're into these sorts of things… or maybe you can examine and see if it has any magical properties," Allodia remarked with a sly smile.

"Hm," Charlemagne grunted. "I'll see about having it sent back with us. In the meantime, let's finish packing, shall we?"

• • • •

Diana and Tristan put the last crate of equipment into the back of the truck. Tristan then jumped down from the back and looked over to Charlemagne as he went to the jeep. Allodia made her way over to the couple as Diana and Tristan looked at each other afterwards.

"Good job," Allodia commended, looking around the beach.

"Do you want to ride with Allodia?" Tristan asked Diana.

"Yeah, I don't mind. Go keep grandpa in check," Diana replied as Allodia went to the driver's seat of the truck.

"I'll see you on the plane then," Tristan replied, kissing Diana on the cheek before going to catch up with Charlemagne as he started the jeep engine.

"Yeah," Diana whispered, smiling as she watched Tristan get in.

Diana moved herself from behind the truck as Allodia turned on the truck. She closed the rear shutter and then went around to join her in the front cabin.

"Say 'Goodbye' to the sunny sunshine of Isla Paraiso," Allodia expressed, "and say 'Hello' to the miserable rain of rainy Harlech."

"We still have a week before we have to be back in school," Diana remarked.

Allodia ignited the engine of the truck and shifted gears. She then drove the truck off the former campground and proceeded to follow Charlemagne as they drove off. The two vehicles went along the beach as the sun started to finally set and hit the horizon. From the beach, they made their approach to the dirt road along the southeast coast of the island.

"So, are you excited to return to Harlech or what?" Allodia questioned, looking to Diana.

"Absolutely!" Diana remarked. "I haven't been there in almost three years."

"Are you worried about school?"

"Kind of," Diana responded. "I'm more worried about living apart from Tristan, but I've had a lot of time to prepare myself, and I think I'm prepared."

"That's good," Allodia replied. "Sorry…"

The car began to hit various rough potholes as the dirt road blended with an old concrete road. The ride was rougher on this stretch than on the dirt.

"All I can say, as if I can offer advice, is that you need to trust each other through and through, because if you don't have trust, then you don't have anything at all."

"I think we certainly have trust," Diana replied. "Tristan and I have had it rough in the last year, but we've worked through it. I've told him this, and we've tried to be more open, and as a result, he's opened up to me and I've opened up to him. The only problem has been that I've had to force it out of him because he hates to initiate conversation… it's like he doesn't want to bother anyone with his own thoughts, or… he's too proud to admit there's something wrong. He's quiet that way."

"Hm," Allodia replied. "I suppose he is short on his words."

"My main worry isn't that we'll drift apart," Diana expressed. "It's that he'll be too alone and have nobody to talk to, and as a result, his psyche will eat him from the inside."

"Hm…" Allodia simply responded. "It's good that you've thought this out. Really, it is. You just need to do what you feel as right. I won't offer any other banal advice or platitudes, but simply entrust this to you. You seem to know what you're doing, and I hope the best of it, because the two of you are perfect for each other."

Act 1, Scene 4

From the southeast coast of Isla Paraiso, Allodia and Charlemagne drove to the airport where the cargo airplane awaited them. They quickly loaded all the cargo that was set to return with them to Harlech and then went to return the vehicles to the rental shop. They soon returned and the plane was set to take off from the island airport before the storm finally hit. It took close to four hours before all of the cargo was loaded, Allodia and Charlemagne to return, and pre-flight checks to be completed for them to leave when it was just about midnight. From the southeast islands of the Caribbean, the cargo plane flew across the continent and back to Harlech in a trip that took most of the night, or roughly twelve hours non-stop.

At the start of the sun's rise over the metropolis, the cargo plane began to descend towards Harlech International Airport. Tristan looked out from a window at the side of the plane to get a view of the bustling three-island plus mainland that composed the City of Harlech. The city outline was familiar to him from the various times that he had flown into the airport, YHL, from the various trips that the family has had.

Nothing more could be said about Harlech in shorter words. The concrete metropolitan jungle could only be described in its entirety. Harlech composed of three islands as well as a mainland to the north which was as dense and large as the three islands together. The south mainland consisted of dense forest along the coast and then dipped down to agricultural land on the flood plains of a deep inlet below where the City of Lennox sat. The Trans-Canada Highway stretched through this rural town before coming up and over the Harlech River via the Grafton Suspension Bridge, a small narrow three-lane bridge that connected the southern coast with the first and original island of

Harlech: Cliffe Island. The first island was where the family was landing now since it had the municipal airport on the eastern tip of this slim and elongated body of land. On the opposite tip, where Tristan's eyes concentrated upon, was the secluded campus of the University of Harlech. The center of the island held three other districts: Southton to the south on the westside from the highway, which was a luxurious beach town on the coast and mouth of the Harlech River; Attlewood to the north of Southton on the westside, which was a modest representation of Old Harlech by the heritage buildings and regional-famous clock tower; and Leicester to the east of the highway and west of the airport, which was an industrial and commercial sector of the island where train yards, warehouses, dry docks, shipping yards, and various small businesses, such as mechanics, body shops, lumber yards, and other likewise businesses operated from.

The density increased on the next island known as Jarsdel Island. The second island was the widest and largest, with a greater surge of people due to the rapid urbanization. Jarsdel could be reached from either of the two bridges from Cliffe Island, either Thames Bridge which ran from a main road through Attlewood to Southton, or Durham Bridge that continued the highway. Thames Bridge reached into the southwest peninsula district of Harthdam, a suburban district with a booming housing market. From Durham Bridge, one came to the southeast of the island known as Northton, a more successful and developed part of the island to the north and then to the south, an industrial and rugged part of the island like Leicester. North from Northton was the largest district, Lincoln, which had a surge of tall skyscrapers at the center and its own bustling metropolitan community that rivaled downtown. To the west, over the highway, the density shrunk in a district surrounding a bay to the north of Harthdam known as Port

Burnes. This area was known for its large shipping yards and train depots as well as the largest harbor in the country that connected Canada to the Pacific. Above Lincoln, on the northeast coast was another port district known as Saffron, which was locally referred to as Chinatown. There, a mixture between three-story structures, suburban homes, and even skyscrapers spread around this northeast portion.

The main highway stretched up from Durham Bridge, through the middle of Jarsdel, with another bridge connecting her with King Island via the Marke Bridge, which was the busiest and densest island. Tristan gazed at the skyline of the downtown with a worried and anxious eye, noticing the tall structures just like the model of the island that Charlemagne had in his office years ago. Cabernet Tower was the crown jewel as the tallest building at the center of the island. King Island was split between its skyscrapers to the west of the highway, which curved through the island, and the chimney stacks of factories on the east of the island on a round district known simply as the Industrial District. The only sign of progress in this old district was the nuclear power plant with its friendly clouds of steam that lifted up from the cooling towers. From Marke Bridge, one came first into Bromley, which was a modest and plain district with lower level structures and the Bromley Stadium at the coast. It had cheap apartments, makeshift living conditions, and an atmosphere that younger generations were calling home. Next to Bromley was a set up in luxury as this district was known as Stoneridge. Condos and expensive apartments lined this seaside area with a boardwalk along the sides and beaches to the sides of that. A similar district known as Camross existed on the northwest tip of King Island, past the downtown area. A small peninsula extended from Camross, to the west, covered in total density of forestry with only artificial structures from the sky being the aquarium and a research facility. The district was a regional park known simply as King George VI Park. To the east of Camross was an extension of the downtown area but separate from the technical district known as Central Harlech. This portion was known as Whitney Harbor and consisted of a waterfront park and trail that stretched around Camross, under the highway as it blended out to form Penultimate Bridge, and then reach down towards King George VI Park. Finally in Central Harlech, various skyscrapers could be found, some with logos of notable companies, such as Cabernet Industries from Cabernet Tower where Allodia's penthouse sat atop of. To the north of Bromley at the northwest corner of the island at the end of Whitney Harbor and to the east of the Industrial District was the contrast to all of the development in the form of misery and impoverishment. There, the slum known as Keswick could be found. The main highway turned between Keswick and Bromley, going underground and beneath Central Harlech before rising up into Camross to cross Penultimate Bridge.

The mainland known as New Harlech was less of a concern to Tristan, who didn't really bother to look at it other than the mountains that were behind and formed the background of this coastal city. In fairness, it was a different kind of weary part of the city than Old Harlech was. In short, New Harlech composed of two sides split in the middle by a small inlet and two bridges. The first bridge was part of the main highway that went across the upper level portion of this section, while the second bridge was part of a main road that went across the lower level of the town and it was known as the Ford Bridge. The western side of Harlech consisted of the following districts: Northhill, Foxwood Vale, Legion Hill, and Westford, while the eastern side composed of Eastford, Northgate, Caledonian Highlands, Iris Heights, Evergreen Plateau, Middlefield, Oakley, and another regional park known as Rosalynn Park. The mainland mountains were four pompous peaks in total: Mount Harlech on the west side and Athlon Mountain, Mount Iris, and Clements Mountain on the East.

"Welcome to Harlech," Diana said to Tristan, grabbing his arm from behind and causing him to jump. "My desolate, hellish hometown."

The cargo plane continued its descent into hell as Tristan turned his attention away from the outside. The plane circled around the airport for several minutes before they were given the clearance to land. Once they had landed, the cargo plane was taken into the private hangar where it was parked.

Diana and Tristan stood up from their seats in the cabin between the cargo hull and the cockpit, which was a small space with only four seats, two facing each other with a window at the side, a small kitchen, and two bedrooms on the other side with two bunk beds each where crew members would sleep in. They went to retrieve their luggage from a storage closet at the side and then exited down a set of steps that entered into the rear of the plane. There, Allodia went through a manifesto with a Cabernet Foundation worker before being alerted by another that her car was parked outside the hangar for her. Diana and Tristan walked through the cluttered cargo hold and then came out into the hangar.

Allodia and Charlemagne met with them, carrying their own luggage. After they had met, the four of them walked to the side of the hangar and walked through a corridor with shutters at the side, through another corridor with lockers, and then to a corridor that went to a set of double doors that took them outside. At the side of the hangar, a luxurious red sedan was parked and awaited them. Allodia went to the car, taking a set of keys from her purse and then unlocking the car and opening the trunk.

Diana and Tristan followed the adults as they placed their luggage in the rear of the car. Allodia then went to the passenger seat door at the front, opened it and then folded the chair over so that the couple could sit in the rear. She then folded the chair out and stretched a hand out for her brother to sit down. Allodia went around to the driver's seat and sat down. She then pressed a button next to the steering wheel and brought the engine to life. Diana and Tristan buckled up while Allodia pulled out and then followed the lane that took them out of the airport.

Tristan looked to the side and through his small window as they went out from the airport and onto the main road that took them into Leicester. He observed the various warehouses that could be seen alongside the auto-repair shops, machine-repair shops, small market businesses, offices, and other industrial businesses. Allodia has soon driven them into traffic, which had them stuck at moving a couple of paces forward every so often. Tristan took notice of a landmark ahead as they sat on the on-ramp onto the highway. Atop of a hill was a small gothic castle with stone walls and red roofs. The castle was surrounded by many trees. He looked at it closely, but not for too long as they were soon on the highway and the castle was behind them. Tristan sat back as there was nothing else to observe.

"Ah, morning traffic," Allodia remarked. "I did not miss this…"

Diana looked to her side and out her window to look over the rooftops of Leicester and the airport ahead. Further ahead, she could see the outline of the south coast and mountains inland.

Allodia drove slowly along the road and by the time they were in Jarsdel Island, the speed began to pickup as it was close to nine o'clock local time. She drove forward through Jarsdel, passing Lincoln and then entering King Island where she exited off the highway in Bromley. Diana looked at Pentateuch Cathedral nearby as they came onto Bailey Drive. From Bailey Drive, Allodia drove north and then turned onto Harleen Street. At this time in the morning, the city was filled with pedestrians on the sidewalks, street corners, and sometimes even the streets. In contrast to Tokyo or Kyoto, there were less neon signs and flashing LED light signs, and more of a mixture of old and new as well as a dirty stench. It was like Marunouchi, the district where Cabernet Electronics was stationed, but with none of the quietness, tidiness, and order. The streets were dirty and there was always some peculiarity, whether it be a street vendor, preacher, or vagrant by the street corner. Allodia soon came to an intersection with Earle Street where she turned right and then went north again.

Tristan took notice at the incredibly dirty and stained streets, the potholes, and the general unpleasantness. His head began to spin at the hectic nature of so many people around him. There were people of all sorts from all parts of the country as this had become a cosmopolitan city similar to Paris, but with less of the history and remnant of culture. Even then, Central Harlech was much larger than La Défense. He moved his head away from the window and glanced over to Diana who appeared to be lost in the environment. Tristan took out his phone and began to focus on that.

Allodia soon arrived at Cabernet Tower where she turned down a causeway ramp that took them into an underground parking garage. She drove through the first level and then went down to the second level where a spot was reserved for her close to the elevators. The spot on her left was closest to the elevator and it was reserved for Charlemagne, while the spot on her right was reserved for Richard Huxley and so on. Allodia gently brought her car in and then shut off the engine.

"We're here," Allodia said with a smile. "Welcome to Cabernet Towers."

"I haven't been the penthouse in years," Charlemagne remarked in a soft voice. "I haven't even seen the renovations that you supposedly did some years ago."

"I've never been to the penthouse ever," Diana added.

"Well, prepare for a view that is the envy of town then," Allodia warned.

"Don't get too used to it though," Charlemagne reminded them. "We're only staying one night and then going to the Windsor across the street until you're moved into your dorms."

"What?" Allodia questioned. "No," she denied. "I am not letting you all run off and waste money at some hotel when you can stay in this home. Family is family. The penthouse has plenty of space and extra rooms for all of us. It may be my official residence, but just as you extend the mansion to me, I extend my home to you."

"You know how much I'd hate to impose on you, especially since you need to rest before chasing dad in Africa next week," Charlemagne replied.

"No – there's no imposing here, Charles," Allodia scolded. "Even when I'm not home, the Cabernet Penthouse is open to those in the Cabernet family, and that includes Diana and Tristan even if their last name is not Cabernet. They're part of the family. We're in a commonwealth here."

Charlemagne didn't dare to argue with his sister for another moment. Instead, he simply got out of the car and brought his seat forward to let the couple out from the back. Afterwards, they collected their luggage from the back of the car and then went to the elevator. The elevator sat in the center of the parking lot around a square where the reserved spots were behind and in front of the lifts. To the left and right were spots reserved to handicapped individuals. Charlemagne impatiently waited for the elevator to descend and then open its doors for them to enter.

"Welcome to Cabernet Tower," a voice announced as the doors opened.

"Hm," Charlemagne grunted, entering "that's new."

"It's been here for as long as I can remember," Allodia expressed, "or maybe it is new... I can't remember."

Diana and Tristan entered behind them, and they all stood together in the elevator car while Allodia pressed the button for the 98th floor. She also took a card attached to her key chain and brought it to a panel. The doors then closed, and the elevator began to lift up.

"We'll have to get Diana and Tristan a key to the penthouse and elevator," Allodia said. "In the mean time, you can use this panel here."

Allodia pointed to the panel at the bottom of the many buttons.

"The override code for the penthouse is 1921."

"What's so special about that year?" Diana asked.

"That's the year that the tower was commissioned to be built," Charlemagne answered. "We really ought to replace that panel and switch it for some biometric security instead. I don't trust an outsider to randomly insert that date and hope to be brought up to the penthouse."

The elevator ascended upwards and the floors on the digital counter ticked up one by one until at long last they reached the 98th floor of Cabernet Tower. The elevator doors opened to reveal a dark room, which automatically lit as the motion sensor triggered and a light switched on.

Allodia walked forward first, letting Diana and Tristan see the vestibule between the penthouse suite and the elevator. The walls were formal with foot-long panels at the base and then painted dry wall in a creamy coffee brown. The floors were of a dark smooth floorboard. Between the rectangular room was a red square carpet. At either side of this carpet, left and right, was a red divan with a painting behind and a narrow table with a pot of false flowers. In each corner from the elevator there were two pots of fake ferns. There were no windows in this room. Allodia fumbled with the keys to unlock the door and then let them inside.

Tristan held the door for Diana and Charlemagne to get in past him. Allodia went ahead and turned all the lights on from the large corridor they came into. Diana and Tristan stepped in and looked ahead. The corridor opened up to a large open space that stretched the entire south face of the floor. Before this space, left and right, were sets of double doors that went deeper into the penthouse.

"Hm," Charlemagne remarked as he stepped forward. "I can't even remember what it looked like before…"

Diana and Tristan moved forward closer as they came into the open space as the door slammed shut behind them. To their right was a living room with a mid-century black three-person couch, a loveseat perpendicular and a large flat screen TV immediately in front. Underneath this furniture was a rectangular white carpet. Before them were a set of wide stairs that went forward to a landing and then came out to a second level above. The steps were simple panels with no sides that rested on a metal frame. To the left was an open dining area immediately behind a kitchen at the far-left side. The dining room had a long rectangular glass table, a cylindrical chandelier above, and simple black chairs. All before this open space were large windows with raised blinds that looked out to a patio around the perimeter. Alongside the patio was an outdoor dining table close to the kitchen, a small garden towards the middle, and then some lounge seats towards the right. This perimeter wrapped around, but did not go all the way around and instead only went halfway. The couple went in closer to get a look around them.

The penthouse composed of two stories as the ceiling in this open space went up two stories and included a loft above. The loft also sort of hung over the space slightly, which created a level protected by glass railing. The stairs that went up to this upper level had a glass railing too which was supported by simple pillars. At either side of the couch were simple rectangular columns that acted as support all the way to the ceiling. Another pair of columns could be seen at the side of the dining room to create a sort of arcade with this overhang. The penthouse was of course larger than this side of the top floor.

"Bedrooms are on the second floor," Allodia said. "Feel free to find an empty one, but don't go picking mine!"

Diana and Tristan went up the first set of stairs to the landing, which gave them a better view of the open space. They then went to the top to the upper level where Diana went to open a set of double doors to the left. The doors led into a two-story library where they had entered the top level. The library was large with bookshelves all around the sides that weren't covered with windows. Below the L-shaped loft that surrounded the top level was a space below, except there was no arcade or overhang, but more of a pit below where the lower level was with a marble statue in the corner, more bookshelves at the side, and a pair of couches facing each other in the center. The stairs that went down to this level were like the ones in the main area with a landing, but these stairs were bent in an L-shape instead of in a switchback design. At the opposite-side of the room were windows that looked out to another rear patio. Diana looked out at all of the bookshelves with an ecstatic expression.

Tristan left her in her own little paradise for a moment while he went to uncover the rest of the penthouse. Next to the library he entered one of the unoccupied bedrooms that Allodia has been talking about. The bedroom had a hotel-like appearance with a bed in the center, end tables at either side, a dresser opposite from the bed with a TV atop, a wardrobe towards the corner, and a tall mirror in the other corner. At the end of the room was a set of doors that entered into a large bathroom, smaller than the one that Diana and Tristan shared, but more luxurious with a square shower space in the corner, large bath in the other corner, and a separate closet for the toilet next to the shower. At the end of the room was a window with blinds that looked down to the rear patio. The bedroom was approximately double the size of Tristan's bedroom. Tristan left the room and checked the one next door to see that it was alike. He then continued through a set of doors that took him into a room as big as his own with glass windows covering the wall at the end. This room had two sets of double doors at either side and was decorated with paintings and frames with photos. Tristan stopped before he could enter either door.

"Careful," Allodia warned. "Door on the left goes into my bedroom. Door on the right goes into my study."

"Sorry, I'm just exploring and getting a grip of the layout," Tristan apologized.

"I take it Diana's already found the library…"

"First room she walked into," Tristan responded.

Allodia laughed.

"Why don't you look downstairs… maybe you'll find a room you can appreciate."

Tristan raised an eyebrow and then saw Allodia off as she entered her room. He went downstairs and returned to the main area. He went through a set of double doors behind the living room and entered another room similar to the one before Allodia's bedroom and study. The room had no purpose other than to display certain objects and act as a bridge between other rooms. It was like a grandiose hallway. Tristan didn't enter the room ahead of him, which he knew to be the ground floor of the library. Instead, he carried on through the door on the left, which took him into the foyer hall, and then went across to enter an actual corridor, even though it was wide and T-shaped. To the left against the walls at either side from the small corridor from the intersection were single doors that went into a laundry closet and a storage closet. Tristan looked through both of these and then turned left and went down the short corridor from which brought him into a sort of recreation room with lots of open space. From the walls that weren't covered by window, they were instead covered by mirror. The only objects in the room were a grand piano in the far left corner and a small bar to the far right with stools and shelves with various alcoholic drinks. Next to this bar were a set of double glass doors that went out to a patio garden. Tristan went to the door to the right of this room and entered a small home gym with the walls similar to the last room. He looked around for a moment, eyeing the equipment, which was more cardio-based as there were only a few dumbbells on a rack, an exercise bike, and a treadmill. He then left to backtrack and see what was in the final room. Tristan opened the door and saw that it was a sort of trophy room with various items from Allodia's own adventures, or missions abroad.

Once Tristan had finished looking around, he returned to the main space of the penthouse and came to the patio. The surroundings of the patio had a tall reinforced glass railing all around that went to about Tristan's mid-abdomen. He placed his hands atop and looked around the city. He looked around and around before giving off a long sigh. Tristan remained here as Diana exited the library. She looked over to Tristan on the balcony and then went over to him as she noticed that he looked contemplative and serious. Tristan hardly reacted to her sudden appearance.

"What's wrong?" Diana questioned, crossing her arms as she joined him.

Tristan sighed and said, "I know this is the city where you were born in, and no disrespect, but it's…"

"A hellhole? If you're getting that impression from being here a couple of hours, then you're not going to like the real desolate parts when I show you them. Trust me…" Diana expressed before turning her head and bringing a hand to Tristan's. "You don't have to like this city. I don't like this city. I wouldn't consider this city my home even if I still lived here instead of Allabrese, and I have no expectation that you'll come to like Harlech and what it offers either, but we have to live here from now on because you have to get your degree, and I… well, less of an expectation is on me. As far as I'm concerned, I'm here for you… even if Charlemagne or even you want me to look out for myself and get my own degree."

Tristan listened to these words and lowered his head.

"Maybe… maybe I'm just being picky…" Tristan remarked. "The contrast from Isla Paraiso and Allabrese is definitely strong, but Tokyo was nicer than this place. Paris was nicer than this place because at least there was culture in that city, and just… I don't know…"

"Don't let it get to you…" Diana cautioned, bringing her hand to his cheek. "You've lived in a quiet part of the world for almost eighteen years… Some would be glad to escape that and come for Harlech and all its amenities, but you're not that person. You want peace and quiet…"

Tristan grunted and replied, "If- If I were four years younger... Hell, if I was a year and a bit younger, before all this crap that's happened... I feel like I'd appreciate all this a bit more, but..."

Diana didn't respond and instead looked at Tristan. She didn't say anything and simply let Tristan be, remaining at his side. Tristan held on and didn't say anything more either. His hands trembled and his face was red. He held on to the side of railing with a tight, forceful grip as he squeezed the bars. He was also biting his tongue. Diana took a deep breath and took Tristan's hand.

"Come on, let's go inside," Diana said. "We've had a long trip and should rest..."

Act 2, Scene 1

By next week, not much had happened as Charlemagne, Diana, and Tristan spent time at the penthouse. Charlemagne watered the potted plant of the dark flower, Sycorax, that he had brought from Isla Paraiso. He set it in the corner of the kitchen and then dried his hands at the kitchen sink. Afterwards, he began to apply some new bandage over the dark marks that had worsened in the last two months. Once the bandage was tied, he put on his leather gloves and then looked over to the couple as they sat the couch watching TV. He gave a frown towards them and made his way over.

"Have you two been out at all yet?" Charlemagne questioned.

"Nope," Tristan simply responded.

"Wouldn't you think some exploration of the city to be beneficial?" Charlemagne asked.

Tristan cringed at the thought of going outside. He didn't reply.

"We could go out now that it's a little bit more cooler," Diana softly said to him.

"This could be your last moment of freedom before the pair of you move into your separate dorms tomorrow. By then, you'll be making new friends and then starting classes, extracurriculars, and you suddenly won't have any time to yourself."

"I guess so..." Tristan muttered, "but what's out there really?"

"Not much," Diana replied, "but it is a big city that you should start to familiarize yourself with. Come on, we'll be tourists, and I'll give you the grand tour."

"Don't be out for…" Charlemagne stopped himself before he could finish. "Sorry, seems a bit foolish to impose a curfew at this point. Enjoy yourselves, but please be careful if you're out late. Knowing the pair of you… you're more like to start or get in trouble than to be the victim of it."

Tristan looked at him and then towards the TV.

"Another thing," Charlemagne said, "don't forget that although you're both fairly mature, you're still seventeen, Tristan, and you're only eighteen, Diana. The legal age in British Columbia is different than in Alberta – nineteen, so don't be getting full of yourselves just because I treat you a couple years older than you really are."

"Well, since our residence is in Alberta, doesn't that mean that I'm technically emancipated?" Diana questioned.

"A good question…" Charlemagne responded.

"It doesn't matter," Diana replied. "Come on, Trist, let's go and see the city."

Diana stood up from the couch as Tristan continued to watch TV.

"Oh, and on the topic, I've just remembered. I promised to present to you a better birthday present once we left the island, and now that we're here and talking about your age, I've just remembered…! Be on the lookout for something that catches your eye, preferably a vehicle. It'll be for the best if you can make use of your license and be able to move around town flexibly."

"You don't need to go that far…" Diana confessed.

"No, I insist," Charlemagne remarked. "I practically gave Tristan the pickup truck (even though he destroyed it), but even then, the new one is still practically his. You should have your own vehicle, so look for one, okay?"

"Hey, speaking of the pickup truck, I didn't get a chance to bring it over here…" Tristan remarked, turning off the TV. "Any chance of that happening?"

"Hm," Charlemagne replied, "you'll have to wait until you can drive it from Allabrese to here, I believe. I'm also partial to having it leave the mansion in case I need it… We'll have to see, but in the meantime, whatever Diana chooses will have to do for the both of you."

"Alright…" Tristan sighed, standing up.

"One last thing," Charlemagne said as the two moved around the couch to face him. "I have an early flight back to Allabrese tomorrow morning and should I not see you, I have some parting words before you go to school. I hope that the two of you can have a tremendous time in university and try to focus, both of you, on your academics foremost. Persevere and know that it is about to get a lot more tough from here on out, but together you can and will be able to push on. You've both entered institutions of the finest minds, the best of the best, and that means competition is inevitable. You are in Harlech, the city of competition at every street corner. All of this will come to hit you hard, and with it, you'll come to think you're not as smart as you thought you were as others inevitably excel around you. This isn't said to discredit either of you, but to give you the reality here and now that you're not the smartest people in the world. I'm not the smartest person in the world. There are others that are smarter than us, some in different subjects, because we have our differences. That being said, these universities are places where people like you of who were eligible to enter, the finest minds, have come together and that is the pool in which you will see yourself against. The key here is that you are among the finest minds, and although you may not be the finest of the finest, you are still fine nonetheless."

"Were you the finest of the fine?" Tristan asked, interrupting him.

Charlemagne shook his head.

"I didn't get to graduate from university to be the finest..." Charlemagne replied. "That aside, I wish the both of you the best of luck, and please, do find the time to enjoy yourselves when you need to, and not when you want to. For example, tonight – enjoy yourselves tonight. Have a safe academic year... Goodnight."

"Thanks, *Charlie*," Diana replied. "Goodnight."

"Have a safe flight," Tristan said.

"Thank you."

Charlemagne turned and then left upstairs to go to his room.

"Alright, come on," Diana said to Tristan. "Let's go and catch the sunset by the pier. We'll make it if you don't slow us down so much..."

"Do we really have to go out?" Tristan complained. "I'd rather just stay here... Let's watch a movie or something, there's nothing out there..."

Diana tilted her head disapprovingly to him.

"Charles was right, Tristan. We've sat on our asses for the last week doing nothing – let's go and make the most of the city and enjoy ourselves. Come on, we live here now, and you're going to have to step out eventually – who knows, maybe you'll come to appreciate the city a little more."

Diana grabbed Tristan's wrists and began to take him towards the penthouse foyer. She grabbed a set of spare keys set for them by Allodia and then the two exited out of the penthouse and went to the elevator. The pair waited for the elevator, got inside, and then went down to the main lobby of the tower, which took them to a large two-story public space with white marble floor and various shops around. The area was like a miniature mall, but with luxurious high-end stores all around, almost none of which were owned by Cabernet Industries as it was not much of a retail company. Close to the entrance of the lobby was an expensive Italian restaurant known as *Lucavelia* and cross from that was a boutique known as *Viljoen*. There were not many people left around as it was close to closing time, eight o'clock, and the tower was at restricted capacity due to the ongoing pandemic. Diana took Tristan around the large fountain in the center of the lobby and to the main doors where water intentionally fell in from the ceiling into the large shallow pool.

Tristan noticed security guards dressed in suits at the front doors as they exited. They went through the revolving doors and then took their first steps out onto the streets of downtown Harlech. Diana let go of Tristan and went forward, extending her arms out as she took a deep breath. She then turned around to Tristan. Tristan looked at her.

"It feels good to be home," Diana remarked.

Tristan looked at her with mild confusion. She held a large smile on her face, which he did not share.

"Come on, let's take the train to Stoneridge," Diana encouraged, taking Tristan by the arm. "We'll need to get train passes beforehand though."

Diana took Tristan down the street, to the east from the entrance of the tower where they passed Dominion Square on the other side before the Royal Harlech Museum. Tristan looked over and noticed a large gathering of people as well as loud obnoxious music coming from the plaza. Diana attempted to ignore it, but Tristan's notice was set.

"Protests?" Tristan questioned.

"There have always been protests on that stupid square," Diana replied. "Even before all that's been going on in the

United States… even then, nobody ever knew what was being protested."

"Huh," Tristan responded.

Diana took Tristan east down Campbell Street and towards the Dowager Street intersection where there were various electronic billboards at the sides of the buildings. The atmosphere was similar to Tokyo, but as Tristan observed earlier, the streets were significantly dirtier and the setting around them was far from pleasant. There were various street merchants at the sides, a hot dog vendor, a street performer, and a vagrant panhandling near the stairs that went down to the underground subway. Diana took Tristan towards the stairs and the pair went down.

The couple stopped at a machine in the underground tunnels, which gave access to various more shops beneath the city, and they each bought a reloadable card that allowed them through the gates to the subways. Diana led Tristan through, and they stopped to tap their cards before pressing on. The tunnel then took them even further sublevel onto a platform with rail lines at either side. The scene here was similar to the Parisian metro, especially the one in La Défense which was new and cleaner. Likewise, the platforms at City Center Station were new and mildly clean, although Tristan did smell an unfamiliar foul smell, potent and earthy like the stench of skunk, but which he knew to be cannabis. Tristan looked at the people around them as they waited, and again, like Paris and as he observed earlier, there were people of all sorts from all corners of the world in Harlech. However, for the most part, these people kept to themselves. He then looked across the platform and towards the many advertisements of brands. The couple waited several minutes until a train finally arrived, which part of the Marine Line that went from Stoneridge all the way below the

Durham River and to New Harlech. However, the train that they had boarded was on return from New Harlech and going back to the station in Stoneridge.

"It's coming back to me," Diana said as they sat down. "If you take the train here and go to Central Station in Keswick you can take the Islander Line which takes you over all three islands through Lincoln and then Attlewood, and then there are some newer lines from the main stations on each island that take you through all of Jarsdel individually, and a line that takes you through all of Cliffe Island individually from the university to the airport – if it's finished. When I left, they were working on that last one…"

Tristan didn't respond. He instead sat down quietly as the train began to move and then shoot off into the dark tunnels beneath the city. They made two more stops before Stoneridge Village where they got off. The couple surfaced from the underground and looked out and around at the modern villa they had arrived in with the many condos around. There were a lot of people around and despite the time, it was still fairly warm out. Tristan looked around and saw that there were a lot of trees and shrubs planted around.

Diana took him through the village and then across a street to reach the boardwalk that surrounded the edge of the district. At the sides of the boardwalk were various businesses, known brands and businesses as opposed to independent small businesses. Even on the boardwalk there were round pens where trees had been planted and decorated the mostly wooden path. Diana took Tristan to the railing where they looked out to the sort of bay consisting of Stoneridge and the north of Port Burnes. The area created a marina with docks on the other side where yachts and private sailboats were parked. In the very distance of Jarsdel, one could see the large port where cargo ships were parked at, which was the Port of Harlech, or literally, Port Burnes. The boardwalk contained the occasional gate which led down a ramp to a low dock where people could be seen with their private vessels, some of them with fishing equipment. Diana and Tristan walked along the pier as the sun almost set.

The couple stopped at a west face of the boardwalk near the end which extended onto a coastal path by a beach. From here, they looked out to the west as the sun began to descend over the horizon.

"I don't want to manipulate you into believing that Harlech is a wonderful place, because it really isn't," Diana expressed, "but it is our home from now on until we can leave to return to Allabrese. We may as well try and seek some comfort from this place rather than avoid it completely…"

Tristan didn't respond. He then let out a sigh.

"Yeah, I suppose so," Tristan admitted. "I'm just not a big fan of change, really, aside from what my views are of a place like this. I know that's easier for you because this isn't that much of a change – you lived in a place like this until you came to Allabrese."

"Even I miss Allabrese, but you're right. This is harder for you, and I know you don't like change," Diana replied, placing a hand on his cheek. "We'll just have to get used to it…"

Tristan gave off another sigh and then asked, "So, what do you want to do now? What's next on the Cambridge Tour of Harlech?"

Diana smiled at him and removed her hand. The two held hands as they continued to walk.

"Let's just wander aimlessly… maybe head towards King George Park…"

"Do you want to go to Keswick?" Tristan asked.

Diana looked at him with slight estrangement and then shook her head.

"I'd rather avoid that place entirely…" Diana replied. "Who knows how much worse it's gotten down there – it's not safe."

"Right," Tristan responded.

The couple proceeded to walk down a path before a wide beach where there were more people, some couples with their children, and some teenagers. The scene was more decent than in Villa Paraiso for the most part. On the other side of the path was a moderate-sized strip of grassland a part of the park with another path on the other side alongside a main road. Tristan noticed a fair amount of cyclists that passed them on the path, some of them cutting them off almost and nearly knocking into them. He quickly became annoyed at them, but by then, they stopped at an intersection, which went to a major street intersection that they walked to instead of continuing along towards King George VI Park. Across the street was a small plaza before a tall condo building. On the other street corner was a two-story luxurious restaurant with many patrons eating outside. The path at the side of the road also came to an end and blended into a sidewalk atop of a minor cliff from the major road that lifted upwards. The couple crossed the street and began to go north up a curved major street known as Turnour Street.

Tristan noticed banners as they walked along this street, which had a rainbow flag beneath them. He looked at this flag with disgust but ignored it as he looked around at the many businesses at the side, most of which were small businesses with the occasional brand business in the form of a shop, restaurant, or hotel. At the end of the curve, they reached an intersection with another major road known as Matilpi Street. All along this street, the banners could also be seen. At the northwest street corner, Tristan noticed a hospital: St. Luke's Hospital. The campus of the hospital consisted of an old structure at the street corner and a tall ten-story skyscraper behind it. Tristan pointed the site out.

"Is that where you were born?" Tristan asked as they waited for the street light to change.

"No," Diana scoffed with a laugh. "I was born in Queen Victoria Hospital over in Attlewood."

"Oh..."

The couple crossed the street and then continued down Turnour Street for several more blocks until they had suddenly returned to Campbell Street. They then proceeded east again along Campbell Street, which largely consisted of the base of skyscrapers with the businesses that occupied them. The closer they came to Durham Street near Cabernet Tower, the taller and busier the street became. There was a light traffic that went through town at this hour, but it was still hectic nonetheless with the occasional honk of a horn or skid. Within about twenty minutes from the previous intersection, the couple soon found themselves before Windsor Hotel near Cabernet Tower.

"Well, this has been pleasant," Tristan sarcastically remarked as they made their way to Cabernet Tower. "We didn't even get a chance to go and look at the cars..."

"We weren't going to find any dealerships around here," Diana replied. "I have to do that in Lincoln or Harthdam. I'm just glad we got the chance to get outside and see the city... It's been three years, but there's certainly a different atmosphere to it than when I left."

"Maybe the change isn't in the city, but in you," Tristan suggested.

"Maybe..." Diana replied. "Well, let's head back up to the penthouse then. We have an early start tomorrow... and I guess this'll be our last night together for a while..."

"Yeah," Tristan plainly responded, stopping before the entrance to Cabernet Tower. "I'm actually pretty tired since I'm still jetlagged... I'd rather go to bed and sleep."

Diana lowered her soft smile as Tristan began to walk towards the entrance. He then stopped as he noticed Diana lag behind him.

"Sure, let's go and sleep then," Diana said with a peaceful and kind smile.

Act 2, Scene 2

Early next morning, Diana and Tristan got up and ready to leave the penthouse and go their separate ways. Allodia called two taxis for each of them and then met them at the base of Cabernet Tower. Tristan finished putting his luggage into the back of his taxi and then went to meet Allodia and Diana. Allodia had her arms crossed as she finished talking to Diana. Diana then looked at Tristan.

"I'm feeling a bit emotional…" Allodia remarked. "I mean, we've been talking about it for the last two months, but I suppose the two of you really are going to university now…"

"We're definitely going to miss you," Diana said, hugging Allodia. "It's been a blast the last two months…"

"I'm going to miss you too," Allodia responded. "Thanks for all the help you guys did… I would have never have been able to do as much as you if I went alone."

"Have a safe trip," Tristan expressed, hugging Allodia. "Say 'Hi' to Everest for us."

"I definitely will," Allodia replied, parting from Tristan. "I'm sorry my brother couldn't sort his itinerary out so that he could see you off with me, but that's just the way he is… He also left that rock that the chief gave to him on the kitchen counter. If either of you want to let him know so he can come to pick it up, please do otherwise it'll stay there."

"Sure," Diana said. "Alright…"

Diana stepped back and looked at the both of them. Allodia looked back at them.

"I suppose you want to have a moment together…" Allodia remarked. "Sorry, I'll just be over here."

Allodia stepped away and left Diana and Tristan alone. The couple faced each other.

"So, I guess this is it then," Diana said to him.

"You say it like we're not going to see each other again," Tristan responded in a plain tone.

Diana tilted her head and replied, "We're going to be spending less time with each other and living at two different parts of town. Doesn't that make you scared, or anxious?"

Tristan didn't respond for a moment.

"Scared of what?" Tristan finally asked.

Diana lowered her head and then looked back up to him. She gave a smile.

"I *am* the anxious one, so maybe that was stupid to ask you. I'm glad you're more confident in this than I am."

Diana brought a hand to Tristan's cheek.

"Please remember that if you feel alone, I'm here for you. I hope you can make some friends over there – and don't forget that I love you, care for you, and will be thinking of you."

Tristan looked back at her.

"I'll talk to you later tonight, okay?" Diana stated.

"Of course," Tristan replied. "I love you too."

Tristan kissed Diana on the head and then parted from her. Allodia waved goodbye to them as they each went to their separate taxis. Tristan got into his and then sat down alone. The taxi driver, a Sikh man, soon parted from the side of the street. Diana got into her taxi and gave a sigh. Her taxi soon parted from the sidewalk and proceeded to take her to Declan Walham University to the north of Lincoln atop of a forested hill. Tristan looked out of his window as his taxi proceeded to take him to the University of Harlech all the way at the other side of town.

The ride from Central Harlech to the University of Harlech took approximately forty-five minutes. The taxi drove down West Queen Boulevard from Attlewood and then reached a part of the road that looked out to a forest on either side, which stretched a fair distance. This forest was known as Island Spirits Regional Park. Once out of the park, the taxi passed a few luxurious homes and reached the campus. On the northwest street corner, Tristan saw a large hospital known as the University of Harlech Teaching Hospital. The hospital was next to various fields that could be seen from afar as they drove down the remainder of West Queen Boulevard. The taxi stopped at a red light at the Davidson Avenue intersection. Tristan looked to his left and saw the University of Harlech School of Medicine across from the School of Nursing to the right. The car then continued and passed the university Sports Center to the left, a parkade and then the Health Sciences building to the right, and finally the kinesiology building on the left. The taxi right turned on University Promenade and then began to follow some signs laid out to people as they moved in to their dorms on Moving Day. They passed the Pharmaceutical Sciences building on the left, crossed a T-intersection with Wilby Mall, the forestry program building, and then continued down before stopping outside of the Robotics building. The ride ended here with Tristan paying the cab driver, retrieving his luggage, and then crossing the street where Residence A and B awaited him.

Tristan walked down a mall, or wide stone path, which looked to the various newly renovated brick buildings that was Residence B to the right and Residence A on the left. There was not much difference between them other than their designated letter. At the end of the path, Tristan reached Residence A Commonplace, which was at the side of a large open field before a major road that bordered the entire campus, Marshall Drive. Tristan entered the commonplace and then followed the signs to a multipurpose room where there was a queue to sign-in and pickup keys.

The queue followed a 'social distancing' rule, which meant that people had to remain at least two meters, or six feet, apart in order to limit the spread of germs given the concern over the ongoing pandemic. Tristan obeyed with this regulation and kept his distance from the people behind and in front of him. With a ten minute wait, he was in the multipurpose room and in front of the table to sign-in. He presented his driver's license as ID and then received his welcome package from the volunteer at the other side, which included a University of Harlech lanyard with two sets of keys, one for his room and another for the mailbox located in the commonplace. The keyring also included a card key for entering the building. The key for the mailbox was like any standard key, while the one for the dorm was a special type of key that was cylindrical with jagged edges. Tristan had never seen this type of key before.

Regardless, with these keys in hand and papers that listed his dorm on the fourth floor of Building A2, Tristan left the commonplace with his luggage and went to find this building. Tristan looked through the papers he was given as he walked to the building and read the procedure for entering the building using the card key. Once Tristan had found the building, he approached the pin pad and entered his card. He then entered the first four digits of his student number and then retrieved the card. It didn't work. Tristan attempted once more until another new student behind him tried the same. Soon it became a hassle as people attempted to unlock the door until a Residential Advisor, one of the supervisors assigned to each floor, exited and taught the people how to do it properly, which was not listed in the instructions at all.

Tristan entered the building and entered the lobby, which was plain and consisted of hard stone tiles. The interior had a hotel-like appearance as the walls were modern and clean, and the carpets in the corridors ahead vacuumed and pristine. From the lobby, the elevator was directly ahead. To the side, Tristan saw a door that went into a stairwell. Next to this door was a large common room seen from outside through the large glass windows. Inside there were already people hanging out together. Once the elevator had arrived, Tristan entered and waited as the door opened at each floor with other people exiting.

Finally, the elevator reached the fourth floor and Tristan was the only one to exit. He walked down the corridor of the dorms, which wrapped around with the L-shape of the building. At the inner corner of this floor was the fourth floor common room, which was medium-sized with a living room that had a flat screen TV to one side, a small dining room at the other, and a kitchenette with a microwave and fridge. Like the common room below, the entire room was visible from the outside through large glass windows. At the end of this same hall were two rooms occupied by the Residential Advisors (RAs) as noticeable by the large signs on the front of the doors.

Tristan continued down the hall and soon reached his bedroom. He stopped before it and attempted to listen to hear if anybody else, such as his roommate, was inside. No sounds could be heard. Tristan took a deep breath and then entered his key, fumbling a bit with the foreign lock until the door unlocked and he could push through. The door was heavy, but not that heavy for him. Tristan looked into the room.

The room was split between a small corridor at the entrance and then a room smaller than the one he had at the manor with a single window at the end. On the immediate left was a door that led into the bathroom that Tristan would have to share with his roommate. On the right was a small enclave with hooks and a larger hook above this. Next to the enclave was a closet. The main room of the bedroom had a bunkbed in the far-right corner, two desks at opposite-corners, and two dressers side-by-side in the last corner. The bathroom was simple and contained a toilet, shower, and a sink.

Tristan looked around and then dragged his luggage in, setting it before a dresser. He walked towards the window and looked out. His dorm had a view of West Marshall Drive and the trees on the other side. He wasn't high up enough to look past the trees though. Tristan held a plain expression as he looked outside and then turned around. He leaned on the window ledge and then sighed.

"Well, I better wait a bit and see who the lucky guy that has to live with me is…" Tristan muttered.

Tristan got a better look of the bedroom and then went into the bathroom to wash his face. When he came out, he heard a knock on the door. Tristan went and immediately opened it to see who was on the other side. It was a Residential Advisor. He was a young Melanesian or perhaps Amerindian man with black hair and brown skin. He wore a red shirt with the university logo on the left side and below the logo it read, 'Residential Advisor.' Tristan looked at him.

"Hey," the RA greeted with a smile. "Welcome to Residence 2A! My name is Manuel and I'll be one of your RAs. I just wanted to say 'Hi' as well as to introduce you to your roommate."

Tristan looked to his left and then felt a piercing jab into his stomach. His face dropped in expression into one of serious shock as he looked at his roommate.

"How do you do?" Finn greeted in his deep Suffolk voice with a charming smile. "Only joking…" he said, looking to the RA. "Tristan and I go way back… thanks for your help. We've got lots of catching up to do…"

Finn pushed past and Tristan stepped back. The door closed on its own and the two former friends looked at each other in quiet from the corridor. Tristan continued to look at him in shock. Finn gave a modest smile back at him. He was dressed in significantly different clothing than from what he wore in Northumbria-Berwick. Finn wore a sweater with a dress shirt, beige pants and sneakers. Behind his back was a backpack, and to his side was some luggage.

"Did you miss me?" Finn questioned.

"You're..." Tristan stuttered. "You're supposed to be dead. What the hell..."

Finn noticed Tristan's expression. His hands were shaking as well. Finn knocked off his backpack and went over to him.

"It's not a hallucination, bruh," Finn remarked. "I'm alive."

Finn looked at Tristan who didn't seem to be convinced. He looked slightly scared. Finn dropped his smile and embraced Tristan.

"I've waited for this moment for over a year," Finn quietly said as they hugged. "I didn't think I'd get to see you again either... after all that happened..."

Tristan only listened. He didn't participate in the hug and instead only allowed Finn to hug him. He took in a deep breath and smelled the odor of this person who was very much real and in his presence once more. He closed his eyes and felt the corporeal touch of the man that was his best friend. Tristan soon raised his hands, but only to part them. He looked at Finn with intent, studying his face. His hair was much the same as it was in the forest, but slightly trimmed. Under his left eye was a scar from when Tristan had cut him with that branch when they were playfighting. He had the same cheekbones that Tristan remembered. The same light blue eyes. Tristan studied his face for another second before closing his eyes, shaking his head and turning around.

Finn looked back at him.

"You know, a 'Hi' would be nice," Finn remarked. "I did just travel thousands of miles to see you again… and you know, go to school here…"

Tristan finally turned around again.

"Sorry," Tristan apologized, raising his hands up slightly before sitting down. "I'm just- I'm in shock."

Finn walked over to him and sat down.

"You thought I was dead, huh?" Finn questioned.

"I saw you fall to your death… Nobody could survive a fall from that height, no less in the condition we were in," Tristan said seriously. "I…"

"Well, by some miracle, I survived it," Finn remarked, looking up. "To be honest, I don't have any recollection of what happened when I hit the water below because I must've blacked out. I've thought a lot about that day… Perhaps I should explain a little more…"

Tristan didn't respond.

"The next thing I remember after the fall from that tree trunk we were climbing over was being on a bank far from the fire. A man had saved me from the river and kept watch of me until I woke up. His name was Damian and he was wandering Kielder Forest when he saw me in the water, so he dragged me out. He offered me food and shelter, and without my stuff I had to accept. We then got to talking and he asked me what I was doing in Northumbria-Berwick, and I told him the excuses I usually give people who inquired. He didn't believe me. I thought that was weird and started to get suspicious of him. He then started to talk about how he was a rich man and then he asked me about what I wanted… and then I got to thinking about that, and I didn't know what I wanted. Over the last day, it seemed like my entire life had been shook about... The man that I despised wasn't even my own kin as I had thought, and then I thought about who my true parents could be. I remembered what you said to me. I remembered about you, and I hoped that you got out and that you were safe, but then I also remembered about the conversation that we had the night before when you told me about your girlfriend. In the end, I told this man that I didn't know what I wanted, and then he asked me where I was going, and I said that I didn't know. He then said that he knew that the Met Police were looking for me, but before I could jump out of there, he told me that he could help me out. I know all of this sounds strange, but it really did happen... I asked what he meant by that and he said that he could help me get out of the forest, hide for a while, but then he offered me to come to the New World, to the United States, where he was from. I replied that I didn't want to go to the United States. I then remembered about you and I said that I wanted to come to Canada. He told me that he could make that happen, but it would take some time. I then asked him why he was willing to help me out, and he said because he sympathized with me, and that was that.

After we had this chat, we hiked out of the woods and then he took me home to the mansion so I could see my mum, or really, the woman I thought was my mother. He told me to keep a low-profile and that his people would be in contact with me, and that's what I did."

"Wait, you went home after what happened?" Tristan questioned.

"Yeah," Finn replied, looking at him with surprise. "She... she was nothing like Aidan. She cared for me in her own way, made sure I had clothes, was fed, and that sort of thing. She cared about me even if it wasn't all that grand. I had to go back and comfort her after what happened to Aidan, so I stayed and kept a low-profile, and I thought about the future… I thought about what I was going to do… I did some research about this man you thought was my father, and sooner or later I began to realize the truth. You were right… this man, Charlemagne, is my dad, or so I think."

"No, he is!" Tristan exclaimed. "You have no idea what Charles was doing and what his plans were. The only reason I was in that forest in the first place was because he was looking for you! He knew you were there because he had people track you down! The only reason why I stayed with you at the start was to keep an eye on you for him…!"

Finn looked back at Tristan with slight doubt. He then looked forward.

"The point is, I wasn't sure at the time, so I started to make a plan for my life. I wanted to start a new life. I was romanticized by the idea… a normal life, so I decided I'd go to school just like I said to you once. I'm in the Applied Science program after all. Some time went by though and I started to lose hope that this Damian guy would ever get back to me. I started to make alternate plans, but knew that if I applied to school in England, the Met would come and arrest me. I felt hopeless at a time, but at the end of all that, I met with Damian again and he went over some ways in which I could come to Canada with a student visa. He gave me an American passport, an American social insurance number, and he set me up with a new life. With my inheritance, I said goodbye to mum and then left for America; to New York. That was the last time I saw Damian, around November, because he had to go leave for some work… He's a busy man and he gave me all that I needed. The next step was to get a flat and continue my plans. I had to apply using my alias and marks from the UK, but that was okay since I hardly thought that'd draw any red flags. In fact, other than my bank cards, I'm still using that passport since the other was just to get me out of the UK. I can't return there with my own passport since I'm technically wanted for domestic terrorism there…"

"Yeah," Tristan replied, "Charles told me that it's likely that I can't ever return to the UK again since I'd be arrested under suspicion of being a right-wing radical and terrorist. He had to thread the needle to get me out after I was discharged from the hospital…"

"Hospital?"

Tristan explained what had happened to him after they had separated.

"Yeah, I had to have a bit of rest after I got out of there too," Finn replied, "but anyways, that's that…"

"What do you mean that's that?" Tristan questioned. "So, you survived because some miracle worker bailed you out of England, took you to New York, and then you're here now? How come you never tried to contact me? To tell me beforehand that you were alive? I've assumed you were dead for the last year!"

"I tried to look into you, but to be honest, I didn't know where you lived, and I could have looked on social media, but a part of me thought that I might just drop it…"

"Drop it? You're here right now!"

"Yeah, and that's because I wanted to be here right now, in person – not online."

"I thought you were dead!" Tristan repeated.

Finn looked back at Tristan as if he was being scolded like a dog.

"I thought, based on what you told me, that I'd eventually come to meet you here, so I took a risk and asked to be roommates with you, and here we are…" Finn simply stated. "What more can I say than that?"

Tristan looked back at him and then shook his head as he looked to the side.

"Eh, cheer up," Finn remarked, sitting back down next to him. "We'll be living together from now on… No use being mad at me…"

Tristan looked back at him.

"What about your dad? Your real dad? He'll want to meet you. You *have* to meet him. He can take you to your biological mother too – I've met her!"

Finn looked back at Tristan with slight discomfort. He then looked down.

"Yeah, maybe eventually, but not now, okay?"

"Why not?" Tristan questioned.

Finn looked to the side and then scratched his head. He looked back to Tristan.

"Because I don't know if I want to meet him," Finn stated. "I've thought about him for a long time. The both of them… even though I don't know who my mother is, and I have a lot of expectations about him, thoughts that I haven't cleared up with myself, and I don't think I'm ready for that."

Tristan looked back at him as Finn looked forward. He then looked back at him.

"If you're in contact with him, please don't tell him that I'm alive, or for that matter that I exist…" Finn requested. "In fact, please don't tell anyone you know about me. Mostly because I'm still a wanted terrorist – I'm going by my middle name around here, just so you know."

"Louis?"

"Yeah," Finn replied with a smile. "It should be a little more subtle than Finn."

Tristan shook his head and responded, "Oh my God… this… this is a lot, man."

Tristan stood up and went to the window. Finn stood up and approached him from behind and then grabbed his shoulders.

"Eh, cheer up," Finn remarked. "I took a gamble and here we are, together again… You thought you'd never see me again, and so did I, but here we are… you and me, Tristan."

Tristan looked back at Finn through his reflection in the window. He then lowered his head and submitted to the fact.

Act 2, Scene 3

The next morning, Tristan awoke in his dorm early at around five o'clock at the bottom bunk while Finn slept on the top bunk. The two didn't spend much time together last night as there were lots of group-oriented events on the fourth floor, organized by the RAs so that everyone could make friends and get to know their neighbors. The event was mandatory although participation wasn't. Tristan lay on his side and looked forward in absolute silence.

By the time that it was six o'clock, Tristan decided to get out of bed and go have some breakfast at the canteen above the commonplace. First, he quietly went to the bathroom to take a shower and get changed. Finn woke up as Tristan exited from the bathroom.

"What time is it?" Finn questioned in a tired voice.

"Six fifteen," Tristan responded. "I have a class at eight."

"You have a class in a classroom? Most of my classes are online because of the kung flu virus," Finn remarked, resting his head on his pillow.

Tristan ignored him and instead picked up his lanyard, phone and wallet.

"Hey," Finn said as Tristan was about to leave. "Do you want to get some lunch together later today, say around twelve? We didn't get much of a chance to talk besides what we did talk about…"

"Sure," Tristan replied. "That's fine."

"Sweet."

Tristan then left the dorm and went down the corridor towards the elevator. He returned to the commonplace and entered. He then followed the signs that took him to a set of stairs and then up to the canteen. Only a few other students were awake at this hour and getting breakfast. The canteen consisted of various stations where a chef sat behind and prepared food. Yesterday, some of the stations already had food prepared and simply served people from what was offered. To the left was a bistro where fast food was served and this morning, it served a standard breakfast while the other station served a more niche, ethnic meal. Tristan went for the standard breakfast and then went to the drink station to serve himself some coffee.

Behind the kitchen area of the canteen was a large dining room with various seats. The kitchen and dining hall consisted of almost the entire second-floor of the commonplace. The dining hall also consisted of a pattern carpet with glass windows that covered the outer walls looking out towards the grass field around the dorms, Marshall Drive, and then the forest beyond. Tristan sat down at a table by himself, ate, and then slowly drank his coffee.

Once it was seven o'clock, Tristan decided to get a move on, so he took his tray and placed it on a conveyor belt that went into the behind the scenes of the canteen where the actual cooking was done as well as the dishwashing. Tristan returned to the commonplace and went around a corner to a small space behind the front desk to find a photocopying machine as well as the many mailboxes. He then returned to the main area to look at all the space with tables, booths, and couches. He then proceeded to the exit where he saw a study room with a sign that regulated quiet within the room. Next to the study room was a corkboard with various events advertised for the residents. Tristan looked at all of this with tired eyes and then left to return to the dorm. He stopped before the door and noticed a sign had been placed over it that said Tristan and Finn's alias, Louis, on it. Tristan simply sighed as he looked at it and noticed that each and every other door had the same.

"At least this must mean I'm not hallucinating…"

Finn continued to sleep as Tristan quietly entered. He walked over to the side of his bed and picked up his backpack. He then placed it around his shoulder and left the room again. Tristan went back outside through the main entrance of their building and proceeded along the path that went to University Promenade. Tristan looked across towards the Forestry building on the right and the Robotics building on the left. He then walked north along the sidewalk and started to pass Residence B on his left, which had an older outer appearance. Ahead of the Robotics building, Tristan soon saw the Applied Science Library and then the Applied Sciences building.

"Finn…" Tristan suddenly muttered to himself. "What the hell…"

Tristan took out his phone as he walked and looked at his screen. He then unlocked it and checked to see if he had any new messages from Diana. There were none since the two had talked last evening. On the left, Tristan saw Residence C, which consisted of ten-story apartment buildings with a restaurant immediately to the left. The road curved out slightly ahead as Tristan reached the Faculty of Science Library & Student Center across the path to Residence C as well as an intersection with another road that went east between the Applied Sciences building and the Campbell Building. This road was Renfrew Mall. Tristan simply continued down the promenade, along the slightly diagonal shift, and then straight again where he saw a large mansion at the end of the road.

Before the mansion, Tristan saw the Nanoscience building, Earth Sciences building, and Physics & Astronomy building to his left and beyond the Campbell Building, the Prescott Building and finally the Chemistry building. Tristan continued down the road towards its end where there was a large plaza before the mansion, which was known as Harlech Manor and acted as the administrative heart of the university with various offices for faculty and staff. The mansion was extremely large and consisted of three stories and two separate wings that were each about the size of Cabernet Manor.

Tristan stopped before he could reach the mansion and decided to jaywalk across to the Chemistry building where he needed to go. The Chemistry building had an older appearance compared to most structures that Tristan had just passed by. It's architecture was sort of typical of the New England college architecture with stone walls. He approached a set of doors and then entered. From there, he took out his phone again and looked at his schedule. Tristan then proceeded to search the lecture hall in which his class would be held in. The interior of the building consisted of square wooden floor tiles, stone walls just as outside, and carved wooden doors. There was a certain antiqueness in its halls. Tristan came to the basement of the building, which was one of three sublevels. He looked around for his lecture hall and soon found the doors that went inside.

The lecture hall was a sort of theater with around two-hundred seats going downwards and looking not to a stage or cinema screen below, but to a podium and desk in front of various chalkboards. Tristan looked at his watch and saw that it was ten-minutes to the start of class. There were a lot of other eager first-year students already sitting down, so he quickly found a seat and then took a notebook out to get ready. The lecture hall soon became full with people who attempted to cross by Tristan to sit at the seats to his left, which required him to raise the small platform with his notebook and allow them to inch across.

At five minutes to the start of class, the professor arrived, wearing a face-mask. Tristan noticed that quite a lot of people in the room wore face masks. A lot of people sat with two or three chairs between each other as was university policy. Some people ignored this rule and sat with their friends. The professor took out a laptop from his backpack and began to set it up with some cables while two screens came down from the ceiling and covered the two columns of two chalkboards left and right. A projector from the back of the room then projected onto these screens.

Tristan looked around the lecture hall again and began to notice almost nobody had a notebook in front of them like he did. They all had their laptops before them, some of them were browsing forums, social media, chatting online, or simply had a word processor open ready to take notes. Tristan frowned and then slid slightly down into his chair as he leaned back and the class started.

• • • •

The lecture took fifty minutes and consisted only of orientation. The professor taught the students how to access resource materials, such as the syllabus, online, and then went through that document, which Tristan couldn't follow along with since he had left his laptop in the dorm. Once they were dismissed, Tristan shot out of the lecture hall and returned to the dorm to retrieve his laptop. He noticed that Finn had left. Tristan retrieved his laptop and then returned back towards the north of the campus so that he could wait for time to pass until his next class in the Campbell Building, which was also the Humanities Student Center, or Art Student Center.

Tristan sat down on a bench in the sublevel of one of the five different wings that were a part of this building. Here, there was a busy café with lots of people sitting at the tables. There were also glass windows that looked out to the courtyard in the center, which was plain and consisted mostly of concrete and a modern sculpture. Tristan then shot his eyes back towards the glass doors at the far-side near the other side of the café.

At the doors, there was a student holding an umbrella to cover themselves despite the sunshine and cloudless skies. Tristan looked at her with peculiarity. This person also wore a baseball cap and a hoodie over themselves. He only got another look at him or her as they passed his line of sight and went behind an enclosed space behind the café.

Tristan continued to wait at the bench as he took out his laptop to have time fly by. At ten minutes to ten o'clock, students began to enter through the doors that went into the lecture hall and took a seat. Tristan put his laptop into his backpack and then joined the pack of people that merged into the doors. There, Tristan saw this person again, noticing their dark blonde hair, almost a light brown as it was a sort of ash blonde hair, tied in a ponytail. He squinted suspiciously towards this stranger and soon lost track of them as they entered through before him.

Once Tristan was on the other side, he went and found a seat, preparing his laptop for the start of class. He then looked to his left and noticed this stranger again, sitting close to the front of the lecture hall on her own. Tristan looked astonished as he realized that this strange and weird person was a female. She had smooth cheeks and extremely fair skin that it was a sickly pale tone, but beautiful with a slight sort of olive color towards it. Tristan noticed her as she held a fist under her chin as she waited for the class to start. He also noticed her piercing emerald green eyes and fine eyebrows. Tristan became slightly astonished at her appearance by his eyes that he looked elsewhere and then to his computer screen.

Throughout the lecture, Tristan looked up from his screen, but not over to the professor, but to this girl. His eyes then soon parted as he began to have them wander elsewhere. At the end of the lecture, Tristan stood up and looked over to the girl again. She stood up and he was able to catch her face again. The girl began to move up the steps to the exit near where Tristan was stood, so he quickly packed his things and then left before she could pass him.

From the lecture hall, Tristan went straight to the bathrooms behind the enclosed space behind the café. There, he went to the sink and splashed some water on his face. He then looked at himself and sighed. Tristan went and dried his hands. He then exited the bathroom and looked down the corridor towards the exit of the lecture hall he had just come out of, but the girl was already gone. Tristan took out his phone and looked at a photo of him and Diana. Almost embarrassed to look at his own phone, he lowered it and turned around. He then proceeded out of the Campbell Building so that he could meet with Finn.

• • • •

Finn and Tristan met less than an hour later at a café near the Student Union.

"Hey," Finn greeted. "How's been day one for you?"

Tristan looked at him.

"It's been an experience," Tristan simply responded.

"You don't sound too thrilled," Finn replied, laughing. "Come on, I'm starving."

The two entered the café, ordered some food and drink, and then went outside to sit down. Tristan looked at Finn before him. He seemed outgoing and jovial, almost always with a smile on his face. However, Finn was not an outgoing person as Tristan had observed last night when the two of them mostly ignored the others.

"So…" Tristan remarked in a plain tone. "Here we are…"

"Yeah, I guess so," Finn replied, lowering his smile for a moment. "It's kind of strange being in this capacity, isn't it? I mean, we spent all that time in the forest together, talking about ourselves, sharing our thoughts and ideas – most of which I still remember, and now here we are in civilization."

"I never thought I'd see you step out of the woods," Tristan stated. "I thought you hated urban life."

Finn shrugged.

"Just because I hate something doesn't mean I'll avoid it completely," Finn stated. "I need to be here for school, and if that means being in the cesspool of society, then so be it. Look at the idiots around us, they're harmless. It's just a city, and since I'm aware of the fact, I have the advantage over these people to not get myself screwed."

"You still believe in all that stuff though," Tristan quietly said. "Right?"

Finn looked back at him.

"What is learned and realized can never be abandoned, Tristan," Finn replied. "If anything, I've had the last year to harden my views and outlook… I have a duty to fulfill, and I'm going to fulfill it."

"What duty is that?"

The duty of every white man to fight for and protect his own people and secure the existence of our children," Finn stated, "and that begins with being able to support a family. In today's day and age, the will and power to fight is more important than ever."

"I get that," Tristan admitted. "Someday, I want to settle down and have a family with Diana, and I'm here so that I can get my bachelor's degree and then apply for medical school... There's nothing more important to me than my family... it's all we have, right?"

"Right," Finn agreed.

"The only truth I've ever been able to discern from the world is that fact, that we are animals too. That's what you told me – we're no different from them, but we're more sophisticated. It's our purpose to evolve forward though... because we aren't meant to be the same."

Finn looked at Tristan and didn't respond for a moment.

"We're not the same, you're right about that, but at the same time we do have our differences," Finn said to Tristan.

"Right, I know that, but in general we're animals, it's like our original sin where the curse is our consciousness."

"Our consciousness is only a curse if you treat it like that," Finn said to Tristan. "Look at what we've managed to do with our consciousness. We've built civilizations and empires, been able to transform and save lives... What makes you believe that we are not meant to be the same anymore?"

"What do you mean? I mean, we've hit the peak of our evolutionary cycle – humans aren't going to progress any more than they have unless we do something about it. We possess the consciousness to understand this necessity, so all that remains is action. Wouldn't it be better if society were transformed completely and overhauled so that only the most perfect humans with higher instincts lived amongst us?"

"Do you think you're one of these people who should be selected for this radical experiment of yours?" Finn questioned.

"What? I don't know – that's not really up to me to decide, I think."

"Don't get me wrong, I understand what you're talking about, the logic makes sense, but I think you're missing out on some key facts about life, such as the fact that you can't control it. Even the most perfect society of our time had its problems, but it persevered by understanding human nature and harnessing that raw power. It never sought to change people, but rode on the moral beliefs that had fundamentally altered Western Civilization for the last two-thousand years. Two-thousand years of which man struggled against these beliefs, but never actively attempted to oppose them until the flood gates were opened, and here we are now. I am of course talking about Christianity and its decline in recent years."

"Christianity is in decline now though," Tristan stated. "We're smarter than we were two-thousand years ago and can understand the important lessons that had created the fabric of Western Civilization through other means, more convincing means. People who talk about Christianity in politics are laughed at nowadays. There's no hope of return to that... it's empty talking points that could have turned society around two-thousand years ago, but not now. What we need now is from facts we can believe in..."

"People are superstitious..." Finn remarked. "If Christianity is in decline, it's not because people are skeptical or because of 'rationalism' but because there's an active movement against Christianity in general rooted in the culture – this wave of malice, and with it, the politicization of Christianity. It's also not because we're more learned than we were, because in sum, we're not. That's an arrogant assumption to make about what there is to learn about the world. If we truly were a secular or atheist society, no religion would be tolerated by the people, but that's not the case. Instead only Christianity is attacked by people, the media, etcetera. Anyways, I don't want to talk about religion because I'm not a religious person. My point is that people will be people, and that's that, but if you attempt to interfere with their liberty, they'll bite back and resist. Don't get me wrong – you should know this about me, but it's tragic what's become of our world and seems irreversible without radical change, but that's not the case. We'll persevere. We always have. And when we're backed in a corner, we'll certainly bite back against those that threaten us. Our way of life, before this cultural revolution through the 1960s, is not the problem. The people that threaten us are the problem."

"Yeah, I know, but… what can we do about it?"

"I already told you," Finn remarked. "Stay the course you're on… When it becomes impossible to do that, then we can talk about direct action. That was my mistake…"

Tristan looked to the side.

"It's not like action to the scale that we did ever did anything," Tristan said. "I mean, look at your own dad – I mean even Cunningham Industries, even though they don't exist anymore, all of their executives probably still make a living. You… you hit the nest and the pests all scattered and made their homes in other establishments, and then there are people like Jeffrey Epstein or Kau Waomoni who have done horrible things and no justice is ever served at all… All that effort to pin these guys, and it blows up because they've got better friends than they deserve… 'Friends' who are looking out for their own asses…"

Finn sighed.

"Yeah," Finn agreed, "I get your frustration because I was frustrated once before. I still am, but you've just got to persevere, Tristan. This is a fight. You can't forget what you're fighting for…"

Tristan looked aside.

"I don't even know what I am fighting for…" Tristan muttered.

Act 2, Scene 4

At the end of the school week, Tristan and Diana sat atop of the penthouse roof, looking out to the rest of the city around them as they spent some time together. The roof had a railing around the edges and was not steep. Even then, the tiles had good traction. The sun had set and it was approximately nine o'clock at night. There was a minor chill in the air, but the couple both wore sweaters to cover themselves. Tristan stared forward and then looked back to Diana as she shook his shoulder.

"Tristan?" Diana questioned.

"Yeah?"

"Did you hear what I said?" Diana asked.

"Yeah," Tristan lied. "It sounds like you had a better week than me. I'm glad you found a bit of passion in your lectures."

"Well, not wholly, but it is interesting to hear some stuff I've never thought about before..." Diana expressed. "It's like a breath of fresh air... some stuff I agree with, and some I find genuinely interesting."

"Yeah."

"How about your classes? Are you enjoying them?"

"I wouldn't say I'm enjoying them," Tristan replied, "as much as I'm keeping up with the material. We learn a lot in a lecture, and a lot of the content is new to me. I think I hate my English class the most since the projects coming up don't seem to be too intuitive. I don't think I find any of them to be interesting..."

"That's a shame," Diana admitted. "Well, I told you about my week, but what else is going for you? There's got to be something..."

Tristan looked forward for a moment. He then looked back to Diana.

"Actually," Tristan said. "There's something I have been meaning to tell you, and I didn't want to text you this and instead tell you in person, but Finn… he's alive. In fact, he's my roommate…"

"What?" Diana questioned. "Are you serious? Of course you're serious… but how? How do you know? How did he survive? What?"

Tristan took a deep breath. He then explained to Diana that Finn what Finn had told him from his fall into a river, meeting someone in the forest who he travelled with, his return to his adoptive-mother, and his plans to come to Canada surrounding a greater plan to start a normal life.

"Does he know that Charles is his father?" Diana asked.

"Yeah," Tristan replied. "He knows about Charles based on what I said to him once and when he learned that his adoptive-father wasn't his actual dad. His plans been centered around that because it's shifted what he's thought about himself and such. I don't know what his inner thoughts are about Charles, and from I've been able to discern, they're semi-neutral…"

"We need to tell Charles about this – this is good news for him!" Diana remarked.

"We *cannot* tell Charles about this," Tristan corrected.

"What? Why not? Tristan, Charles has a right to know that the son he searched for endlessly and mourned is alive. Wouldn't you want to know if Finn was alive?"

Tristan didn't answer.

"Does he not want to meet Charles? What's the deal?"

Tristan sighed and answered, "Finn said to me that he doesn't feel ready to meet his biological father just yet. I also told him that he has a chance to not only meet Charles, but also his mother too since I'm sure Charlemagne would let Manon know in an instant that their son is alive. Then again, I'm not sure if Charles ever spoke to Manon about Finn and his supposed death."

"Oh my God…" Diana simply remarked, looking across to the city. "This is… amazing. Charles is going to absolutely flip when he finds out… and what about you? I can only imagine the impact this has had on you…"

"Impact? What impact?"

"What impact?" Diana questioned. "You mourned his death and it changed you… You can't expect me to believe that this hasn't had some sort of effect on you?"

Tristan shrugged.

"I mean, when I first saw him, I was more than surprised – I thought I was seeing a ghost. I still don't know if it's all real, but it is. I think I'm just shocked at it all…"

"You should be happy – boy, I would give anything if Moira were to talk to me again…"

"I'm relieved," Tristan admitted. "He's alive. He's not dead. He's alive."

"I'm not sure how I feel about lying to Charles about this…" Diana remarked. "It's wrong to withhold information like this to him…"

"You cannot tell Charles, please," Tristan said. "The only reason I'm telling you this is because you're my girlfriend. Finn told me to not tell a single other soul…"

Diana rolled her eyes.

"Charles is not going to be happy if he finds out that we knew this entire time…" Diana stated. "In fact, this might be the worst thing that we keep from him – worse than our own relationship."

"He's understanding," Tristan defended. "He might be so relieved to know that his son is alive that he might not even flinch at this. Besides, it's not like he's dead – he's alive. This is good news. If it were bad news, then I'd get your point."

Diana shook her head.

"It's wrong to lie regardless of the justifications or the circumstances," Diana said. "The action itself is a sin."

"I'm sorry I had to implicate you in this then," Tristan responded, sighing. "I just thought I should tell you if not someone."

Diana briefly closed her eyes and then looked to Tristan.

"I'm glad you told me," Diana said, taking his hand. "If you're not happy about this turn of events, then I'll be happy for you. This is good news, Tristan. He's your best friend and he's now also your roommate. How can you not be happy about that turn of events?"

Diana then took a deep breath and then exhaled.

"Yes, this is good," Diana repeated.

Tristan took his own deep breath and then let out a sigh. He leaned back against the roof and looked up to the dim twilight ceiling above him where there were some clouds and a few twinkling stars. Tristan looked at his deeply and brought a hand to his forehead, not letting go of the solemn expression on his face.

Act 3, Scene 1

Several weeks had passed since Diana and Tristan had met on that rooftop and it was now the end of another week at the start of October. Tristan and Finn were in their dorm and the sun had just set at around six o'clock. The room was heated not by entrapped heat from the sun, but by the heater below the window. Tristan was on his laptop, browsing social media, while Finn sat atop of his bunk bouncing a rubber ball back and forth. He looked through a list of people on the Class of 2024 group page on Facebook, stopping every once and a while to focus on the profile image of girls that were similar in appearance to that peculiar female. Finally, he stopped at the profile pic of a female known as Helen Coleman. The profile image was a bit more mysterious and he had to study it for a few moments before going on to others.

Helen Coleman did not have a lot of other images on her profile, partly due to restrictions that prevented non-friends from viewing her profile. Tristan looked back at her profile image and then typed the name into a search browser to see if there was more about this person. The search browser immediately corrected Tristan from Helen Coleman and gave him Helene Köhlen, which produced several results of a movie and TV show actress. Tristan eyes shot to the right where there was an image of this person. His eyes then widened as he saw the extent of this girl's beauty. The image that was given had the actress with silk-like smooth and straightened light brown hair. Her skin was also as light as it was when Tristan had seen her. She wore a sparkling champagne-colored dress with a black rim. Tristan checked several pages to learn more about this German-American actress.

Finn looked over to Tristan as he continued to bounce the ball. He then stopped and turned onto his side to peek over at what Tristan was looking at. His eyes then went to Tristan's phone as it vibrated. Tristan closed his Internet browser and picked up his phone. He looked at the text message that he received from Diana that read, 'I'm feeling a lot better – it sort of just came and passed.'

Tristan swiped right to unlock his phone and then began to respond to Diana. An earlier message from Diana from around eight o'clock in the morning said, 'Woke up feeling a bit down. I might have to cancel our date tonight…' and Tristan's response of, 'What are you feeling?' Diana replied, 'Nauseous. I think it might have been last night's dinner.' and later Tristan messaged, 'Are you still doing okay?' followed up by what he was messaging now, which was, 'Do you still want to go on our date?' However, Diana messaged before he sent his text, asking the same. Tristan hesitated to respond as he deleted his initial ask.

Finally, Tristan picked up his phone and replied, 'To be honest, I have a bit of work I need to catch up on… I've got a lab due next Wednesday and also a midterm coming up I need to study for. Let's reschedule when we're not swamped with exams. Okay?' Diana replied with a thumbs up and, 'Good idea. I should do some studying too haha.' She also said, 'I definitely will miss you though, but your classes are more important right now.' Tristan read these messages, but didn't respond. He instead sat his phone aside and then looked over to Finn who was looking at him.

"Can I help you?" Tristan questioned, slightly annoyed.

"No," Finn responded, lying back down again and continuing to bounce his ball.

"Don't you have some midterms to study for, quizzes to do, or anything?" Tristan questioned with an even more annoyed tone. "I never see you at your desk."

"Psh," Finn expressed, "no. I'm all caught up – it was all a piece of cake."

Tristan's frown deepened. He re-opened the Internet browser and closed the tabs about this Helene girl before returning to Facebook. He then scrolled through her page and noticed that he was attending an event later tonight. Tristan looked at the location and saw that it was nearby at the fraternity houses to the south of the campus. He clicked on the event and looked closer at the details. Only a student ID with the University of Harlech was required. Tristan scrolled through the rest of the event page and then returned to the main page. He then stood up and went to the bathroom to wash his face.

When Tristan returned to the bedroom, he sat down at his laptop for another couple of hours so that time could pass. At close to nine o'clock, he stood up from his chair and picked up his sweater from the foot of his bed and then looked up to Finn.

"I need some fresh air, so I'm going for a walk," Tristan said to Finn.

Finn, who was reading a book, sat up and looked back to Tristan.

"Hey, I'll come with you then," Finn encouraged.

"You don't have to come with me," Tristan insisted. "I mostly wanted to clear my head..."

"You can clear your head by bouncing back and forth with me," Finn replied. "Come on."

Finn hopped off his bunk and grabbed his pilot jacket. A black leather coat with Sherpa wool inside. He then went ahead to the door.

"Grab your keys, I'm leaving mine behind," Finn remarked.

Tristan looked at him begrudgingly and picked up his lanyard from his desk. He then followed Finn from behind and left with him. Finn stood next to the door as Tristan locked it. The pair then went down the corridor and towards the elevator, going into the staircase instead.

"Don't you have a date?" Finn asked.

"What?" Tristan questioned.

"With your girl? I saw your phone this morning…"

"Oh, yeah," Tristan replied. "No, we canceled. She wasn't feeling too hot."

"That's a shame," Finn responded. "Hasn't been a while since you last saw her?"

"Yeah, it has," Tristan replied, "but it's not your relationship so I don't know why you're so amped up about that."

"I'm not," Finn remarked. "I'm just pointing it out – also a little worried for you. Am I not allowed to be worried for my friend?

Tristan didn't respond. The two exited from the building through the fire escape and then came outside where it was bright because of the many lamps throughout campus. Tristan led Finn along the path from Residence B which took them to University Promenade. Afterwards, they proceed south down the promenade.

"So, what's on your mind?" Finn asked.

Tristan looked back at him. He shrugged.

"I was aiming for a chance to reflect on my own, not talk," Tristan stated.

"You can't talk to me?" Finn questioned, grabbing Tristan by the side. "You need to learn to open up a bit more, I think. I mean, we shared a tent together where we were side-by-side intimately; we shared a moment of terrorism together, and now we share a dorm together. What possible reason could you have for hiding something from me?"

Tristan looked back at him again, annoyed.

"Am I secretive, or is everyone else too invasive?" Tristan questioned

"Fair point," Finn replied, letting go, "but like I said, we're more than friends. We're brothers. Come on, what's really gnawing at you? Tell me."

Tristan sighed.

"I'm stressed," Tristan admitted. "I have a lot of exams coming up and so much to study – I don't know how anyone is expected to keep up with a workload like this. Not to mention the professor goes so quickly that they don't stop to explain, but assume you're on the same track. It's crazy!"

"Have you tried reaching out to any of your professors?" Finn questioned. "Had a chat with them? They're supposed to be there to help you understand if you don't."

"Not yet," Tristan replied. "None of them meet in person anyways because of the epidemic. It's all via video chat and I don't like that."

"I wish I could help, but we're not really in the same classes. Our calculus classes are different since I'm in one for physical sciences and engineering while you're in one for biological sciences. Even our physics classes are different since I'm in one for engineers."

"Chemistry is the biggest pain in my ass right now," Tristan complained, "next to calculus. Don't even get me started on calculus. Luckily this semester's chemistry class isn't a requirement for my degree, but is a requirement for my chemistry class next semester, which is required for my degree. Calculus is a requirement though, and so is physics and English.

The only class I'm doing alright in is my Introduction to Cellular Biology course."

"What's the program you want to get into?"

"CAPS," Tristan responded. "Cellular, Anatomical, and Physiological Sciences."

"Oh, right."

Tristan sighed as they reached the intersection with Queen Boulevard. The pair quietly crossed the street and proceeded down along the path before turning left at the side of the fields. The fields were brightly lit and sprinklers were hydrating the finely mowed grass. Tristan attempted to look across the field and over to the houses far on the other side. He then looked back to Finn and around their immediate area.

"It's important to remember and never forget that in this path we're on, we have to continually fight because life is a struggle," Finn remarked, eyeing some drunken students ahead running to the irrigation system and then grabbing Tristan by the shoulder again. "Look at these chumps – do you think they ever had to fight for anything in their life? Sure, they may have their struggles – everybody has their struggles, but not everyone has the will. It's important to never forget that – that the will is everything. Isn't that what I taught you?"

"You mostly taught me how to howl," Tristan replied, looking up to the sky where the full moon beamed down on them.

"Huh?"

Tristan stopped as he looked at the moon and then to Finn.

"Don't you remember? Before the… shooting, you howled at the moon and told me about how much you loved wolves."

Finn gave a soft smile to him and put his hands in his jacket pockets.

"You really remember that, huh?"

"Of course," Tristan replied. "How could I forget that or anything about the time we spent together?"

Finn looked back at Tristan and the genuine warm smile that he gave him.

"I remember you thought I was a loony," Finn remarked, continuing to walk.

"Maybe we're both loonies," Tristan replied, catching up with him to stop him, "but how about one good howl, you and me?"

Finn looked back at him and laughed.

"Are you actually mad?" Finn questioned.

"Aren't you a wolf anymore?" Tristan questioned. "Don't you have that raw spirit within you?"

Finn raised an eyebrow. He put his hands in his pocket.

"It was all a metaphor," Finn sheepishly explained. "For the state of mind that one had to enter in order to endure and fight, and for myself, to commit the acts I committed the next day. It was about perseverance and manipulating my morale – that's the sort of way my mind works."

"Aren't you a wolf?" Tristan asked again.

Finn looked back at him with slight disbelief. He looked to his side. Tristan looked at him with anticipation. Finn then looked to the ground. He then raised his head up as he howled. Tristan raised a smile and returned the favor by howling with him. Finn laughed and shook his head.

"You're unbelievable. You know that?" Finn said as he continued to walk. "I'm really glad that I went the effort to come all the way here…"

Tristan looked back at him with a smile. The two reached a crossroad over Davidson Avenue to the other half of the fields. Instead of crossing the street, Tristan took them further south towards the frat houses.

"Do you know what's another metaphor I think of that helps me get through it all?" Finn questioned. "Perhaps more than the simple idea of being in nature, it's the idea of being in the wild. It's one thing to be in the neck of the woods, but it's another to know that anarchy where men are truly free. It's something that I can come to appreciate from this New World that I never felt in England, or by extension, Britain. At its heart, all of this... all of this is about freedom, which some might see to be paradoxical, but it is. Freedom comes in many forms..."

"We're masters of our own fate," Tristan remarked to Finn. "We seek to aim for that freedom."

Finn looked over to the houses ahead of them where the loud booming sound of music originated from. There were various students ahead in front of the houses as well.

"There's an example of the paradox of freedom," Finn said. "People seemingly acting of their own freewill to engage in mindless acts of debauchery that enslave them."

"Why don't we head on over and have a peek at what it's all about?"

"What?" Finn questioned.

"Come on, let's scope it out – maybe teach them a lesson?"

"I'd rather not rack up a criminal record in the country I want to immigrate to," Finn replied.

Tristan scoffed and said, "There are a bunch of underage students at a fraternity party and you're concerned about getting caught for a little mischief? Come on, let's have a little fun..."

Act 3, Scene 2

Diana read Tristan's last message and saw that he had left her on 'Read.' She put her phone down at her side and then picked up her book, *The Forbidden Forest*, gifted to her by Miklos and Tanya, placing a bookmark halfway through and then setting it aside on her end table. On her end table there was a lamp, an empty glass, and package of anti-nausea medication. She then looked around her room.

Diana's dorm bedroom was smaller than Tristan and Finn's, but she did not have a roommate. However, she also did not have her own private bathroom, but she did have a sink in the corner of the room. Diana's dorm building was also a lot older and there were more cracks in the corners of the walls, dirtiness in the carpets in the hallways, and stains on the windows. Diana's dorm walls were painted a mustard yellow with white flatboards and mold crownings. Her bed was made of oak wood and the mattress loaded with springs that one could feel as tone laid atop of it. The bedroom included a desk with shelves above, an end table next to the bed, and a wardrobe in the corner. Diana's dorm was modestly decorated, but not overtly so.

Diana sat up and picked up the empty glass on her end table. She then went to the sink in the corner of her room to fill it up and take a sip. She then took the glass and went to the small window that looked out to the side of Declan Walham campus, which included the tall pine forest that the university existed amidst. Once the glass was empty again, Diana sat it down on the end table and sighed. She sat down at the side of her bed and then opened the drawer of her end table, which only had one drawer and a cabinet below. Inside, Diana kept her cherished Bible that she took with her from Allabrese as well as other personal effects, but there was nothing in there that she could make use of right now so she closed it.

Diana then looked across from her bed and to her desk where a set of keys sat next to her laptop. She stood up and went to them. One of the keys on the key ring was a key to the vehicle that she decided to have Charlemagne purchase for her. Diana stood up and went to pick up the set of keys. She then sat them down again and went to her wardrobe. She quickly got changed out of the sweatpants that she wore, but belonged to Tristan, and changed t-shirts for a cleaner one. She also took out her leather jacket and put it on. Diana then took the keys again, went to put on her shoes, and then exited the dorm.

From Diana's dorm, she went down a concrete bridge (most of Declan Walham was built out of concrete and the exterior of structures were pure concrete), and she came to a parkade nearby where her birthday present was parked. Diana took a set of stairs in the corner of the parkade down to the lower level and then turned around to where there were a series of small stalls for motorcycles next to handicap stalls. Amidst these stalls was a brand new luxurious motorcycle from the same Bavarian company as Charlemagne's black sedan. Diana approached the motorcycle and then detached the helmet on the side that was locked into the rear.

The motorcycle was a dark black and not a large bike. It was fairly slim parallel-twin engine dual-sport motorbike made in Germany. The engine capacity was 798 cc. The bike was approximately seven and a half inches in length and little over four feet in height. The seat height was less than three feet in height.

Diana placed her hands over the seat and then over the handles. She brought the helmet over her head and then sat down, switching on the engine and hearing the engine roar to life. Diana sat there for a few minutes, taking deep breaths. Finally, she switched gears and backed out.

"If Tristan's too busy to go out, then I'm going to go out on my own..." Diana muttered.

Once the motorcycle was backed out, Diana switched gears again and then proceeded to drive out of the parkade with care. She took the corners with the bike like someone who was still new to driving a motorcycle, but still knew what they were doing. Diana came down a ramp and then exited the parkade. She then turned left and began to drive through the campus, reaching a major road wrapped around the small campus, going south down the road to pass the fields before going downhill. The motorcycle shot along the road as Diana picked up her speed, the engine keeping up with her demand as they reached speeds on excess of 120 kilometers per hour, or 75 mph.

Diana slowed down as she reached the bottom of the hill and kept right to come onto Riverside Drive. A little further ahead she stopped in the left-most lane at a T-intersection with Shai Street where Riverside Drive ended. Once the lights changed, Diana turned left and continued southward down Shai Street as she entered into Lincoln with its many skyscrapers around.

Lincoln was similar to the downtown area, except it was smaller and slightly cleaner. Shai Street was a wide four-lane road with limitations on left-turns and then forked off at a wide roundabout that encircled a medium-sized circular park. At the outskirts of the roundabout were a series of three curved towers joined together by skywalks. The windows of the towers were translucent and tinted grey and was composed of at least fifty stories. The towers were also wide and large as they covered entire faces of the roundabout. At the southeast corner of where a fourth tower could have been built to complete an entire circle there was instead a large park that took the entire city block and connected to the park in the middle via a pedestrian bridge that went over the road. The towers were known as the Eclipse Towers and the park was known as Elizabeth Jarsdel Park.

Diana made her way around the roundabout once, passing the exit that shot off into the major streets known as W Lincoln Street, Bering Street to the south, and E Lincoln Street before coming back around to Shai Street. Diana exited onto W Lincoln Street and then continued down the curved road past the many skyscrapers, passing a green light at the intersection with the major road known as N Slade Drive to continue right at a fork in W Lincoln Street as she approached the highway. Diana maintained right and merged onto the on-ramp and then she came onto the highway going north to King Island.

On the highway, Diana picked up her speed again, going over thirty kilometers above the speed limit, which was the standard on the highway at this time. In fact, it was the average speed of most cars that she kept up with. The wind that passed Diana as she zipped along was strong. The highway curved leftward as it went around Saffron and then continued straight on approach to an exit just before Marke Bridge.

Diana passed the exit and then crossed the bridge. She was given a glamorous view of the downtown skyline from atop of the bridge where the lights of the condos on the seafront in Bromley mixed in with the even taller skyscrapers behind. Diana passed the exit that either went to Bromley or the south of the Industrial District, and instead carried on as the highway dipped down and became part of a trench in the midst of the city. The walls at the side of the trench consisted of concrete and above either side were cars that drove along a major road known as Main Street. There were no immediate exits from the highway as she drove through Central Harlech. Towards the end, the highway curved and rose up from the ground to return to its overpass form as she entered Camross. Diana passed the exit that went into Camross and towards King George VI Park, but then before she could go onto Penultimate Bridge, there was another exit at the very end of King Island, which she exited from and came onto Maiden Drive in Whitney Harbor.

Diana drove slowly down the road, past the waterfront park, stopping at a red light at a T-intersection with Durham Street on her right. She continued straight, but as she made her approach towards Hardwicke Street, she looked ahead with disdain. She turned right onto Hardwicke and continued up until she reached Main Street. She turned left and continued towards the end of the street at the T-intersection with Bailey Drive. She then turned right again and entered Bromley. Diana passed the intersection with Campbell Street and proceeded to approach Pentateuch Cathedral on the left.

Pentateuch Cathedral was a large Catholic church in Bromley before Bailey Drive. The cathedral was constructed in a French Gothic revival design with two towers at the side. The main doors into the church contained a tympanum and then a large circular rose window above. A small veranda set in stone existed before the entrance of the cathedral with stone steps that went up to this patio. There, there were benches and a pathway that went along the side of the cathedral to a small garden at the rear and the clergy house ahead, which was a small manor in the midst of the city. There were various condominiums built in the land around the cathedral as it was a hilled area between the road to the highway and the highway itself. On the other side at Bailey Drive there was the usual display of downtown with apartment buildings side-by-side, split only on occasion by alleyways and the streets.

Diana slowed down and then moved towards the curb to come to a complete stop. She looked ahead to the cathedral and heard the bells ring. She took off her helmet and looked at the church for a moment longer before she secured her helmet and then proceeded to cross the street. Diana walked up the steps of the church and noticed it to be quiet on the patio as there was nobody else around. She approached the large wooden doors and pulled the door open, allowing herself to come inside to the narthex. The space before the chapel was small and consisted of a small shop at the side that was closed. There were also two separate doors at either side that went into the separate towers. Diana stepped forward and came to the midst of the narthex, looking up as she got a better look of the old cathedral.

Diana's eyes then looked behind her as she spun around and heard the door into the chapel open. A gorgeous woman in a black dress and high-heels stepped out from the chapel. She had very light fair and smooth skin. She appeared to be at least ten years older than Diana. At her side she held a small black purse. Her lips were painted in red lipstick and cheeks were blushed. Her eyes were painted in mascara. Around her head she wore a mantilla, or type of face veil that covered her deep red hair colored similarly to Moira's hair.

The woman made her approach to the exit, but stopped as she noticed Diana looking at her. She looked down at Diana with intent and gave a modest smile.

"Do I know you?" the woman questioned in a foreign accent.

Diana wasn't able to determine from where this accent was from as it was from somewhere in Central or Eastern Europe. She shook her head.

"You look familiar to me," the woman stated. "I feel as though we have met... My name is *Iustina*. Is this your parish?"

"No," Diana denied. "I mean, it used to be. I've recently moved back to Harlech for school and I haven't been here in such a long time... I wasn't really a practicing Catholic back

94

then either, but I'm thinking of coming here to attend Mass now that restrictions are easing from the pandemic."

"This church certainly has its beauty," Iustina remarked. "Beauty that is slipping from the world.... You- you are a beautiful woman... What is your name?"

"Diana."

"You should be pleased with yourself and your beauty, Diana, because as beautiful women we have a duty to present ourselves accordingly to the eyes of the world who gaze upon us. Our beauty is a gift of God and it is a reflection of God."

Iustina looked at Diana and her hair as though she had noticed something.

"Are you about to enter the chapel?" Iustina questioned.

"I was thinking of going to do some praying," Diana replied in a quiet voice.

"Here," Iustina remarked, taking off her veil and presenting it to Diana. "Go on and take it. It's important to remember that although we are beautiful, it is important that we cover what may distract men in the house of worship for we are the glory of man, and man is the glory of God."

Diana took the veil. It looked expensive and brand new.

"I won't impose where you should attend Mass, but I will encourage you to travel to Lennox if you're able to, and attend the Mass at the Church of the Beloved Disciple in town. They have a beautiful Mass in Latin... Have you ever experienced a Mass in Latin?"

"Only once," Diana replied. "In the United States."

"You should come when their doors open soon," Iustina insisted. "Perhaps we will see each other there, if not here. I come here every once and a while for confession and to pray sometimes because it is more accessible to me. They used to offer Latin Mass here, but not anymore. However, this church is also one of the few that is still built facing east – it's hard to come by that as well."

"East?"

"To the east," Iustina explained. "It's important that we face east when we pray. Have you not heard of that?"

"I thought that was an Islamic practice," Diana replied.

"Muslims pray to the east because that is where Mecca is," Iustina replied. "We do not pray to the east because that is where Jerusalem is. Christians have held this tradition since before the Muslims, although the reasons have not been all that clear. It is a mysterious tradition, but some believe that this is the direction in which the Mount of Olives was in Jerusalem to which the disciples and later followers prayed to as they awaited the Second Coming. Another explanation is that the sunrise is symbolic of the rise of New Jerusalem over the dark days of that is the end of time."

Diana was silent.

"It would be a pleasure to speak more with you, Diana," Iustina remarked, opening her purse, "but I won't hold you any longer. I hope that we meet again."

Iustina gave a warm smile and then left the narthex. Diana looked at the veil in her hand and then over to the doors that went into the nave. She put it on and then walked over to the doors, dipping her hand into the Holy Water and then making the sign of the cross before she went inside to pray, facing the altar, which looked to the east.

Act 3, Scene 3

Finn and Tristan crossed Cole Avenue at the end of path besides Davis Field on the right and Sutherland Field on the left. The fraternity and sorority houses were stretched across a strip of land at the bottommost part of the campus, in front of a gated community behind along Coyle Street. To the left were the sorority houses, while on the right were the fraternity houses. Finn and Tristan crossed Davidson Avenue and went eastward along the sidewalk where various students could be seen going away from and towards the frat houses.

The screaming and shouting that came from these voluminous houses got louder as they got closer to the three homes that were hosting parties. The closest house, Kappa Phi, was a three-story home with loud rock music coming from within met with the banging of pots and pans. Finn and Tristan stopped and looked into the house from the windows and saw people lined up in a circle, shouting with the loud clank of metal, almost as if they were aiming to create as much noise as possible. The screaming was worse from the middle house, Delta Beta, which was accessible past a front garden that connected all three of these party houses. From this house, much was the same, except there was no banging of pots and pans, but the sight of lots of people drinking from the porch and within. The screaming was non-existent from the third house, Alpha Kappa, where instead there was the vibration of loud techno music and flashing of lights.

Tristan eyed this third house as it was the same house from the Facebook event post.

"Where do we begin, Tristie-boy?" Finn questioned, looking at all three houses. "House number one, two, or three?"

"Let's get one thing clear here," Tristan replied to him. "We're here for a bit of fun of our own. No homicidal terrorism, okay?"

"Well, that's taken a bit of the wind out of my sails," Finn sarcastically replied, patting Tristan on the back. "I knew what you were talking about, so let's go…"

The pair continued down the sidewalk and stopped before the archway that led into the front garden of the three houses. A fraternity brother stopped them before they could enter. He held a red cup in his hand, appeared to be a lot older than Tristan by his face and size, and was also significantly taller than the pair of them.

"Let's see some student ID," the fraternity brother requested.

Tristan took out his from his pocket and showed it, while Finn took his wallet out from his jacket and took out his own university ID. Tristan looked at Finn's ID as it quickly passed him, seeing that it had Finn's full legal name, Finn Louis Cunningham. The frat student allowed them to pass him, ushering them into the front garden. From there, they stopped in the midst and looked around. Tristan looked to Kappa Phi begrudgingly.

"Let's mess with those guys," Tristan suggested, looking around. "They seem obnoxious and wouldn't be missed."

"I like the way that you think," Finn responded, leading him towards the front door.

The pair entered the house and looked around at all the yelling students. The house lights were switched on and from the back of the large group in the large open space of the house were several students serving drinks where there were other students getting drinks in red cups from them. The pair moved over and attempted to remain discrete as they got drinks and then moved around the back of the large group to where there were a set of stairs.

Finn moved back and then proceeded up the steps. They stopped just at the bottom of a turn in the stairs as a heavy door opened ahead and three frat students came galloping down the stairs. Tristan watched them as they went down while Finn looked to the door that slowly began to close. He quickly went up once the boys were down and then grabbed the door to maintain it open. Tristan saw and followed. Finn led Tristan into the second-floor of the frat house where it was quieter.

Tristan observed the environment around him in the wide corridor that they had come to. The walls were tall and there was a sprinkler system and a vent system across the entire corridor below the ceiling that went into the separate room ahead. The pair were approximately in the middle of the house towards the west-side. A second door immediately next to them provided access to a second set of stairs that went up to the third-floor. At the end of the corridor, there was a small space or lounge towards the east-side of the house. The lights were dim across the entire corridor and it was dark up ahead. Tristan looked to Finn.

"Well, what then?" Tristan questioned.

"Let's split up," Finn suggested. "I need a better idea of the place we're working in. I'm going to check out the third-floor. Stay here and look around to make sure we're alone."

"And?" Tristan asked.

Finn shrugged and replied, "I don't know. Look for something that we can use – be creative. We'll meet back down here in a couple."

"Alright," Tristan responded.

Finn left him alone and then Tristan proceeded down the corridor. He came to the end and entered the small living space with a kitchenette at the side. At the other side of the house was a large flat screen TV with a video game console and large leather chairs. The room was amess with bags of chips, clothing and all sorts of garbage lying on the floor. Tristan looked around the immediate area with minor disgust and then moved to the kitchenette to look through the cupboards. The frat barely had any cups or anything in the bare cupboards over the sink. There were minor scraps of cooking ingredients, salt and other assorted items, and a few glass cups and mugs. Tristan opened the fridge and immediately closed it due to the smell that overcame him. He then crouched down and opened the cupboards below. Under the sink, he, perhaps ironically, found various cleaning items, including a bottle of bleach, an almost empty bottle of rubbing alcohol, and some ammonia. Tristan took a mental stock of the items in the cupboard and then stood up again. He began to open some drawers where he found some cutlery in one and another with a random assortment of items. Tristan rummaged through the drawer and managed to find some matches. He took them out and looked at them. The box was almost empty and there were about six left. He picked these six matches and laid them on the counter. He then continued to rummage through the drawer as he realized that a lot of the matches in the box must have fallen out as they were randomly around in the drawer. In total, he was able to collect about twenty-two.

Tristan quickly shut off the lights as he heard a noise from the other side of the corridor. He then peaked his head over and attempted to see what was going on ahead. Finn had returned from down the stairs. Tristan stepped out from the side and looked over to him. Finn waved over to him and signaled him to come over. Tristan grabbed the twenty-two matches and dumped them into his sweatshirt pocket. He then crouched down and picked up a bottle of ammonia from the cleaning supplies and then made his way over towards Finn. Tristan suddenly and quietly jumped back into the darkness as the door to his side opened.

A frat student left his room and proceeded down the corridor. Tristan's eyes widened and focused. He set down the bottle of ammonia on the counter and then began his approach from behind. Finn, who was hiding around the corner, peaked out as he saw this person on approach. He quickly took cover around the corner while Tristan moved in from behind and then grabbed the student before he could lay eyes on Finn. The student struggled as Tristan pressed his bicep into his arteries and within a few seconds, he passed out. Tristan then quietly laid him on the ground and began to drag him back to his room.

"Don't just stand there," Tristan whispered to Finn. "Help me!"

Finn moved in and began to help Tristan with moving the body back into the room and then closing the door.

"What the hell was that?" Finn questioned.

"What was what?" Tristan asked. "I've always known how to do that. My uncle was a police officer, remember?"

Finn looked at Tristan unconvincingly. Tristan walked back into the living room and picked up the bottle from where he had left it.

"I managed to find this and some matches," Tristan expressed. "If we mix this with the sulfate in them match heads, we should be able to make a *really* bad smell. What did you find?"

"Not much," Finn responded. "There's only one bedroom up there and then a mechanic room. If we mix these two though, we might be able to reach the entire house without dropping it off anywhere if we lower it into the vents. Hm…" he paused for a moment. "I have an idea. Come on."

Finn led Tristan upstairs and to the third floor. They entered the bedroom there and then went to the mechanic room that branched into the surrounding attic. The ceiling was low in this area and the sides of the attic consisted of the sloped sides of the roof. Finn took Tristan to a vent gate that went into a tunnel system along the floor. He crouched down and passed a hand through. Finn took out his smartphone and flashed a light down.

Tristan took a look and saw that the vent went forward and then dipped down ahead. Beforehand there was a fan blade that was motionless.

"I'm going to need a glass bottle, preferably a thin one," Finn said, looking at the ammonia. "I'm also going to need some string."

"There are a couple of beer bottles laying around downstairs," Tristan replied. "I'll also see about getting some string."

"Preferably some fishing wire," Finn clarified.

Tristan left and went back downstairs. He returned to the kitchen and collected two empty beer bottles he had seen on the floor. He then rummaged through the drawers to collect some thin canvas string. Tristan then returned upstairs where Finn was waiting.

Finn took one of the bottles and then raised it up. He dropped it from his hands and saw it shatter on the ground. Tristan flinched as it suddenly happened.

"What was that for?" Tristan questioned.

"I'm just testing the material," Finn replied. "Let's see those matches."

Tristan took the matches out from his pocket and placed them on the floor. Finn began to snap the heads of the matches off and then filter them into the second bottle. Tristan helped him and they easily fit them all in. Afterwards, with the cap ready, Tristan began to pour in the ammonia before Finn closed it.

Finn picked up the bottle and gave it a shake. The two solutions began to mix.

"Alright, so here's the plan," Finn stated. "I'm going to attach some string to the neck of this bottle, lower it down just over the edge and then tie it to the grate. When someone turns on the AC, such as ourselves before we leave, the fan will cut the wire and the bottle will drop and shatter as long as the drop is greater than four feet."

"Solid," Tristan replied, looking at the bottle.

"And we'll be far from the aftermath…" Finn noted. "First though, I need to measure how much of a drop we have."

Finn picked up a socket wrench from the floor and began to tie some string around it. He then tossed the wrench through and began to gently lower it. The wrench hit the sides of the thin metal walls and made some minor noises, but Finn was not concerned. He lowered the string down and down until it finally hit the bottom at almost three meters. Finn then withdrew the tool and took off the string. He proceeded to apply a shorter length of less than a meter and tied it to the other side. Finn promptly left to retrieve a hockey stick from the other room and use it to push the bottle down until it hung from the edge, waiting to drop.

"Perfect," Tristan noted.

"Yeah," Finn replied. "Let's get out of here…"

The pair of them left the attic and returned downstairs. Finn stopped on the second-floor and eyed the heating and air-conditioning knob.

"You go," Tristan said, moving his hand to the knob. "Get a head start and I'll meet you back at the dorm, okay? We better split up, right? Here."

Finn looked at him and nodded. He took Tristan's dorm key. "It's been a pleasure scheming with you," Finn remarked.

Finn proceeded down the stairs and Tristan waited a few minutes before he turned the knob and then heard the shatter of a bottle from the echoes in the vents. Tristan cringed at the sound and then proceeded downstairs. He quickly left the house from around the back, but did not go all the way down the alley to a gate that exited off the property. Instead, he went around the backside of the house and returned to the front garden of the village.

Act 3, Scene 4

Tristan looked over to Alpha Kappa and then turned around to Kappa Phi as he heard the shouting stop and be replaced by uncomfortable chatter as people began to filter through. Tristan took a step back as he noticed crowd of people exiting from the house and then heard some loud boyish shouts. Tristan then turned around and quickly went through the front door of Alpha Kappa.

Tristan stopped in the middle of the foyer and looked around. Alpha Kappa was different from the former frat house as it had a small foyer that went into separate rooms at all five-sides, including the ceiling. To the left there was a room where there was a large dance floor with people dancing to the tune of a loud DJ. Bright lights flashed from that room, while from the other more people could be seen dancing and drinking. A set of stairs went to a balcony above that went to the rooms upstairs. There were a couple of boys loitering by the railing looking down. Tristan also observed there to be some awkward boys standing in the corner, sheepishly drinking beer from red cups.

A couple of young girls in less than modest clothing passed Tristan and made a glance towards him. They giggled as they passed him and then disappeared to the back. Tristan went to the left room and went to get himself a drink. He downed the first drink quickly and then got a refill before he began to circle the entire first floor of the house, eyeing every person he came across in the darkened house as he attempted to identify Helene amongst them. Another pair of three girls looked at Tristan from a corner as he passed a room in the top right corner. He then went around the side of the DJ room and returned to the foyer.

Tristan made another pass before returning to the foyer, stopping under a door frame. He looked both sides and took a deep breath.

"This is hopeless," Tristan muttered. "I shouldn't be here."

Tristan turned around again and looked to the corner of the bottom left room. He then eyed a girl talking with two other girls before making her approach away from them. She held a red cup in her hand and was dressed in a pinstripe white dress with a black bow around the waist. Unlike the way Tristan saw her in lectures, she didn't wear a hat over her head, but instead her silk-like light brown hair was at its freest.

Helene waved goodbye to the girls that she was with and then passed Tristan, ignoring him as he looked at her. She moved into the foyer and then went up the stairs. The boys at the railing had left. Tristan stepped into the foyer and looked at her. She disappeared to the right-side of the second floor. Once she was out of sight, Tristan followed from behind and then peaked around the corner. Helene disappeared through a door on the right again, but didn't close the door.

Tristan walked forward and made his way towards the door she had gone through. The door had been left ajar with the lights on. Tristan approached the door and then flipped around to the other side as he peaked in. He then gave an embarrassed look as he realized that the room was a bathroom, but his expression soon turned to shock as he looked at Helene through the door.

Helene had her mouth wide open in front of the mirror where she showed sharp fang-like upper canines, which gave her an appearance like a vampire. Tristan's eyes widened and then looked down to the counter next to her where there was a vial of a reddish-black liquid sitting atop. The breath from Tristan's mouth caused the door to widen slightly, which gave off a creaking sound. Helene's eyes shot towards the door, but Tristan quickly rushed out of the way and returned back downstairs.

Tristan noticed behind him the door open wide and a woman rush out. By the time Tristan was downstairs again, however, Helene was stopped before she could reach the stairs by the same group of three frat students that had been loitering by the railings earlier.

"Hey, what are you doing up here, sweet cheeks," a frat student taunted.

Tristan turned around and looked as Helene was confronted by these three men. She took a step back.

"Do you think it's funny? Perving on a woman when she's in the bathroom?" Helene questioned in her North German accent.

"You should watch the way you speak to us," one of the students warned in a threatening manner.

"Yeah, you should do something about that attitude of yours," another cautioned.

"Anyways, babe," the third frat student said. "What are you doing up here? You should be down there where we can all appreciate you."

Helene stepped forward and slapped the man. He caught her hand afterwards and looked at her menacingly.

"Hey!" Tristan shouted from below. "Ease off her!"

The frat student let go of Helene as Tristan rushed up the stairs. Tristan caused him to back up a step as he rushed towards him.

"I don't think I will, chum," the frat student replied. "You think you're tough, posturing up to me? Back off, you simp."

Tristan caught the man's hands as he was about to push him back. Tristan exerted his own force against him and threw him back against the wall in a brutish manner. Helene stepped back as it happened. The other two looked at their friend and then looked over to Tristan begrudgingly. Tristan raised his hands up and took a ready stance as the others raised their fists.

The second frat student threw a punch to Tristan, which he caught and then threw back. Tristan then went in and grabbed his arm, raising it up and kicking him down onto his knees. He then bashed his head into the railing before tossing him over. Tristan ducked before the first frat student could punch him. He then stood up and grabbed his arm, picking him up by the torso and then throwing him over the railing. The first frat student smacked onto the floor below, causing some people below to scream.

Tristan was panting by the end of the brief fight. He looked at all three of the frat brothers and then behind him to Helene who simply looked back at him, stunned. Tristan soon realized that onlookers were looking at him from below, which forced him to move out of the way and downstairs. He left the house, the property, and then came to the sidewalk where he began to pick up a light jog as he made his way away from the frat houses, especially as he saw flashing sirens from behind.

Act 4, Scene 1

Tristan sat in the cafeteria of above the commonplace, towards the far corner furthest from the canteen at a wide booth table with half the seats against the wall in the form of an elongated sofa. He sat with his arms crossed, a serious face, and tired eyes. Before him was his open laptop, while to his side were some notebooks and textbooks as well as some different colored pens. Tristan looked straight at his laptop as he listened to Charlemagne speaking to him via video chat.

Charlemagne could be seen in a small window on Tristan's laptop from his study at the manor house in Allabrese. He sat with his hands together before him, fingers intertwined, but hands flat.

"If you have any more questions about those models, feel free to ask me," Charlemagne stated. "I'm always happy to lend a hand – it's been remarkably quiet without either you or Diana here."

Charlemagne moved his hands apart and picked up a glass off camera with some scotch and ice.

"Thanks, Charles," Tristan remarked. "You've been a big help, really…"

"Don't feel discouraged," Charlemagne replied. "I didn't know all the answers. I had to learn, and the best learning is done the way we've done it now. The best learning has always been the tutor-mentor model… It's been the basis of craftsmanship for thousands of years, and since I've taught you properly (which your professor has failed to do), you now know something that is very complicated."

Tristan gave a light smile.

"You sure do know how to make me feel better about myself," Tristan replied.

"How have you been otherwise?" Charlemagne questioned. "Have you been sleeping okay? Eating? How's the dorm?"

"Yeah, I've been okay. I mean, I'm eating – I can't promise you that I'm sleeping a lot, but I do sleep at least a couple hours a day. The dorm is fine…"

"What about your roommate? You haven't told me much about him, or her… I imagine they paired you with a boy."

"Yeah, they pair you up with the same-sex," Tristan responded. "F- fine. He's been fine."

"That's good," Charlemagne expressed, sitting back. "I'm glad to hear that."

"Hey, Charles?" Tristan asked. "I have one more thing to ask from you…"

"What is it?"

"In your long life, and all the strange, morbid things that you've come across as we've come across, such as Yetis, aliens, and cults, have you ever come across something as bizarre as vampires?" Tristan questioned.

"Vampires?" Charlemagne repeated, stroking his chin. "What has you thinking about vampires?"

"It's just an inquiry," Tristan remarked. "It's part of my English class and I was hoping to do some real-life influences to beat around that."

"Hm," Charlemagne responded. "You shouldn't look into that, Tristan. It's not very politically-correct content and it could get you removed from school."

"Huh?" Tristan replied. "What do you mean?"

Charlemagne struggled to answer and then replied, "To answer your question, no, vampires do not exist, or at least as we know, or read, or see them on the TV. All of this nonsense about fanged individuals that can turn into bats is utter bollocks. Instead, the myth comes from ancient beliefs in medieval times that came from horror stories of blood ritual sacrifices, the drinking of human blood, and such. The majority of these actions of which were committed by Jews and are described as 'blood libel,' today. Of course, for this reason the mention of Jews and these roots of the tale could get you suspended, so this is between you and me only."

"Yeah," Tristan agreed, looking to his side.

Tristan was more or less alone in his immediate area. The volume projecting from his computer was quiet.

"These blood libels are dismissed as anti-Semitic, and nobody really cares about them anymore except, well, I suppose, Anti-Semites and Jews. However, there is some truth to these ancient tales from medieval times, such as the fate of Little St. Hugh in England, St. William in Norwich, or St. Simon of Trent, and so on, various infant children who had been kidnapped by a group of Jews, tortured, and sacrificed. For this reason, and many other reasons across Europe, Jews were expelled for their actions, one-hundred-and-nine times, but that is beside the point..."

"Why?" Tristan questioned.

"Hm?"

"I mean, why do they do that? It doesn't make any sense why people do these things..."

"Because they're not people, Tristan. I mean, the people who do these things are not people. They're monsters," Charlemagne remarked. "You know that. You've seen that. However, I can understand your perplexity. The group of people in this medieval time we know as the Jews are the same people who only a couple hundred years ago had been kicked out of Judea and rejected Christianity. They feared the change that had come and despised it in all its roots. These people are the descendants of the Pharisees that had Christ crucified. A vendetta against

Christianity has always existed between the Jews against the Christians, in this sort of feud between these two groups that even goes on today... even if Christians have become limp. The Catholic Church used to hold in doctrine that Jews were responsible for Christ's death and that this fact should be held against them until the 1960s – that turbulent time in which the Second Vatican Council overturned that sentiment in face of the Second World War."

Tristan gave a deep sigh and replied, "Okay... but what about all this 'blood libel' and bloodsucking crap? You said this still goes on today, didn't you?"

"Reports of this practice have been recorded since the start of the last century, and before then well-recorded into the (ignored) fabrics of history, but in recent times has become a sort of 'conspiracy theory.' However, and of course, while we have talked about Jews, the ritual today is not exclusive to them nor is it specific to them, but has become and always been a sort of satanic practice of the elite, and elite among Jews. It would not surprise me to know if those people that I had seen at Isla Paraiso also partook in this vulgar act. The most recent research into the practice, and possibly the current reason for its practice, comes to the theory of the harvesting of a chemical known as adrenochrome, which becomes potent in the blood of a victim who is in a state of fight or flight. The adrenaline releases into the blood and forms this chemical and it is thought that when blood is collected from a suffering victim, it is rich in the blood and can be consumed to give a euphoric high. Of course, it is empirically accurate to suggest that blood becomes potent with this chemical when in a state of adrenaline, but whether it gives off the euphoric effects when consumed... even I have no idea because it is so morbidly horrid that nobody in their right mind would test it out. However, some rumored tests state that consumption of this substance really does give off a high similar to LSD. Some other rumors around this drug also state that the elite of the world practice these same blood rituals as in the past to collect this blood, and in return it gives them mortality. Come to think of it, while Kau's motives for practicing human sacrifice may have been revealed in court to be because of psychodrama, I would not put it past him to have been into that sort of thing."

Tristan didn't respond. Instead, he kept his arms crossed in a slightly uncomfortable manner.

"Anyways, the point is that these are the roots of the vampire myth. In it is also the overlap in the idea of the 'Wandering Jew,' which connects to the curse of Cain, Ham, and Esau, which provide a lot of overlap with the stereotypical vampire you see in Dracula as an outsider suffering from persecution."

"Right..." Tristan replied, tired. "Alright, thanks. That's been... a really informative lecture. Maybe you should be doing the teaching over here, Charles..."

Charlemagne smiled.

"Sorry I had to ruin your English topic for you," Charlemagne replied. "I hope you can still write a paper on the topic without getting suspended because of me."

"Don't worry about it, Charles," Tristan assured him. "Listen though, I got to go. I'm dead-tired, and thanks to you, I might be able to sleep early."

"Well, in that case, I hope I haven't given you any nightmares," Charlemagne remarked. "Goodnight, Tristan... Oh! And do not forget that I'll be in Harlech on Saturday to have lunch with you and Diana. Do not forget it!"

"I won't," Tristan assured him. "Goodnight, Charles. See you in two days."

Tristan brought his laptop screen down and then started to pack his stuff into his backpack. Once he was done, he took his backpack and then proceeded to cross the cafeteria before looking into the kitchen as they were about to close. Tristan re-entered the canteen and made his way to order some food from the fast food kitchen. He put in his order for some curly fries and then waited while the chef finished grilling a hamburger. Tristan mindlessly waited with his head up as if he was about to fall asleep, or was dazed. He then jumped as he felt a hand on his shoulder. Tristan looked behind him as he gave himself some space.

Helene looked back at him.

"Sorry," Helene apologized. "I didn't mean to startle you."

Helene spoke in an elegant German accent, speaking English without a single struggle or flaw. Tristan simply looked back at her with shock as she spoke.

"You're that boy, aren't you? The one from the party earlier this month…"

"My name is Tristan," he said in a surprised voice.

"I'm Helene," she greeted, offering her hand. "Or perhaps not."

"Curly fries," the chef said, placing a bag atop of the display glass.

Tristan went to pick them up.

"I wanted to give you my thanks for what you did the other day," Helene expressed.

"Thanks?" Tristan questioned.

"I'm usually not too eager to see a boy defend me like that, but you gave those jerks what they deserved," Helene said. "Thank you for that."

"You're welcome," Tristan quietly replied, holding the bag of curly fries in his hand.

Helene began to twirl her hair. Tristan eyed her mouth and then looked back at her green eyes.

"If you're not busy this weekend, would you like to maybe go out for dinner sometime?" Helene proposed.

"Dinner?" Tristan questioned.

"Yes, dinner," Helene repeated with a smile. "Are you interested?"

"Dinner..." Tristan repeated again, looking to the side. "I can't... I'm having dinner with my – my family on Saturday, and then I have a midterm on Monday."

"Okay," Helene responded. "What about Friday? You can't say 'No,' to Friday, can you?"

Tristan looked at Helene's mouth again as she spoke. Her mouth was normal and her canines were flatter than Tristan's two upper meat-eaters. Tristan then looked up to her eyes again and her light brown hair. She had a coy smile on her face and her cheeks were blushed. Tristan was lost in her eyes, however.

"Yeah..." Tristan quietly agreed. "How about that..."

Helene giggled.

"Friday it is then," Helene replied. "Do you live in Residence A?"

"2A," Tristan said.

"I actually live in Residence B, across from here, but I just came over because your after-hours marts has the candy that I like..." Helene said.

"Yeah?"

"Anyways, I'll text you before our date," Helene remarked. "What's your number?"

Helene handed Tristan her cellphone. Tristan took it into his other hand. He then looked at the numbers and he sheepishly put in his cellphone number in. Helene looked at the area code.

"You're not from here?" Helene questioned.

"No," Tristan replied. "I'm from Alberta – to the east from here."

"How interesting," Helene flirted. "I'll see you on Friday then, Tristan. Talk to you later..."

Helene then placed two fingers on her lips and blew a kiss towards Tristan. Tristan's heart became flushed and he watched her off, around the opposite-corner that went to the exit as she went around near to where Tristan was sitting earlier as there was a mart that opened at nine o'clock that connected to the fast food kitchen and where people could make late dinner orders. Helene presumably went there, while Tristan went to pay for his cold fries.

Once Tristan had left the commonplace, he walked back to his dorm, awestruck and continually stunned, walking past the common room where Finn was with some of his newer friends from his faculty, studying. He ignored them and went straight to his room, walking to his bed and placing the fries over his desk. He took out his phone, looked at it, and saw that he had no new messages. Tristan then flinched as he received a text message from an unknown number that said, "Hey, Tristan! It's me, Helene!" followed by an emote with its tongue sticking out. Tristan let out a sigh and then sat down. He then picked up his phone.

Act 4, Scene 2

Diana answered Charlemagne's video call and looked to her laptop screen as his face appeared before her. She gave a warm smile and waved back to him through her webcam camera.

"Hi, Charles," Diana said in a soft voice. "How are you?"

Diana sat in her dorm, atop of her bed with her laptop on her lap.

"I'm quite alright," Charlemagne answered. "I had just finished speaking with Tristan as I was tutoring him on some chemistry models he was struggling with, and then our conversation sort of detracted onto the topic of vampires, and now I'm here, speaking with you."

"Vampires?" Diana questioned. "How did that come up as a topic?"

"He basically wanted to know if they were real, if I knew anything more than the average person might know, and I told him what I knew. I told him that they're not exactly real, but that they're based on old tales of bloodthirsty parasites that used to prey on young women and children, which resulted in their persecution."

"Hold on, what do you mean?" Diana questioned.

Charlemagne let out a sigh.

"I don't think I have the energy to repeat what I said to Tristan," Charlemagne confessed, laughing. "In short, I told Tristan that the people we had seen at Waomoni's mansion are the same sort of people who practice vampire-like actions through human sacrifice and the harvesting of adrenaline-rich blood for consumption as a psychotic stimulant."

"Oh…" Diana responded. "Of course, his mind must be focused on that stupid island still…"

"No, I believe his curiosity came from an English paper he thought to write about the origins of vampire myths on," Charlemagne defended.

"Hm," Diana responded. "Maybe my mind is still on that island then... I definitely won't forget what we saw at the mansion... and then there's that story the chief told us before we left."

"What story?"

"The one about the shapeshifters that came to the island and began to prey on the people, women, and children," Diana replied. "I've always felt it to be a metaphor for the sort of things that we had uncovered, and now that you mention vampires, perhaps the two are interconnected."

"Perhaps in one way or another," Charlemagne remarked, clearing his throat. "Anyways, what's new with you? How's your semester gone so far?"

Diana reflected a warm smile again.

"It's going," Diana confessed. "I'm almost done. I have no more midterms, but I do have two papers due next month. I've been able to manage my time effectively, and that's really helped me stay on top of my work."

"Good," Charlemagne replied. "Very good."

"I'm not fetching the best grades, but that hasn't bothered me. I'm passing all my courses, so I'm happy."

"I'm glad you are, but has anything you've taken interested you in the slightest? Perhaps given you a sense of idea in what you want to take on as a career?"

Diana thought for a moment as she looked across the room. She then looked back to Charlemagne and raised her shoulders up and down, shaking her head.

"I'm sorry, but to be honest, I don't think I have any vocation," Diana remarked, giving off a sigh. "I'm only really interested in my literature course, but that's expected. I could never make a living off of being interested in books. I'm not a writer either. I have no skills in storytelling whatsoever."

Diana sighed.

"I don't think I'm meant for anything, to be honest, except to be a mother, which I hope one day to do..." Diana said.

Charlemagne took a deep breath.

"It's difficult to know what you're interested in, especially when your own parents never made careers for themselves for you to understand what it is that you'd strive well in. My family, for example, have always been the way we were – entrepreneurs foremost with an interest in helping others out. You though, you come from a royal bloodline. Leadership is in your blood, as well as integrity and faith. You have a special bloodline, Diana. Never forget that."

Diana raised her smile again.

"I'm not a leader," Diana modestly replied.

"You've shown remarkable leadership and initiative in your part-time work as a lifeguard from what I've heard, and don't forget that you were once also one of the finest athletes in Allabrese when you used to race with that horse of yours."

"How's Zephyr? I miss him a lot... I haven't seen him in almost half a year!"

"Zephyr is well... I'm sure he misses you too."

Diana sighed.

"Maybe you're right," Diana remarked, "about my family path, but being a monarch isn't a realistic job expectation. I can't strive to become the queen of an entire kingdom, and it's not like my ancestors beyond my great-grandfather ever held jobs other than being the king or queen of England."

"Don't be so sure," Charlemagne responded. "They were political leaders, military leaders, and many living descendants of other former monarchs have turned to business and taken their skills to the global market. There, they've been able to continue their thrill-seeking games of conquest and domination, but in a less violent way. For us men, the path has always been clear for us… Of course, I had my grandfather's direction, but my father was less sure. His time with Cabernet Industries, in his opinion, were wasted years where he attempted to help people, but never felt satisfied by the results. My mother and grandmother's interest have always been in the family, especially my grandmother who made the home her territory more than my mother. In the end, this path is what a woman fits naturally in. Diana, whatever path you seek to take is your decision, and I know wholeheartedly that you will make the right decision because you're a clever girl. You don't have to finish university either if you don't think that this degree benefits you or interests you in anyways. However, I will encourage you to think more about yourself, who you are, and what it is that impassions you for you to set your heart on that. If children with Tristan is what you want to focus on, then by all means place your energy into raising your children with him. I know for sure that if you choose to do that, you will have very lucky children. However, my intentions in sending you to school have always been with an idea in my about expanding your skillset and knowledge for better or for worse. In other words, I've wanted you to expand yourself because an expanded women is worth double to her children than a woman who has no experience in anything at all."

"I want to have kids," Diana confessed, "but I feel like I'm getting ahead of myself in that regard and that you're right. I'm too hasty and need to be like Tristan – preparing myself for what is to come by 'expanding' myself. I know Tristan doesn't want to be a father right now, and he shouldn't be one either. His entire mindset is in getting to a point where he can support us independently, and that'll be in years to come."

Diana sighed and looked back to Charlemagne.

"Thanks for this insight," Diana admitted. "It's been nice being able to talk to someone about this and get some reflection. I haven't really been talking to anyone because of the pandemic restrictions, and it's been a bit lonely..."

"What about Tristan? You are still talking to him, right?"

Diana hesitated to respond. She looked down at the keyboard and then back to Charlemagne.

"The last time I talk to him was about three weeks ago..." Diana confessed.

"What?" Charlemagne questioned. "Are you serious?"

"He's been busy," Diana deflected. "I've been busy. We were supposed to go on a date at the start of the month, but that's been postponed indefinitely, or until further notice."

Diana sighed.

"I haven't been that worried about him because I trust that he's in good hands with his roommate, but at the same time now that I'm talking to you about it, all of the anxiety is coming back to me..." Diana remarked. "I should probably message him..."

"Yes, you should," Charlemagne replied. "From what I've seen from him, he is focused on his studies, but you are not doing him any favors by leaving him alone," he said. "One is never too busy to reach out to the ones that they love. If I could speak to him just now, so can you."

Diana did not respond.

"You are the sole key to Tristan's subconscious," Charlemagne stated. "If you don't speak to him so that he can drain his inner thoughts, then the bubbles will simmer and he'll start to lose touch with reality. Do not forget what that boy has been through over the last year... and more-so, don't forget what this boy's brain is like. If he has not spoken to you, it could be more than just forgetfulness."

Diana did not respond to that either. Instead, she picked up her phone and began to send Tristan a message.

"Please speak with him," Charlemagne requested. "I had no idea you've been so distant – this distance isn't good. Even I'm now worried for him even though I had just seen him."

Diana put her phone away.

"I just sent him a message," Diana responded. "Aren't we meeting this Saturday for lunch anyways?"

"Yes," Charlemagne replied. "We are, but even then, please speak with him beforehand just to be safe. I'll be in touch. I'm going to leave so that you can focus on this task at hand. Goodnight."

"Goodnight," Diana responded.

Charlemagne hung up and left Diana alone. She looked to her phone and saw that she hadn't received a response yet. She picked up her phone and then began to phone Tristan. Diana sat at her bed. No response.

Diana put her phone down and became whiter than usual. She stood up and went to get a glass of water. She then sat down and looked towards her phone.

"Dammit..." Diana cursed, picking up her phone again.

Diana attempted to phone Tristan again, but when he didn't pick up, she dropped her phone on her bed and then growled.

"Okay..." Diana muttered. "It's fine..."

Diana picked up her phone again and sent Tristan another text message that said, "I want to make sure you're doing alright and breathing. Please message me back when you can. Love you," followed by a heart emote. Diana then turned off her phone and sat it down at her bed. She proceeded to pace the room as she waited for a response.

When almost half an hour passed, Diana looked more than worried. She appeared as though she might cry. She took a deep breath and then picked up some clothes to get changed. She found her leather jacket, put it on, and then took her wallet and phone with her as she left the dorm.

Diana drove off from the university and swept through the island at a hefty speed. Finally, she arrived at the outskirts of Pentateuch Cathedral in Bromley where she went to and entered inside. Diana began to shed tears as she stepped through the narthex. She quickly tied her hair into a ponytail and then brought the veil that Iustina had gifted to her over her head, covering her hair before she entered into the nave. Diana dipped her two fingers into the holy water and then made the sign of the cross. She then proceeded down the aisle and came to a pew at the front of the church. Diana knelt down to make the sign of the cross again and then sat down.

A faint tune of some organ music could be heard in the ambience. Other than that, it was more or less silent. Diana whimpered and kept her head down. Tears rushed down her eyes. She then looked forward towards the aisle and up to a representation of Christ on the Cross. The sound of footsteps could be heard behind Diana as she wept. The footsteps presented in a manner as though they were high-heels.

Diana looked to the side and found herself in the company of the mysterious woman, Iustina. Today, she wore a fashionable white blouse with a matching skirt and dark leggings. The edges of the suit blazer and skirt were bordered in a solid black. The blazer was worn like a cape around her shoulders. At her left shoulder were the straps of a matching purse. She wore black high heels and a wide-rimmed hat that covered her head. Diana looked at her and wiped the tears from her face.

"Why are you crying, child?" Iustina questioned, placing a hand on her shoulder.

"It's really complicated," Diana confessed, looking forward.

"That is just a deflection by your words," Iustina replied. "Tell me what burdens you…"

Iustina knelt down and made the sign of the cross. She then sat down next to Diana. Diana let out a sigh and then proceeded to explain her situation, starting with the recent months and then going back into the past year and then the year before that with Tristan. She finished off by wrapping up the entire past two years with the present, explaining her anxiety and her loss of control in the situation with Tristan. Iustina did not interrupt throughout the explanation, but did ask occasional questions as she listened to her story.

"I feel as though I've brought this upon myself," Diana remarked. "It's been nice in a way being apart because I haven't had to focus so much, but at the same time, I feel like I've been neglecting my duties to him and avoiding the problem just like he has. I thought I was better than this – I was trained to be better than this. I confronted these problems, my inner demon, last year, and I felt better, but now it's all coming true… my worst fears, and it's horrible."

Iustina took a deep breath. Diana lowered her head as she continued to cry.

"Tell me, my child," Iustina remarked. "How important is God to you?"

Diana raised her head up and looked back at her.

"M-more important than anything, I suppose."

"And what do you believe it is that Christ wants from a child of His like yourself?"

"I- I suppose my total devotion to him?" Diana answered, "but…"

"My dear Diana, you have not given to Christ what is rightfully owed to Him. What I have heard from you is a beautiful tale, but it is also a confession of a relationship that was doomed to fail from the start. What you have told me is that since the age of fifteen, you have been in a premarital sexual relationship with a boy that you have also cohabitated with for the last two years. Although as you have expressed to me that a lot of good has come from this relationship, in particular to the healing and comfort that you have felt since the loss of both your parents, you have replaced a dependence on the love of your mother onto the love of this boy. The only love that we can depend on is in Christ, my child, because Christ will never fail us. The good that have received from this relationship with this boy you must take with you to the next destination in your life's journey, but you must also realize the wrong that was in this relationship. The mysteries and joys of marriage have been spoiled for you and left nothing behind. This boy, if he truly loved you, would not have placed you in this situation that you are in – of desperation and fear. And that is another point… you have fallen in love with a boy, and not a man. How could you have expected to meet the next point in your life with a person like this? The only reason why your relationship has succeeded has been in these temporary circumstances where the two of you, of conflicting personalities, have been together in unison under the guardianship of this Charlemagne. The instant that the two of you separated, you entered into a state of your natural selves where he has come to avoid you, while you have entered into despair. While you expressed to me that you confronted this inner demon earlier this year, since then, you have not made the changes that you could have made, and instead given this demon space to rise up again, but there is good news. While you have defeated this demon of yours once, it has not fully developed so it is easier to smite the second time. You have that chance, and I encourage you to take that change to right the wrongs and do what it is that Christ would want from you?"

"Would Christ want me to leave Tristan?" Diana questioned with immense fear.

"Christ wants you to understand what is truly important," Iustina replied. "He asks us to be in a state of preparation where we are willing to abandon all of our worldly possessions in a heartbeat in order to follow him. For some, such as St. Francis of Assisi, this is a necessary sacrifice in our lives to make to show our devotion and to prove to Christ our love to Him. For others, it is not a necessary sacrifice to make because there are some that do not value the material, worldly things, such as objects and people, more than Christ and would easily make this sacrifice, but do not have to. Christ does not want us to abandon what we have unless it is necessary, is the point. The same was true for Abraham, whose test of faith was in sacrificing his son Isaac, but when Abraham proved his devotion, God stopped him and blessed him and his descendants. Therefore, if this boy that you love is an obstacle to your love of Christ, which from what I have heard, it is, then it is the choice you must make. He will make his way in the world, and from what I have also heard, he is not worthy of your love and devotion. He is a boy, not a man, and remember, women were made for men, not boys. Mothers are meant for boys and that boy needs his mother, and not a wife."

Iustina looked forward.

"In your search for what Christ wants, you need not look too far, but only towards the Holy Mother, sweet Diana. You seek to become a mother, but you are not ready. The path to motherhood is a noble path. The Holy Mother placed her faith in God and love in her son before her husband. If you wish to become a mother, you must be willing to do the same and cannot place your partner between the two. You must love your future child as Mary loved her son, with the same faith in God, and if your man is as faithful as Joseph was called to be, then you will have the blessed family you desire. You cannot, however, interfere in the life of Joseph for it was not Mary's place. Instead, Holy Gabriel went to Joseph and spoke with him, and when Joseph received the strength to understand his calling, he returned to Mary and never parted from her side or in her son's side."

Diana's phone vibrated. She took it out from her jacket and looked at the message on her screen from Tristan, which simply read, "I'm alive." Iustina saw and placed a hand on Diana's shoulder.

"If you truly love Christ, you will do what is necessary," Iustina remarked. "Place your life and sufferings in God's hands and trust in him. He will guide you…"

Diana looked to her phone and at Tristan's message. Another tear rolled down her cheek. Iustina stood up and looked to Diana.

"Do what you must, child," Iustina remarked. "May the Lord be with you."

Diana nodded and she was left alone. She put her phone away and continued to look forward. She took a deep breath and brought her hands together. She then knelt down onto the kneeler and began to pray for guidance from the Holy Spirit.

Act 4, Scene 3

Tristan met with Helene on Friday evening at her dorm at Residence B. He dressed himself in a polo and in jeans, and knocked on her room. The door opened and Helene stood before him in a sparkling crème-colored dress that went just over her knees. Her hair was straightened and fell on one side. Tristan looked at her with a plain, but astonished face.

"How do I look?" Helene questioned.

"You look," Tristan responded, hesitating. "Beautiful..."

"Come on, I'm starving," Helene expressed, closing the door behind her and locking it. "I want to eat at that restaurant by the school of business. I hear it's very good."

"Okay..."

Tristan seldom spoke as the two of them walked across campus to the faculty of business building. On the ground floor, there was a luxurious restaurant where the couple sat in. The restaurant was quiet and there were very few spaced out seats. The furniture in the restaurant was modern. The tables were black and dimly lit by a lamp above them.

"I've heard good things about this place," Helene remarked with her hands on her lap.

"Yeah?"

"So, tell me more about yourself," Helene expressed in a positive attitude. "You said you are in the Faculty of Science?"

"Yeah, same as you... Although I don't understand why or what you're doing here... considering you're an actress."

Helene blushed.

"So, you know about that? Hm? Were you doing a bit of research about me?"

Tristan blushed.

"No… I mean, I wanted to know more about you, but I didn't expect that you were an actress…"

"I was pushed into acting when I was a child by a good friend of my father… Well, he's not really my father. I'm adopted."

"Adopted?"

"Yes," Helene replied with a lower smile.

"What about your biological parents?" Tristan questioned.

Helene shrugged.

"From what I've heard, I really don't know," Helene expressed, "but I was very fortunate to be raised by the couple who adopted me, although I've recently lost one of them…"

"I'm sorry to hear that…" Tristan replied, looking aside and pausing for a moment. "You wouldn't believe it, but I'm adopted too. I've lost both my mom and dad, and my uncle and aunt – the latter of whom raised me almost my entire life."

"That's horrible…" Helene expressed.

Tristan shrugged.

"That's life, I suppose," Tristan plainly replied.

Helene squinted at him.

"How could you say something like that," Helene remarked. "These are the people that have loved you, and you make little of it?"

"I loved them too," Tristan expressed in a chalky voice. "I'm sorry, sometimes people don't like to hear about these things, so I try not to burden them…"

"You do not need to be courteous with me," Helene responded. "I know your pain."

Tristan nodded.

"I must admit though… we share a class together, you and I," Helene said. "English. I've known for quite some time, but have been slowly building enough courage to ask you out…"

"Really?" Tristan questioned. "Wow…"

Tristan went quiet.

"If we're being honest, I've been aware of you for quite some time too..." Tristan said with a light laugh. "That day, at the frat party, I was keeping an eye on you, and that's why I was there when the fight happened. That day... I saw you with a pair of fangs in your teeth too..."

"Oh?"

"Yeah," Tristan remarked. "You looked like a vampire with them."

Helene smiled and replied, "It's a fashion-piece. I sometimes do some modelling for my mother, and they're supposed to be part of a new vogue, but I do not like them that much..."

The waiter soon attended to them, and then the two made small chat until dinner arrived. Once they had eaten, Tristan paid for the meal and then he proceeded to walk Helene back to the residence. He remained quiet and only spoke when prompted to, which even then were fewer than two sentences. Tristan took Helene back to the front of her residence building where he looked to her.

Suddenly, Helene looked across to the field between the two residence blocks and took Tristan's hand. The field had various flowers in it, mostly black-eyed Susans.

"Ah, it's such a clear night," Helene remarked. "Come and look at the stars with me."

Tristan did not object and went with her. The two laid down on some grass on a field between their two residence blocks. They looked up to the sky above where there was not a cloud in sight, but only the few twinkling stars that could be seen through the barrier of light that emitted from the city.

"Isn't the night sky a thing of beauty?" Helene questioned.

"It's more beautiful away from the city," Tristan responded. "In the middle of nowhere... where one is freest."

"Is one truly free when they are subject to their primitive needs?" Helene asked.

"Is one truly free when they are subject to their unnecessary urban needs?" Tristan questioned.

"A good point," Helene replied. "I was not trying to contradict you... The topic of freewill when it comes to our basic needs are really not a question of liberty if you consider that we are more than just the command center that is our brains. We see, we hear, and we process all that information in these little minds of ours," she said, pointing at her head. "We develop egos that are centric to the needs and demands of our central nervous system, while we are an entire human body and all its other organ systems even if they are not as powerful, they are certainly as important. We are our muscle fibers, our heart muscles, our bones, and even the littlest of cells in unison. I was taught this in the home that I was raised in, where we were told that the most stable of societies are to act in this same manner where they are not centric to the demands of the elites, being our brains, but of all the small, different specialized groups as they all contribute to the success and wellbeing of the whole, whether the whole is a human body or an entire nation."

Tristan did not respond and instead simply looked back at her.

"I like that," Tristan muttered. "I've never thought about it before."

"Our minds are like a computer," Helene expressed. "What we see is what our eyes see, the information that they provide, and our thoughts are the processing of that information and other information. We believe that we are just this, this mind, but we are more. We are a body and a soul; a whole person."

Tristan did not respond and instead sat up. He kept his knees bent as he sat. Helene raised up to and folded her legs, placing a hand in the grass. The air was cold, but they were not bothered.

"Tell me," Helene said. "Do you believe in God?"

Tristan looked back at her. He then shook his head.

"No," Tristan answered. "I don't. I'm an atheist. I don't believe in God."

"How come?" Helene questioned.

"Because there is so much suffering in the world that I can't push myself to believe that there is an all-powerful, almighty deity that is watching over us and doing nothing. Either there is a God and he is very cruel, or there isn't. I'd rather believe in the latter."

"Wouldn't it make more sense for there to be a God because there is so much suffering in the world?" Helene asked. "Would it not be better to believe there is a God in a cruel world like ours?"

"If God existed, the world wouldn't be so cruel... What would be the point in that? It's insane. It's psychopathy..."

Helene looked down to the grass and picked a flower.

"It seems that you don't understand God," Helene remarked, dropping the flower. "You place your feeble expectations into a being that is infinitely larger and more powerful than you. A being that has more than just this little world of his to even care about, and all its people, but choses to love every one of us even if he does not like some of us, if any of us at all."

"You haven't seen the cruelties that I've seen," Tristan said coldly. "You haven't experienced what I have..."

"Try me," Helene challenged, looking intently to Tristan.

Tristan began to shake. He brought his arms around his legs and placed his hands together. He shook his head.

"What do you have to say about all the children in the world that are taken from their homes? Who are forced to perform acts against their innocence? Who are sexually abused and exploited because of the lustful desires of a bunch of miserable, old men? What do you have to say about the fact that thousands of children are abducted and forced to undergo this, and the fact that there is never *any* justice for these men?"

Helene was silent.

"Epstein. Waomoni." Tristan said. "They're all dead, while the network lives. It's like a monster who severs its own head so that the rest of the organism can survive. It's horrible... How can I not feel frustrated about that? After all the effort I went to save those children, the looks in their eyes, and there is no justice? What about those that I didn't get to save? What about those that I was too late to save? What about those who I did save, but their lives have been forever changed?"

"These people will one day have to come before God to answer for their crimes," Helene remarked, "and the glory of these children are in Him."

"That's not good enough though!" Tristan shouted. "That's not reassurance. That's a banal platitude that stupid people go by to make themselves feel better about themselves, and not to mention that those same people also believe that these men can be saved simply because they repent?! I want answers! I want death – I want them dead!"

Tristan smashed a fist into the dirt. Helene frowned at him.

"You think you are a good person, don't you?"

Tristan looked back at her. He looked confused.

"I- I don't know," Tristan responded. "I don't think so... I'm better than most people, I'm sure though."

"Do you want to be a good person?"

"I suppose."

"Do you believe you are a bad person?"

"No."

"So, you do believe you are a good person then?"

"What is your point?"

"My point," Helene said, "is that when you come to sin against God and realize the calamity of sin, then you will begin to sympathize with all people and rejoice in the Christian message of reconciliation. You believe that you are better than most people. You believe that none of your actions have had consequences? You believe that everything is right in your own world when you want to change the world around you?"

"I never said I wanted to change the world around me..."

"You do though," Helene stated, "but you don't understand your own place in this world, your own effects, and your own sins. You are not conscious about yourself. You are in this ivory tower where you look out to the rest of the world, but cannot see before you."

Tristan did not respond. He frowned and looked straight instead.

"Do you know what punishment God has in store for these men and women who have harmed God's precious children?" Helene questioned.

Tristan was silent until he responded, "No, I don't."

"You cannot judge God then, because the punishment of Hell is more than an eternal hellfire. It is simply hell, the struggle and pain of an endless battle between oneself and God. You, Tristan, are in hell."

Tristan gave a sort of half-laugh and half-grunt.

"Yeah, that's what I've heard Harlech to be called..." Tristan remarked.

"But I am serious," Helene stated. "You are in hell, and if you do not understand that, you will only sink deeper until you are fully submerged in its deepest pit, for eternity. Rejoice that this is the time you have on earth to change that direction in your life..."

Tristan shook his head.

"Sorry, but I'm not falling for that mumbo jumbo."

Helene rolled her eyes.

"And so, you have all these idealistic expectations, but you are too lazy to have hope?"

"Hope? Lazy? Idealistic?" Tristan questioned. "I've lived a life and a half in the last three years! I've nearly drowned in icy cold water at the top of the Ural Mountains when I was fifteen to almost being half-beaten to death in Siberia earlier this year! I have the most realistic expectations of life, because I have *lived* life. I've lived a horrible, terrible life where I once had an inch of hope that my mother was alive, only for her to be taken from me after only just meeting her. The same with my father. I had the belief that my only friend, my best friend – my brother, was dead, but turns out he's not... but for God's sake, I wish he was because this stranger who's my roommate is nobody, not even close to the person I spent two-weeks in the middle of nowhere in England with..."

"You spent two-weeks with someone, and you're surprised they are not who you thought to be?" Helene questioned. "You've obviously constructed a false image of someone and carried that with you through the burden of loss – there's no doubt that this is why this real person confuses you."

"He's not Finn, though," Tristan argued. "He's not. He's nothing like the radical I loved! The boy that I looked up to!"

"And your parents, two people that were hardly in your life, but you have come to mourn them as though they had always been with you forever?" Helene stated, shaking her head. "Do you not even listen to yourself? You have established three idealistic representations of three different people, and you've come to cry over them when they haven't even existed in this manner. You live an idealized life, Tristan. Ideal does not necessarily mean utopian, but it means optimal in your eyes, and that is what these people have become to you in your mind. These are the representations that you have crafted, and it is wrong…"

"Stop!" Tristan shouted, grasping his head. "You're wrong!"

Helene hit Tristan in the shoulder as he lowered his head.

"Do not talk to me like that!" Helene remarked. "Who do you think I am?"

"I'm sorry…" Tristan muttered. "I'm… so screwed up…"

"You are very much," Helene said, shaking her head. "You have created a world around you that is darker than the world really is. This is the world that fits into your worldview, and whether there is a lick of truth towards it is not my concern. The people, however, in your life, have come to be known in this light. The ones that you have lost, you have held a candle to shine the brightest features and exonerate them in this light while ignoring the darker features. You do not have to be this way, however… You can pick yourself up again…"

"I can't…" Tristan muttered in response. "I see no reason to… What's the point in anything? There's no meaning to anything… It's all a sham. It's all pointless…"

Helene lowered her head and then looked to Tristan, slightly annoyed.

"If you do not pick yourself up, nobody will," Helene stated. "You need to find what it is that invigorates you, or you can sit here and be as useless as you want to be. I for one, will not pick you up. You are like a small child, and not even in the sense of holy innocence, but in the sense of simple childishness and the banging of your fists on the floor while you cry. You are like a roach in the dirt, stuck in the ground, and only able to see around you and criticize the world, while you yourself do nothing or even look at yourself in reflection, believing in lies you have constructed and hoping for death..."

Tristan did not respond. Helene took a deep breath.

"I for one, will not watch you die if you will not act," Helene expressed, standing up.

Tristan watched her stand. He then quickly stood up and took her by the wrist. Helene turned around and Tristan kissed her. Helene was surprised at the kiss, but she quickly calmed down and the two continued to kiss while Tristan moved his arms around her waist and she did the same. Helene kicked up her leg back as the two continued to kiss. Tristan leaned in towards her as they continued to kiss for almost a whole two minutes.

Act 4, Scene 4

Diana tidied her hair, bringing the front left-side of her hair around her ear as she looked at herself in the reflection of the window that looked into the lobby of Tristan and Finn's building at the University of Harlech. A couple of girls passed outside and held the door for her to enter. Diana smiled to them and went inside. She looked at her phone in one hand as she walked to the elevator. She held the strap of her purse with the other hand. Tristan had not responded to the messages she had sent last night.

Diana entered the elevator and hit a button for the fourth floor. She then sat inside and took deep breaths. Once the elevator reached the fourth floor, she proceeded to walk down into the first corridor. The dormitories were quiet, especially on the fourth level. Diana looked into the common room as she made her pass by the glass window that looked in. She saw half-a-dozen boys inside, sleeping around on the floor. Amongst them, she recognized the boy known as Finn. Diana stopped at the entrance into the common room and then went inside.

The common room was a travesty with pizza boxes littering the floor, tin cans and party cups everywhere, and the sink loaded with a dozen unwashed dishes. Diana looked judgmentally around and then approached Finn who was on the couch. She sheepishly nudged him and then stood back as he gave a mild thrash around.

"Hm?" Finn remarked, opening his eyes. "What? Who are you?"

"My name is Diana. Diana Cambridge. I'm Tristan's girlfriend."

"Diana?" Finn questioned, sitting up. "Diana! Yes, of course! You're Tristan's woman."

Finn stood up and offered his hand. She took it and shook his hand. They then walked towards the exit so that they could talk in the corridor outside.

"How do you do?" Finn greeted. "I didn't expect to see you here... What are you doing here?"

"I came because I need to talk to Tristan before we meet our guardian for lunch," Diana expressed with an anxious voice, "but I saw you through the glass, so I thought I'd say hello."

"Yes, well... Hello then," Finn said with a nervous laugh, "but seriously, it's good to finally meet you. I was just... well, with the boys and such and it was a late night..."

"So..." Diana remarked. "I guess you're the great son of Charlemagne then..."

"Well, I wouldn't say, 'Great,'" Finn replied, "but definitely up there," he jestered. "You, uh... know about that though?"

"Of course," Diana responded, "but don't worry. Tristan told me not to tell Charles about the fact that you're alive and not presumed dead... You know, getting to meet you is more than just getting to meet Tristan's best friend."

"Oh yeah?"

"Yeah," Diana replied, "because Charlemagne and I are cousins, which makes us cousins as well."

"Oh... I didn't know that," Finn remarked. "I like that. I guess that means that if you and Tristan ever marry, that'll make him my brother-in-law... Wait, no. I don't think that's how it works... Sorry, I'm really tired and didn't sleep much last night. What time is it?"

"It's eleven o'clock," Diana answered, looking at her phone.

"Really? Wow," Finn replied, starting to walk down the corridor. "Well, my point was that if you and Tristan get married, then we'd all just be one big happy family... I suppose you want to see him, that Tristan of ours… I'll go take you to our lovely chateau then."

Diana followed Finn down the rest of the corridor and they stopped at the door. Finn took out his keys to open it, but Diana stopped him, placing a hand over his wrist.

"Before we go in," Diana expressed, "since I have you here. I actually wanted to talk to you about Tristan before we see him."

"What of?"

"Tristan's had a very hard year ever since he thought you died," Diana expressed. "Like I said, you had a big impact on him, and that included your supposed-death. Not to mention, later that same year, he finally met a man he later found out to have been his dad after he had died, and then his mother who also died. After that, we had an experience in Asia where he was brutally beaten, tortured, and his mind-altered… but he endured it, and a lot of that had to do with you… and then recently we had an experience during our summer vacation where we saw a lot of child exploitation, and my point is that Tristan's had it rough, and coming to Harlech, the big city, was hard for him too. I know that school must be affecting him negatively too, and the problem with Tristan is that he finds it hard to cope with his pain because he doesn't talk to anybody about his problems. It took me a lot to get him to open up to me, and I'm still surprised we managed to get over that, but you're his best friend. I'm worried about Tristan, especially after the talk we're about to have, which frankly, could go either way for us, but it might hurt him. I'm all the way at the Declan Walham university and don't have the time to come see him… we haven't really been speaking that much, so I'm wondering if you could do me a big favor…"

"Oh?"

"Could you please watch over Tristan… as his best friend? He's very close-minded about his personal problems, so it might take you some time to break into his subconscious, but I think you just have to force yourself in no matter what. Even then, please keep an eye on him for me... I'm worried about his safety and his psyche. I'm worried he might hurt himself."

"Don't you worry, love," Finn said with a smile. "I love Tristan like he's my own brother. I won't let anything happen to him, and I'll do anything to make sure that all is well with him. Thanks for reaching out to me about this – You're right, that nutter doesn't talk much, especially about himself. It drives me mad."

"Here," Diana said, opening her purse and taking out a piece of paper. "Here's my cell number. Please message me if there's ever anything I should be worried about."

Finn took the piece of paper and smiled to Diana.

"Certainly," Finn remarked, "but let me put your eases to rest, because as long as I'm watching him, he won't ever do something to hurt himself."

"Thank you," Diana replied with a soft smile.

Finn unlocked the door and then opened it. Diana walked in behind him.

"Tristie," Finn greeted. "We have company..."

Finn stopped at the end of the corridor and looked across to Tristan's bed with slight shock and horror. Diana stopped next to him and immediately dropped her reassuring smile in exchange for one of equal shock. Her change in expression was met by the visible pounce of her heart as her heart-rate soared and her face became flush. Finn's expression had quickly swapped from shock to anger as he looked to Tristan before him.

Across from them, in Tristan's bed, Tristan was bare-chested with Helene at his side. She too was bare-chested. The extent of their nudity was unaware to them, but it provided the assumptions. Diana's hands trembled. Tristan looked at them with fright, while Helene was mostly confused and shocked as she covered her breasts.

Diana blinked and the tears fell down. She immediately stormed out of the bedroom, knocking into Finn who attempted to go after her, but was stopped as the door slammed shut. He growled. Tristan simply looked forward with a pale face. His head span and he grew a neutral expression of shock and contemplation as his eyes fixated ahead of him. Helene placed a hand on Tristan's shoulder.

"What is going on?" Helene questioned. "Who was that?"

Finn turned around and looked at Tristan with disapproving eyes. Tristan looked at him with guilt. Finn shook his head at him. He then opened the door and went after Diana.

"Diana!" Finn shouted, rushing to catch up with her. "Diana!"

Diana arrived at the elevator and began to stamp her finger into the call button. Finn caught up with her as she rummaged through her purse.

"Diana…" Finn said, reaching her.

"Please," Diana expressed. "I'm going to be fine…"

"Diana, please," Finn remarked. "I didn't know…"

"I believe you," Diana replied, turning and pushing through the fire exit door. "It's okay though, because this… this is the answer that I needed. To know that all these years have been a waste! To know that… after all the…"

Diana began to weep. Finn followed Diana out into the fire escape and trailed behind her as she went down the steps. Diana stopped just between the ground floor and second floor clearing.

"To know that after all these years," Diana said, weeping louder. "I've been a fool in a relationship where I didn't matter. Where I poured my soul into a person I thought I loved, and I thought loved me in return…"

Finn stepped slowly down the final steps as he caught up with her. Diana put her weight on a steel railing as she held a hand to her face. Finn walked over and placed a hand on her shoulder.

"Please, just go…" Diana requested. "I'll be fine… to be honest, you should go and do what I asked you to. Go and see him, or not, who knows anymore. As far as I know and understand now, he's nothing but a sociopath with no consideration or regard for the emotions of others…"

Diana continued down the final steps and returned to the lobby. Finn followed her to the exit. Her tears began to pick up again. She sat down. Finn sat down next to her.

"I'm still your cousin, am I not?" Finn remarked. "What kind of a cousin would I be if I just left you on your own?"

Diana wiped tears from her cheeks. She then looked back at Finn. He placed a hand on her back. She dropped her head on his shoulder. She continued to cry.

"The last thing that you need right now is to be alone," Finn stated. "No matter how strong you think you are…"

"Bastard!" Diana shouted, hitting Finn in the shoulder. "That sociopath! That asshole!"

"Ow…" Finn muttered, grinding his teeth before looking ahead to the front door of the residential block. "Oh no…"

Ahead, dressed in a black coat for the mid-autumn weather was Charlemagne. He wore black gloves and black leather boots. Diana looked and wiped her eyes. She then placed a hand on Finn's shoulder.

"You should go…" Diana said in a coarse voice. "I'll be fine…"

Finn did not respond. Instead, he went and opened the door for Charlemagne. Charlemagne looked back at Finn and nodded.

"Thank you," Charlemagne remarked, entering the foyer and then looking straight towards Diana.

Charlemagne squinted.

"Diana?" Charlemagne questioned, looking over to her.

Diana had a darkness under her red eyes from the tears she had been shedding. She stood up.

"I'll, uh… leave you two alone…" Finn remarked in a quiet voice.

Finn left through the fire escape as Diana looked past Charlemagne and at his side.

"Diana, what's happened? Have you been crying?"

"Tristan…" Diana simply said.

"What about him? Is he okay?"

Diana scoffed and looked back at Charlemagne.

"He's more than okay, it seems…" Diana said with a coldness. "He's upstairs right now… in bed with another woman…"

Tears fell down Diana's eyes and she resumed to cry. Charlemagne dropped a look of shock and sadness for Diana. He opened his arms and embraced her. Diana stretched her arms around him and proceeded to cry even more.

"There, there…" Charlemagne hushed. "Let it all out… Shh…" he hushed.

Diana continued to cry.

"Everything is going to be okay, Diana," Charlemagne said in a quiet voice. "Believe me, it may seem like it is the end, but it isn't… You will overcome this. Please though, don't fret. Be strong, my dear. Please, be strong…"

Diana squeezed harder as she cried more and more. All Charlemagne could do was stand there and comfort her.

Act 5, Scene 1

Diana shortly fled from the University of Harlech after Charlemagne had gone to see Tristan. Likewise, Tristan had fled, leaving Charlemagne alone at Residence 2A. Diana spent most of her day alone in Keswick where she had managed to find a rooftop she could be huddled in and under the cover of an abandoned shelter. The rooftop gave a view of surrounding rooftops, and one of the buildings was the old four-story apartment building that Diana had grown up in. She looked over to it with saddened eyes.

A minor rain fell over the city and the skies were bright, but a light grey as they all covered in the fluff of nimbus clouds. Once Diana had enough of the rain, she stood up and climbed down the fire escape at the side of the building to return to the alleyway where he motorcycle was parked. The rain continued to fall down as she placed her helmet over her head and then drove back onto the streets.

Diana arrived at Pentateuch Cathedral and parked her motorcycle across the street. She then rushed through traffic to get to the other side where he slowly made her approach to the front steps of the church. Diana pushed against the doors and entered in to the narthex. The lobby was quiet. There was not even the sound of music coming from the organ. Diana passed into the nave and dipped her hand into the holy water, making the sign of the cross on the front of her body with her fingers, and then going down the aisle to the front of the church. The church was quiet and there was nobody inside, including Iustina who was absent as far as Diana could tell. Diana knelt down, made the sign of the cross again, and then sat down at one of the front benches. She promptly dropped onto her knees and brought her hands together. Diana closed her eyes.

"Lord," Diana said in a fragile and very quiet whisper, "even after I had made my decision, it did not matter. Even then, it shook me, and even now it has still shaken me... I can't believe he's gone..." she remarked, eyes tearing up again. "Just like that, the last three years appear to have meant nothing to him when they meant the world to me. I'll never understand him. I don't want to understand him. I want to know, why... after all the crap I went through, I thought I was done... Why again? Why did you make me feel like this again? My Tristan... the only one I thought I was allowed to have... Am I not allowed to have anything? Am I not allowed to be with anyone? Am I supposed to be alone? And what that woman said, about me valuing Tristan over you... Is that why? Is that why I'm not allowed to have him? Because I treated him like an idol? I assure you, Lord, that I have always worshipped you and you alone. I have never worshiped Tristan. I've only loved him with my body and heart. I thought he was all that I was allowed to have... but if this is some sort of punishment... Were my parent's deaths some sort of punishment too?"

Diana stopped.

"No," Diana replied to herself. "I'm in such a disoriented state, I can't even think logically or rationally about it. My suffering was a way of life... and even if I thought Tristan and I being together was a holy gift, I... I could have... I *was* wrong about that. It was wrong... It was all wrong."

Diana shook her head.

"After all we've been through... The dilemma between him and Arturo, Tristan's confession of his love to me – was it ever sincere? Was I nothing more than an object to him? Was I nothing more than a convenience to him because we lived together?"

Diana opened her hands and placed them on her face as she cried harder.

"I gave myself to him… something I can never have returned to me. My God, Iustina was right… I've sinned against you and I've paid the price. Even though I was so confident that we'd be together, forever, it was struck down with a terrible wind. I… I'm in shock."

Diana parted her hands from her face and returned them together before her atop of the wooden railing before the pew.

"How could he do it?" Diana questioned. "How could Tristan have done this to me? Is he even human? Is he even the same? No… not my Tristan… Why… Why did he have to become like this? I refuse to believe that this Tristan is the same Tristan that I fell in love with, the sweet boy that I once knew. The boy that risked his life to prevent me from (ironically) coming here… He was such a sweet boy. He smiled. He laughed. He had a sense of humor. He was open, even if it still took him a lot to open to me about his parents. I always hated that side of him. That moment by the fire in the cabin in Russia… my least favorite moment, and yet it was our first intimate moment together… I strived to never see that Tristan ever again, but that's who he's become in the last year. Dammit… ever since he went into that forest. What happened there? Why did you have to change him? Why couldn't I have the Tristan that he formerly was? Why did you have to let him suffer? He's broken. He's defeated. His mind is shattered. He probably doesn't know who he is either…"

Diana lowered her head. The tears dropped to the floor below.

"Tristan… My sweet, sweet… Tristan…"

Diana wiped her mouth.

"I feel like a part of me has been torn in half. I thought he was my other half. I felt the connection – the mental connection. I felt as though I could read his mind, as if in all our intimacy, we had become one. We were one... Dammit, I gave myself to him..."

Diana shook her head.

"I refuse to believe that this was a punishment..." Diana expressed. "You've done something to my Tristan, and I don't know why you've done it, but he's gone and torn us apart... Then again, I suppose I was about to do that too... If I had the courage and wouldn't have caved like that last time. All I wanted was... to be with him, to get married and raise our family, but his mind...! Dammit, why did you have to screw with his mind – nothing good has come of it...! Don't I deserve some answers?"

Diana stopped speaking for a moment. She closed her eyes and took some deep breaths. After close to five minutes, she opened her eyes again and looked forward.

"Lord, if you could tell my mother.... Mom... if you're listening, I'm sorry I haven't spoken to you before like this. A part of me knew that you would never want me to live in regret of what happened, or to be focused on you indefinitely. I had that liberty when Tristan stepped into my life... you would have loved Tristan... as I knew him though. I'm nostalgic for that boy that I knew, and perhaps it's for the best that I look back at those moments rather than the last year. I was lucky enough to have a good year with him while it lasted... that woman, Iustina, was right about everything and I knew it, but I didn't want to believe it. We were doomed from the start, but that's beside the point.

What I really want to say to you, mom, is that I hope you're looking down on me, your little girl. You'd be so proud of me."

Diana's eyes began to tear up.

"I'm all grown up. I'm eighteen now. I'm going to university, even if I don't know what for or if I'll stay. I know that you want me to focus on what I want to do, and to be honest, I don't think a university education can get me where I want to be. Even then, I'm not sure I know what I want to do with my life anymore…"

Diana sighed. She wiped the tears that had fallen from her eyes.

"You would want me to do something with my life though… If I let this drag me down, we'll end up being the same. You were never the same after dad died… I won't make the same mistake… You want that from me… You've always wanted the best, even if you were never able to deliver… You still tried through and through… You were the strongest woman I ever knew, and I owe it to you to be stronger to show that we can triumph. It's you and me."

Diana snorted and wiped her nose. She then looked up to the ceiling of the church and took a deep breath. She gave a light, but insecure smile, and then looked forward again.

"Okay, God…" Diana muttered. "Here I am, torn from my other half. I have nothing more than you, and it's just you and me now. Iustina told me to entrust my life and fate into your hands, so that is what I'm doing. Guide me, Lord, and take me where you want me to go next…"

Diana prayed a couple of Hail Mary prayers and then a single Our Father before she made the sign of the cross and stood up. She made the sign of the cross again as she exited from the pew, kneeling down, and then she returned to the narthex where she wiped her eyes. Diana carried with her a sunken and depressed look, and her face shined by the tears that had left her skin moist.

A clergyman in red stepped out from the office next to the gift shop and proceeded out before stopping as Diana passed him.

"My dear child," the cardinal expressed in either an Italian, Iberian, or Hispanic accent. "Why have you been crying?"

Diana looked at the cardinal. He was an old man she had not seen before. He wore a black cloak, or cassock, with a Roman collar around the neck. Around his waist he wore a scarlet red piping. He also had a pectoral cross around his neck. The man was balding and only had grey hair on the sides. He had various wrinkles at the bags of his eyes that stretched out to form crow's feet. His skin was fair, about the same tone as Diana's if not a degree darker. It was also wrinkled and withered. The man was shorter than Diana. He wore gold-rimmed glasses and had a large, pointed nose with wide floppy ears. Diana raised a look of surprise and then curtsied.

"Your eminence," Diana greeted.

"Save your formalities," the cardinal assured her. "Tell me, what has brought you here in pain?"

"Oh…" Diana responded. "Personal trouble, your eminence… Please, don't let me burden you or take up your time…"

"Nonsense, do you think that because I am a cardinal that my time is worth more than yours? My time is meant for the children of God, so please, let me take the moment to hear of your pain. Please, step into my office…"

The cardinal extended his arm towards the room that he had come out of. Diana looked and then nodded.

"Okay…" Diana whispered, wiping her eyes.

Diana followed the cardinal into the room. He then closed the door behind him and then went around to sit down behind his desk. The office was a large space at the base of the left tower. There were various bookshelves with many old books, a cabinet with some photographs in frames and other artefacts, a fireplace with a mirror above, and a large painting behind the desk over a wide bookshelf. The painting was from the Romantic Era and depicted a scene where people were frightful and being chased by people in black and red cloaks. A fire was set in the background against a windmill and there was a lot of fright, some people hung in the background, and others crucified. It was like a scene out of the Spanish Inquisition. Diana sat down in the seat before the desk.

"I have not seen you before," the cardinal expressed. "Are you baptized?"

"Yes," Diana replied. "I was baptized in this church as a matter of fact, but I haven't been here in a long time. I moved away to Alberta and came back last September for university... something which I'm beginning to regret..."

"The only regrets one should have is for the sins that they commit," the cardinal expressed. "What is your name?"

"Diana," Diana answered. "Diana Cambridge."

"Well, Ms. Cambridge," the cardinal replied. "I am Cardinal Mario Francesco Calavera Rojas, Archbishop of the Metropolitan Archdiocese of Harlech, which oversees the many dioceses of northern British Columbia. So tell me, child, what ails your heart?"

Diana took a deep breath.

"I was recently cheated on... by my long-time boyfriend," Diana said. "He... he cheated on me with another woman."

A tear from Diana's eye again.

"We've been together for almost three years, and... he was never the same after he returned from England."

"Oh dear..." Cardinal Calavera replied, presenting a box of tissues for Diana to use. "I'm terribly sorry to hear that."

"I... I thought that the life I had growing up with my parents was the pinnacle of the suffering that I would have to endure... the suffering of which brought me closer to God as I rested on the faith that my mother was in Heaven... but, I guess... I was wrong..."

"The breadth of suffering knows no bounds, dear child," the cardinal replied.

"I... I had a tough upbringing with my parents. We're from Keswick, and I... I had an abusive father who used to hit me... and my mother, she was a heroin addict. I just... I thought I had caught a break, but... now this has happened, and I don't know what to think anymore..."

"Has your faith been shaken by this incident?"

"I... I don't think so," Diana remarked. "My faith in God has never really been about him, Tristan, but about me and my mother. Even then, over the last three years, I've come to love God for so much more... Before Tristan cheated on me, we were becoming distant since we lived so far apart from each other, and I thought that God was testing me to see if I'd chose Him or Tristan..."

"No..." the cardinal denied. "God does not do that."

"The point is though," Diana expressed, "that my faith has not been shaken although I'm clueless about what to do next with my life. I was in school, but I was thinking of dropping out because I don't really like being in school. All I wanted was to get married with Tristan and live our life... to have children and raise them. We were both orphans, and what we could both agree on, at least when we met, was a principle of family... to have and construct a family to replace what we had both lost... but now, I guess..."

Diana began to cry again.

"It's lost..."

"I'm sorry," the cardinal apologized. "Dear Diana, your suffering is not a plight that you must endure, but all this trouble with this boy must be let go because if you hold on to it, you will only harm yourself. No good comes from letting yourself suffer like this. God bless you and your unshakeable faith, and I will pray that this faith of yours continues through as strong as it is, because it is this sort of faith that will allow you to triumph. However, what you must do is to let go of this boy and make peace with the situation and his decisions. How old are you?"

"Eighteen," Diana answered.

"Eighteen," the cardinal repeated. "So young, and yet you are such a strong, independent woman. You must continue to be strong and continue to be independent. My dear Diana, now is the time for you to not stop, but continue going as Christ would want you to be. The church here and all of our parishioners are here for you. Make a name for yourself and make us proud. Do not abandon your studies, but remain in them and continue to explore the different options that you have in this blessed world of ours. Somehow, perhaps, you will find what it is that Christ wants from you to make this world a more peaceful place. I am sure of it…"

"Yeah?" Diana replied, wiping her eyes. "Maybe I'm not in a right mindset to make any major decisions right now. I don't know… we'll see when the semester ends… Thank you for your help."

The cardinal stood up and walked around the table as Diana stood up.

"My office is always open for you to drop-by," the cardinal expressed. "I've recently returned from Rome to visit the Pope, but I do not have any travel plans for the next while… Feel free to visit whenever you want and we can chat."

"Thank you, your eminence," Diana replied, being led out.

The cardinal opened the door for Diana and she walked out. He then closed the door behind her.

Act 5, Scene 2

"You didn't tell me that you had a girlfriend," Helene said with an upset look.

Helene and Tristan sat in a small restaurant south from Harlech in Lennox. She had driven him away from the university after Finn kicked him out of the dorm with Helene, calling him out for his fornication, to which Tristan did not respond to. Helene stayed with Tristan throughout and she drove her own car when Tristan asked if they could go somewhere away from the city.

"Had I known that you had a girlfriend, I would have never have approached you..." Helene remarked. "I feel terrible for that poor girl of yours..."

"You- you didn't do anything... voluntarily..." Tristan replied in a quiet voice. "It's not like she's mine anymore. If anybody should feel bad about anything, it's me... I... I'm so screwed up... I- I don't know what to do."

Helene did not look back at Tristan with pity, but instead annoyance.

"It's pretty obvious what you should do," Helene said. "You need to speak with her and apologize... She may not accept that apology, but it is better that you let her know what she deserves to know even if it won't provide you with any gain. It's the least you can do, or owe to her. It won't bring her back – but it is what is right..."

Tristan did not respond. He simply looked out the window. The rain was harder in Lennox than it was in Harlech.

"Why are you even with me? After what I did to you too? I basically lied to you... We didn't even have sex... We only slept together... You're in the clear, and you can go about your life as if this was nothing..."

"No, this is not nothing," Helene rejected. "You are so dismissive to grand situations as being nothing. You can lie to yourself that this is 'nothing,' but please, do not lie to me. I have been a part of an insidious affair, and that hurts me too, to hurt another woman like that. What I should do is slap you across the face, but I will save that pleasure for your woman. No, if I am with you, it is to make sure that you do what is right for all our sakes, and be sure that you don't choose the coward's way out."

Tristan's hands trembled. Tears fell from the side of his eyes. Helene shook her head at him and then raised her hand as she spotted a waitress nearby.

"The bill, please," Helene requested.

"Certainly."

The waitress left and later returned with the bill. Helene paid for the meal that Tristan didn't eat. The time was currently a quarter past two o'clock in the afternoon and Tristan had not eaten a single bite of food. His hands had been trembling all day.

"Can I pack that up for you?" the waitress questioned as Helene tapped her card on the machine.

"No, thank you," Tristan remarked.

"Okay, enjoy your day and have a happy, safe Halloween!" the waitress cheered.

"Thank you," Helene said with a smile, getting out of the booth. "Come on, we're leaving," she then said to Tristan.

Tristan stood up and held his face down as he walked out of the restaurant. The pair of them entered the parking lot and returned to Helene's luxurious white SUV. Tristan got in the other side while Helene got in the driver's seat. She started the engine and then looked to Tristan.

"Where am I going to take you now?"

Tristan gave a weak shrug. Helene shook her head and shifted gears.

"I'm taking you back to the university," Helene said. "I'm going to leave you with your guardian, and you are going to apologize to him, your roommate, and then your beloved before the day is over. Do you understand?"

"I- I can't talk to her," Tristan said in a dead voice. "I…"

Helene slammed on the brakes before she left the parking lot.

"You pitiful man!" Helene lambasted. "If it was not for the fact that I sympathize with your woman, and empathized with you and your woes, I would have left you in your room… If you want to die, then you can die later like the coward you are, but right now you are going to go home and apologize to all those you have wronged… I will not leave you until that is done."

Tristan looked out his door window and gave a scorned look. Helene continued to drive and proceeded through town, turning left to bypass traffic and take an alternate coastal route back to Grafton Bridge. Once they had reached the highway, the car began to accelerate and decelerate inconsistently with the amount of inertia that was being thrusted around. Helene drove beyond the speed limit, over one-hundred and twenty kilometers per hour, and with a temper of rage seen in her eyes. The road that they took was just above some cliffs that looked out to the Pacific Ocean. The waters were as grey as the light grey clouds in the sky and they were mildly choppy. Tristan continued to look out from his window and towards the cliffs next to them.

The car skidded slightly as they reached a slippery slope, causing Helene to tap the brake gently. Tristan raised his head up with cause to alarm, gaining a worried expression, but lowering back into his somber look as Helene regained control. Tristan dropped his head again and continued to look out. The SUV passed the cliffside as they descended downwards to be close to the water below. A forest of dense coniferous trees replaced the rocky side on Tristan's right. Helene hit the brake again at a turn, but the car began to shake as they decelerated.

Tristan picked up his head as he felt the car swerve left and right. Helene attempted to regain control. Suddenly, a large truck passed them and brought a large wind against them alongside a large puddle of water that blinded them briefly. Helene hit the brakes even harder, which caused the swerve to worsen and for the SUV to hit the concrete post on their right. The car rose up at its front and hit a tree at the other side, which caused the rear of the car to swing around and vault over the concrete ledge and hit against another tree. The car then tipped over on its left before smashing against the side of the hill. The glass windows in the car shattered. Tristan covered his head as he felt shards of glass fall over him.

The car fell onto its roof where it then began to slide down the muddy hill and hit all the trees in its path. At the base of the hill, it rolled once more and then came to a rest. Smoke rose from the engine. Tristan and Helene were passed out in their seats.

• • • •

Tristan opened his eyes minutes later. His face was wet from the rain that poured in and the blood at the side of the face from the cuts he had suffered. He held a painful, sorrowful expression on his face and breathed slowly. He was upside down, suspended from his seat and held in place by the seatbelt that had locked in. The air bag before him had blown out. He looked straight before him until his eyes slowly and on their own began to look around his immediate area without moving his head. Once the immediate shock passed, he started to move his neck to get a better to look around him. Tristan saw Helene next to him. She was unconscious, almost smothered by the airbag that had blown out by the steering wheel with her arms around it. Her face and neck were tilted to the side as her left cheek rested on the airbag like a pillow. Tristan looked away from her and then looked down below to see all the debris under his head. There were a few shards of glass, which he moved out of the way before detaching himself from his seat and collapsing onto the ceiling of the car.

Tristan yelled out as he landed. He brought a hand to his stomach and then looked at his hand as it was covered in blood. He looked down at his shirt and saw that his stomach was damp in blood. He breathed more sharply as he saw the obvious major wood he had sustained. Tristan brought a weak hand to open his car door and then he kicked it open wider so that he could crawl out and get out of the vehicle. Tristan crawled out and made his way into the wet, damp forest to rest against a tree. His hands, trembling even more than ever, carefully lifted up his shirt to see the major wound in his lower abdomen. Tristan took off his navy blue zip hoodie and began to use it to absorb some of the blood, but his hands were too weak and the area was too sensitive for him to even touch. He gritted his teeth with pain and breathed slow, painful breaths. His eyes were wet from tears as he began to cry. He simply tilted his head back against the trunk and continued to cry.

Helene soon opened her eyes and looked around. She was slightly dazed. Her arms began to move around and she picked up a shard of glass, which she used to pop the airbag. She then let herself go and fell to the ceiling, grunting at the impact. She attempted to climb out of the window at her side, but stopped. She then went to Tristan's side where she stopped again. A brightness of sunshine that cut through the forest and trees separated the car with where Tristan was. Helene looked over to Tristan who had his eyes closed as he looked up, grabbing his side with both arms. He was still conscious as he let out labored breaths.

"Tristan..." Helene said. "You're injured..."

Tristan ignored her. He opened his eyes and looked to the side. He had no energy. He was almost paralyzed in place with his muscles barely functioning. Even against his stomach, his arms had no force to apply pressure. Helene looked around and then came back into the car.

"Let me find a phone and call for help..." Helene said, looking around. "I can't find my phone... Tristan, do you have your phone?"

Tristan opened his eyes again as he had closed them. He couldn't move.

"My... my pocket..." Tristan replied in a weak voice.

"What?" Helene questioned.

Helene sighed and took a deep breath. Tristan closed his eyes and his neck muscles gave in. His head went back all the way and his muscles ceased to contract, including those of his lower lips as his mouth was left slightly open.

"Tristan!" Helene shouted.

Helene took another deep breath and then looked side to side. She closed her eyes and then she proceeded to crawl through the sunshine, which instantly caused her extremely fair skin to burn as if the sunshine was being focused onto her by a magnifying glass from above and she was an ant. Even her hair burned as she entered the sunlight. The heat was too much for her and she collapsed halfway. Helene looked ahead and over to Tristan. A small puddle of blood formed around him. The top half of his jeans were soaked. Helene crawled on her stomach towards him. Her skin turned cherry red. She grabbed fistfuls of dirt as she reeled herself in. Her skin began to tear slightly as she finally reached Tristan. Helene took her last bits of strength and raised Tristan's shirt, exposing his abdomen. She then brought her face over to his skin and opened her mouth. Helene bit into Tristan's side, biting down against the muscle and through the skin with a hard bite that pierced the flesh.

Helene screamed out in pain as her face became covered in Tristan's blood. She moved her head away from his abdomen, leaving behind a sizable bite wound in addition to the other major wound. Helene fell onto her back and began to seize in pain. The sun that hit her from above added in to that pain as her skin continued to burn. Her face became covered in blood, including her own blood, which ran down the sides of her face and onto her neck. Eventually, the pain was too much for her and she passed. Helene's muscles gave in and she relaxed while her skin continued to burn as she was cooked alive and nano-sized cuts formed all around her inner and outer mouth, bleeding out.

Meanwhile, the bite wound that Tristan had on his side miraculously had healed on its own, while the larger wound began to stop bleeding. Tristan opened his eyes and picked up his head. He moved his arms and looked around. He saw Helene collapsed on the floor next to him and saw that she was burning. Tristan attempted to stand, but it was too difficult. He brought his hand to her hand and felt that she was hot. Puzzled, he looked up to the sun and then took his hoodie and placed it over her face. He then looked at his abdomen and saw the remnants of the bite wound and the other wound that gradually healed in real-time.

Tristan continued to experience a weakness, but the muscles in his arm had a wider range of motion than before. He took out his cellphone from his jean's pocket and wiped his wet hands so that he could swipe over and place an emergency call, dialing Charlemagne's cell number.

Act 5, Scene 3

Charlemagne sat at the table in the common room of Residence 2A with Finn nearby. Finn looked at Charlemagne from across the room with crossed arms and intent. Charlemagne held a worried expression on his face. He brought his phone up to his ear and listened to it ring before it went to the voicemail of Diana's phone. Charlemagne withdrew the phone from his ear and then looked at his phone. In the blink of an eye, his screen changed to show that he was receiving a call from Tristan. Charlemagne looked at the screen with an annoyed expression. He looked at the screen for several seconds until it was too late to answer. He then sat his phone aside and scratched the back of his head.

Finn approached Charlemagne.

"Mr. Cabernet, is it alright if I have a word?" Finn expressed.

"Certainly, Louis" Charlemagne responded, looking to Finn. "Whatever about?"

Charlemagne's phone went off again. Finn looked at it.

"Your phone is going off," Finn noted.

Charlemagne gave a sort of disgusted grunt as he looked to see that it was Tristan attempting to phone again.

"Sorry, hold on a moment," Charlemagne remarked, picking up the phone.

Finn took a deep breath and then left the common room as Charlemagne picked up. He brought the phone to his ear and answered.

"Hello?" Charlemagne greeted with low morale.

"Oh, thank God," Tristan praised with a sigh of relief.

"What is it Tristan?" Charlemagne questioned. "Where are you? I'm with your roommate and we're both very much concerned for you…"

"You need to help me…" Tristan begged with a panic.

"What is it?" Charlemagne replied, gaining worry.

"I- I was in a car crash. I'm out of town. I'm… I'm bleeding badly… Helene is passed out and I don't know how long I have until I pass out too. I- I don't feel too good and I'm starting to get feverish…"

"Good Lord," Charlemagne responded. "I'll be down as soon as possible. I'll dial 911 once I get your immediate location."

"No," Tristan denied. "No police. No paramedics. Just you, alone, please."

"What? Why?" Charlemagne questioned.

"Helene… she's… she's not normal," Tristan explained. "I knew it all along… she… her skin was burning because it was in sunlight. She never goes into sunlight without covering herself. She… she bit me in the side and for some reason, my wounds have been self-healing, but I feel terrible. I think… I think whatever she did to me, it isn't agreeing with my nanomachines. I have a fever… I've never had a fever in my life and I feel sick, nauseous…."

"I see," Charlemagne responded. "Hold on then. I'll be on my way as fast as I can."

"We're on the way to Lennox, along the coastal highway," Tristan explained. "Hurry."

"Don't you worry, just sit tight," Charlemagne said, standing up and leaving the common room. "I'll be there as soon as I can. Keep calm, Tristan."

Charlemagne hung up and rushed down the fire escape to the foyer of the dorm building. He then went along the path and to the sidewalk where a black SUV was parked with Lacplesis and Elegast chatting together outside. They were in their urban combat uniforms, but without any visible arms and instead the words 'Security' across the back of their uniforms. Charlemagne rushed to them.

"Get in the car, hurry," Charlemagne said to them. "There's been an accident and we need to rescue Tristan ASAP."

Lacplesis rushed into the driver's seat while Brandan opened the back door. Charlemagne got in the front with Lacplesis and the Baynard roared to life. Finn rushed outside as he saw the SUV drive by and then zip off before he could say anything to his father. Lacplesis drove as fast as he could to reach SW Marshall Drive.

Charlemagne brought his phone to his ear.

"Come on... pick up..." Charlemagne muttered.

"Hello?" Diana responded in a dull tone.

"Diana!" Charlemagne replied. "Where are you? I need you to meet me somewhere... There's been an emergency!"

"I'm at King Island," Diana answered. "What's going on? Are you okay?"

"I'm fine, but it's Tristan," Charlemagne said. "Tristan's had an accident. Please, make your way towards Lennox and meet me at my location. I'm going to need your help..."

Diana sighed.

"And why should I care?" Diana replied. "Tristan has Helene. He's not my boyfriend anymore. I have no reason to care about him, or his wellbeing..."

"Helene is part of the problem – the two of them have had a fatal crash and Tristan's currently bleeding out. He could die..."

Charlemagne listened to silence from the other end.

"Diana?"

"I'm busy," Diana replied.

"Diana," Charlemagne responded in a disappointing tone. "I can understand that you are mad at him for what happened today, but now is not the time to let your emotions cloud your judgement. Even if he wasn't your boyfriend, or even your adoptive-brother, he is still a human being. Both of them. Two human lives are in danger right now. Tristan can die..."

Charlemagne could hear Diana's breathing from the other side.

"I've made my peace," Diana replied. "He's not my problem anymore."

Charlemagne waited for more, but there was nothing more. He moved his phone from his ear and realized that she had hung up on him.

"Damn that child!" Charlemagne shouted as they almost reached the highway. "Hold on, I'm going to get Tristan's location. Do we have a first aid kit?"

"Yes, sir, Mr. Cabernet," Elegast responded.

Tristan looked at Tristan's location on his phone. He then placed a marker on the GPS computer at the side of the driver's seat. Lacplesis drove over Grafton Bridge and went south, coming off the Trans-Canada Highway and onto the coastal highway that bypassed the urban center.

"I'm going to have to take them to a secured location," Charlemagne remarked. "I'm going to give Heavner a phone call."

Lacplesis continued to drive and eventually they reached the location of the car crash. He pulled the car over and the two immediately went off with flashlights to search over the edge of the other side. Once Charlemagne had finished talking with Heavner, he joined them and attempted to look down the steep hill. Lacplesis pointed downhill with his flashlight.

"I see them!" Lacplesis shouted, jumping down and sliding down the hill.

Elegast took a rope and tied it around a tree before he joined Lacplesis. Lacplesis had made his way to Tristan's body and immediately went to perform first aid as he checked his airway and breathing. Charlemagne slowly made his way down via the rope that Elegast was securing. Elegast soon touched the bottom to where Lacplesis was cutting off Tristan's shirt to expose the wound.

"He's breathing," Lacplesis reported, "but he's cold... very cold..."

"We'll have to get that wound dressed before we get him out," Charlemagne said.

Charlemagne looked at Tristan. His skin was very pale. He looked at the wound and saw that it was half-healed, but still in the gradual process of healing, although it looked like it had stopped midway. Lacplesis cleaned it so that they could have a better look. He exposed the bite wound, which had left a faint scar on the side as he cleaned off the blood. Charlemagne then turned around and looked at Helene.

Helene appeared to Charlemagne to be a perfectly normal girl, although her skin was covered in third-degree burns and mouth in blood.

"She's not responding," Elegast said as he checked on Helene. "She's also not breathing... I'm going to start CPR."

Elegast proceeded to attempt to resuscitate her. Charlemagne then looked back at Tristan and brought a hand to his forehead.

"He's as cold as ice," Charlemagne remarked, checking his pulse at his wrist. "I can barely get a beat... Heavner will call me back with a location, but we need to get them out of this rain and into the SUV."

Charlemagne turned around as he heard some murmurs from Helene.

"She's alive," Elegast reported.

Charlemagne touched her arm and felt that her skin was warm. Helene continued to murmur, almost as if she was in pain.

She held her eyes closed. Elegast wiped her face and saw that her mouth was covered in cuts and gashes. Charlemagne looked at her in horror.

"Good Lord," Charlemagne muttered.

Charlemagne looked to Elegast.

"We'll have to bandage her in the car and cover all the exposed skin," Charlemagne said. "See if you can wake Tristan too. Tristan? Wake up!"

Charlemagne shook the boy, but he didn't wake up.

"No use," Charlemagne remarked. "Right then. Let's get them back to the car now... We have to clear this area before emergency services poke their heads in. Double time..."

Elegast and Lacplesis picked up each of the two and then began to fireman carry them up the hill with the help of the rope that Elegast had secured. Charlemagne looked around the scene and picked up Tristan's cell phone. He then looked around and followed his two bodyguards up the slope and back to the SUV where they were brought into the back of the SUV.

"Lower the seats in the back," Lacplesis told Elegast. "We'll have to lay them out."

"The pair of you ride in the front," Charlemagne ordered. "I'll take care of the bandaging... Just get us back to Cliffe Island and Heavner will give us a place to keep them."

"Yes, sir," Lacplesis replied.

Charlemagne carefully hopped into the back of the SUV and then Lacplesis closed the door behind him. He then went back to the driver's seat while Elegast went to the passenger seat next to him. Charlemagne looked at Tristan with worried eyes, placing a hand on his forehead while Lacplesis took the car and began to drive off.

"Please, Lord," Charlemagne muttered. "Save this poor boy's life..."

Act 5, Scene 4

Diana watched the sunset from atop of another rooftop, this time within Bromley with Pentateuch Cathedral behind her. She held her cellphone in her hand and took a deep breath. Once the sun was down, she moved to sit down so that she looked over to the church, looking at the streets and the cars that passed by as it became late. Diana stayed here for almost two hours, peacefully looking out.

In the time that Diana had spent alone, she had received numerous text messages from Charlemagne on Tristan's condition, his preliminary analysis, and his initial theory that Tristan's nanomachines are in conflict with a rare artificial virus. The messages went into Helene's mutated condition and how Charlemagne's slightly familiar with the theory behind meta-humans like her, but has never encountered one. The final message read, 'Tristan condition is critical. If someone doesn't help me, he may very well die.' Diana's eyes looked at this message. She tilted her head down with sadness and turned off her phone. Diana stared down at the ground.

A red sports car then passed along the road below and parked on the curb in front of the church. A woman stepped out from the driver's seat and Diana recognized this woman as Iustina. Diana's spirit perked up and she stood up, immediately moving to go down the alleyway she had climbed up and going across the street to meet up with the mysterious woman.

Diana entered the cathedral and looked around for Iustina, entering the chapel and seeing her at the front of the church, praying. Diana made the sign of the cross and then went in, joining her and kneeling next to her. Iustina looked over to Diana.

"Diana," Iustina greeted. "A pleasure to see you here…"

Iustina then stopped as she looked at Diana closely.

"Is something wrong? You seem depressed…"

"It's been a rough day for me…" Diana admitted.

"Have you made your decision?" Iustina questioned.

"I didn't have to," Diana replied. "He made it for me, and cheated on me with another woman."

"Oh…" Iustina responded. "Diana, that's terrible to hear… You must be devastated…"

"I was… yes," Diana remarked, "and now, I've just heard that he's been in a car crash… whether that is divine intervention and justice, I'm not sure."

"The only divine intervention where God takes back the life he has given one of his children is against men who are so far gone as being lost that their eradication is the only solution so that they can meet with Him personally and answer for their crimes," Iustina explained. "I very much doubt that a young boy such as your lover could have been as vile to deserve that fate. You should be ashamed to think that this is what the boy deserves, simply because he broke your heart. Shame on you."

"I'm sorry…" Diana replied.

"Do not apologize to me, but that boy," Iustina noted. "What is his condition?"

"He's in a bad place," Diana answered. "It's 'critical,' apparently."

"Come then," Iustina remarked, taking Diana's hand. "We will say a prayer for him, because that is the least that can be done…. Every night since my husband left me, I have prayed for his return. Tonight, we will pray for both of the men in our lives so that they can return to us. *In nomine Patris, et Filii, et Spiritus Sancti, Amen*," she said, making the sign of the cross.

Diana joined her.

"Lord, we have joined together to offer a prayer to you so that you can save the life of the dear boy that has hurt your poor daughter's heart, little Diana. We cannot know for sure what your plan is with this boy, but we can be certain that death is not one of them. We beg for you to help stabilize this boy's medical condition and return him to those that love him, and we also pray that should he return, he may repent for his sins and turn to you. And on this day, Lord, we also pray... one-hundred and eighty-four days since I last saw my beloved husband, that you return him to me, and that until then, he may still be alive and safe."

Iustina then transitioned into an Our Father, which she said in Latin. Diana followed in English as soon as she realized that it was the Our Father, and then they said another one before making the sign of the cross again.

"You lost your husband?" Diana questioned, looking to her.

"Yes," Iustina replied. "I've spent every day since then coming here and praying for his return, and although it's been that long, I have yet to lose faith because God has not answered my earlier prays asking to know if he was dead."

"You understand then," Diana said. "The loss and the pain..."

"Of course," Iustina responded, standing up and helping Diana up. "Come, we shouldn't converse in His temple. Let us take this conversation outside."

Iustina and Diana walked off and entered the narthex. There, they removed their veils and went to sit down at a bench.

"When I told you to make your decision about your love, I had faith that you would have made the right choice, but I never expected this," Iustina said. "I also thought that if your faith were as strong as I believed it to be, God would have realized your loyalty and helped you. We can spend a lot of time analyzing our lives, trying to see if there is a deeper meaning behind such and such travesty, but I'm sure that a lot of our sufferings are merely part of the nature of this Fallen world and not coincidental to His plan. Regardless, what matters is that we are steadfast in our faith to Him through and through, and I am sure that you will be, and in return, he will reward you with double of what was lost."

Diana nodded and then sighed.

"I used to think that the life I entered with Charlemagne and Tristan was the reward for my faith, but at the same time, I never had faith when I was suffering… It's easy to grow into despair… but I've thought a lot about what you told me… about placing my confidence in God's plan, and that's eased my pain. I'm prepared to accept whatever it is that God presents to me as long as it's something, because to be honest, I have no idea what to do with my life anymore. It's a load off my mind if he takes the reins and guides me, because whatever I try to do blows up on me."

"Remember to not take in too much sloth though," Iustina warned. "It's good to trust in God, but it benefits nobody to be dormant about your life, expecting something to happen. God gives us opportunities and moments we can act on, and we must do our part. We are instruments in God's orchestra, and sometimes, His work and intervention is done through us by the inspiration of the Holy Spirit in willpower, wisdom, and strength."

Diana looked to the side. She then looked back to Iustina.

"Can I ask you something?" Diana questioned. "It's a moral question, and I'm sure I already know the answer to it, but… Tristan is a critical condition, and currently, my guardian, Charlemagne, is looking after him, but Charlemagne's asked me to help him. He told me that if someone doesn't help him cure Tristan, then Tristan may die. I have to help him, don't I…?"

Iustina looked at Diana as if Diana had stated the obvious.

"Of course," Iustina remarked. "Just as I said, we can pray for God's divine intervention, a miracle, but many times He has already blessed us with the tools or capabilities to overcome the obstacles before us. We are instruments… and if you in some way can help save Tristan, then that is the way that it will need to be done. God helps those that help themselves."

Iustina looked past Diana and over to the door into the cardinal's office. The door had opened and Cardinal Calavera stood in front of the door, looking over to the two of them. Iustina stood up and looked down to Diana.

"Go and save the life of this boy, Diana," Iustina entrusted. "You know the pain that it will cause you, and the overwhelming regret, should you stand idle. I must leave now though… I'll see you soon hopefully."

Diana looked at Iustina confused as she quickly left. Diana stood up in an attempt to go after her, but she then looked at the cardinal next to her. She faced him.

"Your eminence," Diana greeted.

"Ms. Cambridge," the cardinal responded, "do you know that woman?"

"Yes, your eminence," Diana replied. "She's a friend of mine. We met here and we've been talking over the last month."

The cardinal brought a hand to Diana's arm and ushered her away and towards his office. He then quietly spoke to her under the door frame into his office.

"I must warn you," the cardinal said, "that this woman is a dangerous individual. Come here. Close the door behind you."

Diana followed the cardinal into his office out of curiosity. She closed the door and then looked to him as he poked at the fireplace.

"Sit down," the cardinal insisted.

Diana sat down.

"Ms. Vaduva has been excommunicated from the church for holding dangerous beliefs, Ms. Cambridge. We have asked her in the past to refrain from coming to this cathedral and other churches in the diocese until she renounces her beliefs, but she has held her head up high with pride and refused to submit to the Church's wishes."

"What sort of beliefs does she hold?" Diana questioned.

"Beliefs of the old," Cardinal Calavera replied. "For example, she has been seen teaching to children as young as old that the persecution and various pogrom of six million Jews by the Church over the years was just because of their role in Christ's death, counter to statements established by the Church in Vatican II which forgave the Jewish people, and has insisted that much of Church-led persecution was justly done."

"What?" Diana remarked. "I don't believe you."

"Ms. Vaduva also runs a dangerous organization, I'll have you know, but the location of this organization's home is unaware to us. She is rumored to be the head of a sort of cult, placing the lives of children at risk and in danger, and practicing in what I can only describe to be, unholy practices."

"What do you mean?"

"I'm afraid I have said far too much," the cardinal replied, straightening up and going to his desk. "Promise me that you won't speak to this woman again."

"I- well, I…"

"How have you been?" the cardinal then suddenly questioned. "Have you found peace?"

"No," Diana responded. "I had a bit of peace this afternoon, but I've just learned that my ex-boyfriend's been in a car crash, and I've been asked to help."

"Why's that?"

Diana hesitated to answer. The cardinal looked at her expectantly.

"You wouldn't believe me if I told you," Diana admitted with a laugh.

"Try me on for size," the cardinal responded with his own hearty laugh. "Go on, tell me."

Diana took a deep breath. She then explained Tristan's immune system, his condition, and the condition of this girl as a 'meta-human,' as Charlemagne told her. He then said how the girl had injected him with a virus that sustains the condition of the girl, but that this virus has come into conflict with Tristan's artificial immune system and forced him into a critical condition. At the end, the cardinal was very much interested with a finger over his mouth and the rest of his hand at his chin.

"Interesting…" the cardinal expressed, "how our two worlds have collided. Ms. Cambridge, what if I told you that I may be of some help to you?"

"How so?" Diana questioned.

"Your ex-boyfriend, Tristan, was a terrible man to do what he did to you, but it may not have been his fault. It seems that the two of you have been led astray by vampires…"

"What?" Diana questioned.

The cardinal stood up and placed his hands behind his back.

"I did not want to say it, but it appears that you're more informed than I imagined. The unholy practices that Ms. Vaduva and her followers practice are vampiric practices. I am not sure if they are worshipers of demons, but they certainly are themselves, demons not of this world that take part in devilish and cult-like practices. It is their narrow-minded beliefs that threaten the integrity and survival of the Church, so it has been my mission, as granted by his Holy Eminence, the Pope, to see to it that they are taken care of."

Diana was silent.

"Now, the decision is yours whether to help this boy or not," the cardinal said. "However, you can let your infatuation and lust of your former partner chain and force you to act to save him, or you can move on. You are not in his debt, as I am sure that you will move on and find someone else…"

"He might die if I don't help him…" Diana stated.

"No," The cardinal denied, "his death would not be your burden to carry, but his. It is his actions that have placed him into the situation he is in, and therefore he alone is responsible. He made the decision to cast you out of his life, so you must respect that decision…"

Diana looked unsure.

"I don't want to be with him again…" Diana admitted. "He's not the man… boy that I fell in love with…"

"Then let go of him."

"I have to save him though…"

"You are not obligated to save him," the cardinal repeated, stopping in front of the door. "However, this comes to my proposition… the girl. We have only known of Ms. Vaduva's existence, but she is evasive and secretive. The existence of this girl and her role as a vampire may prove of some use to us, so if she were to survive, she could be a key of sorts into locating this hive of vampires that I've been pursuing."

Diana looked to the side. She closed her eyes and shook her head.

"I- I can't believe it… I can't believe that Iustina is a vampire. She… she's been my bestest friend. I've confided into her. I've felt… so warm around her."

"These are the tactics that they employ," the cardinal warned. "They lure you into a false sense of security, and then either abduct you as their prey, or indict you as one of them."

"She said that she had a husband that she had lost… She said that she always prayed for him, and we even prayed together…"

"Lies! All lies!" the cardinal shouted out. "She is a wolf in sheep's clothing, that woman! And I'll have her on a stake for the crimes she has committed against women like you! It wouldn't surprise me that the two of them have been in cahoots since the very beginning, her targeting you, and this other girl targeting and luring your beloved from you. The forces of evil have attacked you, so are you going to sit by and let them get away with it?"

Diana felt a tear drop from her eye.

"Are you going to let more be hurt as you have been hurt? Or are you willing to take on this task for me, to help me purge the world of this evil and rise beyond the duty that you owe almighty God?! Are you ready to bring to justice these monsters and send them back to hell?!"

Diana looked back at the cardinal who was impassioned.

"I… I'll always put God first," Diana replied, "and if God wants me to rid the world of this evil with you, then by God, I will do it…"

Act 6, Scene 1

Diana left the cathedral and found herself atop of the steps of the church, looking out towards Bromley as the sun had long set and Halloween night settled in. She began to muse as she looked around and then she took in a deep breath. Diana stepped forward and then made her way to her motorcycle in an alleyway. Diana took out her phone and phoned Charlemagne.

"Diana?" Charlemagne answered.

"Hi," Diana sheepishly replied. "I'm going to help you save Tristan, Charles. What do you need me to do? Where are you?"

"Come to the University of Harlech," Charlemagne responded. "I'm going to send you our location... we're in a secluded location that's a part of a closed-off building that's under construction. You'll have to maneuver over a fence to get in, but I'm sure you'll manage."

"Okay," Diana replied. "I'm on my way."

Diana made her way from King Island to Cliffe Island, and then to the University of Harlech. She stopped outside of the building that Charlemagne's location came from and saw that it really was a closed-off construction site with tall fence around the perimeter. Diana took her bike and parked a block away. She then walked back to look at the site.

The building where Tristan was being kept in was unfinished, but almost finished. The site lacked proper landscaping as all around was just dirt, but the exterior walls had been finished and windows placed in. The inside was dark and there was no sight of security around the perimeter.

Once Diana had a good look of the grounds, she began to run across the street and then jumped atop of a roof of a parked car, using it to give her a boost as she jumped over the fence and landed on the other side unscathed. She rolled at her landing and then ran to take cover. She then moved to sneak around the front of the building, coming to the installed doors at the entrance. Diana brought her hand at the handles, but the doors were locked. She then continued to sleuth around the side of the building, looking up to see some holes in the building where windows had yet been installed. Diana also saw a bulldozer parked nearby.

A campus security SUV passed by the street as Diana hid behind the bulldozer. She watched it off and then proceeded to climb atop and then jump to the unfinished window ledge. She grabbed the ledge with her fingers and shimmied her way so that she was just under the opening before bringing herself up. She then slipped into the building and found herself inside.

Diana took out her phone and followed Charlemagne's location to the opposite-side of the building. Once she was directly above the center of the radius, she came out to an unfinished open corridor and jumped. She then proceeded to wander around until she reached a set of transparent sliding doors with a light on the other side, within another room, or stairwell. Diana pulled the sliding doors open and then ran towards the stairwell and went down to the sublevel.

A cold breath could be seen before Diana's mouth as she came into the basement of the building. The walls were unfinished here and there was a dropped ceiling above, but only the frame of it as the tiles had yet to be installed. A mesh of wires and piping could be seen above. Only the lights were installed and on in this sublevel corridor.

Diana followed the lights and entered a corridor that turned to the left with a window at the end. Diana walked to the wide window and looked inside to where she saw Charlemagne on the other side in the center of a large circular chamber with two bodies strapped onto two separate operating tables, hooked to various equipment. A variety of seats could be seen around the arena-like room that was cordoned off by a tall plastic glass wall, sort of like a circular hockey rink. Diana continued around and then reached a set of doors that brought her into a room ahead where Lacplesis and Elegast were on guard outside of a set of doors. They looked and waved to her. Diana waved back and then went through the doors to join Charlemagne, catching Charlemagne's attention.

"What is this place?" Diana questioned.

"It is an expansion to the University of Harlech teaching hospital being built by Cabernet Construction," Charlemagne explained. "Heavner gave me access to this place to hide Tristan and the girl from the authorities, and to give them medical treatment."

Diana looked at Tristan. He had an oxygen mask over his face and had intravenous needles hooked to a dialysis machine. An oximeter displayed his low heart rate and a blood pressure cuff was wrapped around his arm and showed his last readings, which were low. His skin was pale and he was unconscious.

"How is he?" Diana questioned.

"I'll cut right to the chase, because we don't have much time. He is poor," Charlemagne bitterly answered. "His wound hasn't healed, so I've gone ahead and sutured it myself, but his body temperature has dropped and his blood pressure is low. He... he has heart failure. Currently, his body is at war with the virus, what I've dubbed to be V2-M, and for whatever reason, this virus is so powerful that it is giving the nanomachines that make up Tristan's immune system a run for their money."

Diana looked over to Helene. Her face and arms had been wrapped in bandage. She looked like a mummy.

"At first, it seems like the virus was able to offer what I can only describe to be a natural healing process, but then it came into contact with the nanomachines and they've been at it ever since. This virus… it has an incredible exponential growth rate, and in its rush to survive, it has been developing millions and millions copies of itself to fight against the nanomachines. The last blood sample I took had an estimated fifty percent loss. If this continues, Tristan might not have an immune system left because the nanomachines are not equipped to replace themselves. However, in order to achieve that, the virus has torn so much of Tristan's organ systems that there might not be anything left to save."

"And what's her problem?" Diana questioned with a disgruntled voice.

"She's been burned," Charlemagne responded, "and severely cut. When she bit into Tristan to give him the virus, the nanomachines attacked back at her and treated her entire body as a foreign agent. It began to destroy her face and it's left her with a multitude of cuts as well as some burns from, what I assume to be, from the sunlight. I'm not sure what her condition is, but I'm curious as to why her body has not healed on its own. I don't fully understand this virus and its purpose, so I'm continuingly learning…"

"So, she bit him and this has happened to him…"

"Yes," Charlemagne affirmed.

"Do we even know if the virus was responsible for Tristan's heals? I mean, Tristan's never suffered any major wounds other than the lashes on his body, a few cuts here and there… How do we not know that his mother's nanomachines were responsible for the healing, and that this virus just ruined everything…"

"Why would she bite into him?"

Diana shrugged.

"To save herself?" Diana suggested.

"She is clearly not well, if you can see that. She clearly has not saved herself," Charlemagne remarked.

"She's gotten what she deserves…" Diana muttered under her breath.

"Nonetheless, I'm glad you're here to help… I'm in the works for a cure, or more accurately, a poison that would eliminate the virus. I've taken apart the virus and been able to find a weakness… There's a chain in the RNA that codes a protein, which if I apply to a venom found in a plant I discovered at Isla Paraiso in late-August, I believe I could create a poison that targets the virus. I've spoken with Lukas and he's on his way from Allabrese with the canister that contains one of the copies of Tristan's nanomachines that I developed, and once he is clear of the poison, I'll begin treatment to return his immune system as it was, or I should say, as his mother left it. However, I need you to go and fetch this plant."

"Where can I find this plant?" Diana asked. "It's not like I can just fly down to Isla Paraiso right now and hunt for it."

"You won't have to," Charlemagne responded. "There's a pot of it in Allodia's apartment, in the kitchen. I brought one over and left it there."

"That's it? You need me to fetch a flower?"

"I'm sorry it's not as brave as a task as you were hoping, but I really cannot leave at the moment, and only you have access to the penthouse at this immediate moment."

"Alright, I'll be right back," Diana replied.

"Do not take too long," Charlemagne remarked. "At his rate… he won't make it through the night, and it'd be a shame if he died after midnight… It will be, after all, his eighteenth birthday."

"Of course."

"And Diana," Charlemagne said, stopping her in her urgency. "I'm glad you came back for him..."

Diana turned to him and shook her head. She replied, "I didn't come back for him."

Charlemagne looked at her straight.

"Regardless, I know that you won't let him die. If you're not doing this for him, then I'm sure you're doing this for some sort of reason that I know to be noble. I appreciate the help nonetheless, because in the same way, you are helping me."

Diana nodded and then proceeded to leave.

"I'll be right back," Diana expressed.

· · · ·

Diana drove back to King Island and then made her way into the Cabernet Tower parkade, bringing her motorcycle to the curb just before the elevators and then getting off. She removed her helmet and carried it with her as she went to enter into one of the cars. Diana then inserted the pin code, 1921, and then rode up to the 98th floor. Once the elevator doors opened at the 98th floor, Diana stepped out and took her keys to open the front door.

The penthouse was eerily quiet. Diana stepped down the entrance hall and then went into the kitchen, eyeing the pot where she remembered the plant was. She quickly came to the plant and grabbed it by the pot.

"Oh no..." Diana whispered.

The black flower had wilted. Its leaves were crisp and dry, and all of the metals had fallen to the floor. The main step was bent over, hard, and lifeless.

Diana took her phone out from her pocket and phoned Charlemagne.

"Charles," Diana immediately said as he answered. "It's dead. I'm at the penthouse and the flower is all dried up."

"What? How is that possible?"

"I don't know," Diana responded with a bit of panic in her voice. "Maybe because nobody's watered it since it got here two months ago?" she growled. "What do we do?"

"There's nothing I think we can do... that flower was all I've spent my time focusing and hoping on," Charlemagne remarked.

"You must know of something else," Diana insisted. "You have a Plan B, don't you?"

"I'm sorry, Diana, but that's really all I've come up with," Charlemagne stated. "I've been researching that plant for its potential to treat cancer, and the idea was fresh in my mind... I had no other idea other than that. I'm simply not that knowledgeable into this sort of thing to be able to provide an instantaneous idea..."

"Okay..." Diana muttered. "Okay, but what if I knew someone who was knowledgeable about this sort of thing..."

"If you do, then I insist that you go and speak with them at once," Charlemagne replied. "We need as much information as can hope to retrieve."

"Okay..." Diana responded. "Hold on, I'll get back to you."

Diana hung up and left the apartment. She returned to her motorcycle and raced back to Pentateuch Cathedral. Once there, she parked at the curb and went up the steps. She then banged on the door of the cardinal's office and looked at him as he opened the door. Diana then rushed in.

"I need your help," Diana said.

"Ms. Cambridge, what is it?" the cardinal questioned.

Diana explained the last hour since she was last here.

"Is there anything, in all of your years of research and knowledge into the topic of vampires that could help me? I can't let Tristan die, and I know what you've said, but this is my choice…"

The cardinal raised his hands.

"It is not up to you to play God," the cardinal warned. "It is not up to you to decide life or death."

"If you want my help with these vampires, then you'll help me save Tristan. That's my only condition!" Diana ordered.

The cardinal raised his head up and pointed his chin at her.

"Well then," the cardinal expressed. "I'm afraid that I simply do not have any solution, or remedy to this virus."

"What? So, what was the plan then? What's the Church's plan to save these people?"

"Save them?" the cardinal questioned, going to his desk and sitting down. "My dear, Diana, these people are unholy demons. There is no cure to what ails them except the fate of what every demon deserves. I've told you that already, so this shouldn't be a shock to you."

"There has to be something, anything," Diana remarked.

"Have you spoken with the girl yet? She may have information that you seek," the cardinal stated. "Go to her, and if need be, make her talk."

Diana looked back at the cardinal.

"Go," the cardinal said, "and remember… we need to know where this hive is. When you have that information, please come to me."

Diana nodded. She then left. However, before she returned to the University of Harlech, Diana returned to the penthouse to retrieve an object from a small wooden box with carvings on the side. Inside, Diana picked up the dark pinkish-red stone, which she took and placed into her pocket. Diana then raced back to the university so that she could confront Helene.

Act 6, Scene 2

Diana returned to the University of Harlech and went back into the under-construction expansion of the hospital to meet with Charlemagne in the operating theater. Charlemagne looked over to her as she arrived with haste.

"What do you have?" Charlemagne asked.

"We need to wake Helene up," Diana stated. "I need to talk to her."

"Why?"

"Because she might be the only person who knows of anything that can save Tristan's life," Diana explained. "And if she doesn't tell us, then Tristan could die. Can you wake her?"

"Yes," Charlemagne answered, "but it would be very painful for her."

"Good," Diana muttered, looking around at the bed to notice a set of leather restraints at the side. "Help me restrain her so that she doesn't escape."

Diana started to tie Helene down while Charlemagne took out a drug from a drawer nearby. He then set it on a metal table next to Helene and helped Diana finish tying the restraints. Once that was done, Charlemagne took a syringe and extracted the drug from the vial, and then brought it to the intravenous apparatus so that he could slowly give Helene a dose of the drug. Diana watched and slowly Helene began to wake. She moved about with painful moans.

"Helene," Charlemagne said, "can you hear me?"

Helene's consciousness rose as she began to squirm and start to thrash.

"Where am I?" What's going on?" Helene questioned in a panic.

Helene attempted to break out from the restraints as she flexed her arms and legs.

"We need information about your condition," Charlemagne stated. "Can you answer some questions?"

"Who are you?"

"Let me ask her," Diana said to Charlemagne. "Helene, we know about your condition and we know that you tried to infect Tristan. Tell us what we want to know, or this is going to become extremely painful for you."

Charlemagne looked at Diana with worry.

"Let me go!" Helene replied. "Let me go!"

"Where does Iustina Vaduva hide with the others? What is the location of her stronghold?"

"What?" Charlemagne questioned Diana.

"Where are they?" Diana repeated to Helene, ignoring Charlemagne.

"Let me go!" Helene shouted, continuing to the thrash about.

Diana grabbed Helene's wrist where there were she had been burned. Helene cried out in pain as Diana squeezed her arm.

"Tell me what I want to know," Diana yelled. "Where are the others?"

"Let go of me!" Helene replied.

"Where is Iustina? Where can I find her?"

"Diana…" Charlemagne remarked.

"Diana…" Helene grunted. "Let go of me…!"

Diana looked at Charlemagne with slight disbelief.

"Let go of her," Charlemagne muttered. "You're causing her too much pain, she can't even concentrate…"

"Tristan is dying because of this woman, and you think I care that she feels a little pain?" Diana remarked, tightening her squeeze. "What about what I've felt?!"

Helene yelped.

"Tell me where Iustina is!" Diana shouted. "I need to find her so that we can cure Tristan!"

Helene didn't respond. She continued to cry out in pain. Diana didn't remove her grip.

"I..." Helene finally said. "I... didn't try to kill him..." she muttered. "I... tried to save him."

Diana let go of Helene's wrist and then grabbed her neck. Helene shouted out and began to choke.

"You liar!" Diana yelled. "We know all about your lies! The collusion between you and Iustina! Where is she?!"

"Diana, stop!" Charlemagne said, attempting to force her off.

Diana let go of Helene's neck and then pushed Charlemagne back. She then continued to apply pressure to Helene's neck.

"You... you'll never know where we hide..." Helene said in a choked voice. "Tristan..."

"Diana, that's enough," Charlemagne said, moving around and grabbing her. "Seriously, what has gotten into you?"

"Let go of me," Diana remarked, brushing Charlemagne off. "I need her to tell me where the others are so that we can cure Tristan. Don't you see? There are more of these witches out there, and unless we find them, we might not be able to cure Tristan."

"I'd rather take my chances at sending someone off to Isla Paraiso to retrieve another flower than hope for some information about a supposed-coven."

"You'd rather risk Tristan life like that for this shapeshifter?" Diana questioned. "Don't you see? People like her... they're what's wrong with the world. They lured Tristan away from me! They manipulated us and tore us apart! She's just like the shapeshifters from that story we heard..."

Charlemagne shook her head as he took a drug and injected Helene with it. Helene was attempting to break out of her restraints as the two fought.

"No," Charlemagne denied, "she's not. She's far from it."

Diana frowned at Charlemagne.

"I'm going to send word to Heavner to send people to Isla Paraiso by any means possible to retrieve a flower," Charlemagne said. "In the meantime, I'll attempt to stabilize Tristan's condition as best as I can."

Diana walked forward to Helene and took her hand placed it on the opposite-side from the elbow, in the elbow pit. Helene yelled out in even more pain than before.

"Diana!" Charlemagne shouted.

In a quick burst of force, Helene lifted her left arm up in a flex and broke out of her restraint. She then pushed Charlemagne backwards while Diana attempted to hold her down. Helene quickly pushed Diana back and then broke out of the other arm restraint. She then untied the leg restraints as Diana and Charlemagne stood up. Diana took caution and stood back as she stood onto the table and crouched down. Helene looked at Diana.

"You're a fool," Helene said to Diana, "and Tristan is better off without you. I won't let you harm my brothers and sisters. Never."

Helene then hopped off from the table and ran towards the glass that surrounded the arena. She jumped up and vaulted over, making her escape.

"Do you see what you've done?!" Charlemagne shouted. "You've allowed her to make her way off instead of getting what we needed from her! Good job!"

Diana scowled and looked around. Helene was bleeding and there was a stain of blood on the floor, going the way that Helene went. Diana looked at it and then eyed Tristan's cellphone nearby on a table. She grabbed it and then looked at Charlemagne.

"I'm going after her," Diana stated. "Do what you want, but try to keep Tristan's condition stable for as long as possible. I'm going to follow the original plan. I won't let Tristan die."

Diana then went off, jumped up, and then pulled herself over the reinforced glass around the operating theater so that she could run after Helene.

Act 6, Scene 3

Diana entered the corridor that went around the operating theater and followed the trail of blood that took her to an exit. She then came to the end at a junction and looked both ways. The stains of blood could be seen going onwards to the right. Diana followed and then reached a stairwell. She went downstairs and reached a small corridor where the blood continued through a vent. Diana climbed up and began to crawl through.

The trail of blood took Diana to the other side of the sublevel at a corridor at the other side where she continued to follow Helene's path. She went into another staircase and followed the blood to the second floor. There, she entered the large corridor with an open floor in the center that looked down to the ground floor of the lobby. Diana followed the trail down and then around to the other side. She then hopped down and went around a central corridor at the front of the building, and then a set of stairs that went into an open sublevel. Diana observed the trail of blood going from exit to exit as Helene attempted to get out of the site. The trail soon ended at the end of this corridor.

Diana looked around and then fell to her knees as she was hit in the back of the head. She fell over, but quickly turned around to see Helene running off. Diana ran after her, coming around to the front corridor and then the central space of the lobby. Helene jumped onto some crate and then climbed up back onto the second level. Diana followed from behind.

Helene ran down the corridor and around a corner as she went along the second-floor balcony platform turning and going through a door. Diana entered through the door and stopped as she lost sight of Helene. She then proceeded with caution through the interconnecting rooms. Diana moved her sight out of reflex as she spotted some movement from the room to the left. She then followed suit and turned again to the right as she saw Helene moved to the left. Helene then appeared to the left again.

Diana rushed to the other side and saw Helene running down a corridor to the rear of the site. She ran after her and they soon entered another maze of unfinished rooms. Diana took cover at a door frame and looked at the other side. She saw Helene pass, running around with a hand at her bleeding arm. Diana moved in.

Helene saw and ran away from her. She went after her, from room to room, before eventually coming out at the other side. Helene ran towards a stairwell. Diana was closely behind her. They ran up the stairs and came to the third-floor where the windows were not covered. Diana chased her down to the end of a corridor and then Helene turned around the corner. Eventually, they stopped and faced each other at the end of the line.

Diana brought her hands up and readied herself to fight. Helene went ahead and attacked Diana. Diana deflected and countered her attempted punch, bringing her arms down, and then with swiftness, took Tristan's phone from out of her pocket and slipped it into Helene's jeans. She then let go and Helene pushed her back. Diana jumped back and maintained her pose.

Helene looked back at Diana and then took careful steps back. She then turned around and ran off, through the window, and onto a container below where she promptly made her escape. Diana watched her run off and then made her own exit as soon as she couldn't see Helene anymore. She returned to a stairwell and went down to the ground floor. She then walked around to one of the open doorways where she stopped to take out her phone. Diana unlocked her phone and opened a map application. Helene's location was shown under Tristan's name, continually updating as she moved further from the university.

Diana put her phone away and then proceeded to return to her motorcycle. She took her phone out again and saw where Helene was. She was slowly moving southeast on foot. Diana watched for another moment and then put her phone away again, taking her helmet and then placing it over her head. She started her motorcycle and then made her way off, not towards where Helene was, but instead north to Jarsdel Island and then King Island. Diana stopped in front of Pentateuch Cathedral, but continued around up a street that went at the side of the property and came to a small manor.

Diana parked her bike at the curb and then went to the front gates of the small manor. She pressed a hand on a callbox in front of the gates and waited as it rang.

"Archdiocese of Greater Harlech Rectory," a man greeted. "Visiting hours are now closed. Please state your business."

"I'm here to speak with Cardinal Calavera," Diana said. "Tell him that it's Ms. Cambridge and that I have the location of the people he is looking for, as well as a gift."

The man did not respond. The feedback from the microphone cut off and Diana was left outside where she stood, waiting for a response. Five minutes passed and then suddenly, she saw movement from the front of the house. Two men in black suits stepped outside and went towards the front gate, opening it and then confronting Diana.

"Cardinal Calavera will see you," the man said. "If you'll please wait here, we have a car coming to take you to him."

"A car?" Diana questioned.

Diana waited outside and sure enough, within another five minutes, a limousine pulled up and parked at the curb. One of the private security guards went and opened the door for Diana to step in. Diana walked over with hesitation and her phone in her hand. She stepped into the car and then sat down. The man closed the door behind her.

Diana sat in the empty cabin of the limousine and looked out the tinted windows. It was hard to see outside, but she was able to see somewhat. She was taken through Bromley and then they turned left to go into Central Harlech. Based on the buildings around, Diana saw them turn north on Durham Street and continue down all the way to the end. The car then turned east again on Maiden Drive and went all the way around, into the outskirts of Keswick before turning west onto a causeway that took them down and towards the seafront by the rails. The car soon stopped with a view of Walham River on one side and the side of the sublevel of a concrete structure built into the side of the island on the other. Diana looked as the door opened for her and she then stepped out onto some gravel.

Diana looked around and saw that she was at the railyard to the northwest of Keswick, near the expo center, or between the expo center and Bradford International Hotel, and Waterfront Station. The building they had taken to her had a façade of a warehouse, but with a long overhang over them of structures that faced Maiden Drive on the other side, and an orange glow from the lights that lit the surrounding area. The façade of the building ahead consisted of two platforms with shutter doors for trucks to park their rears to. To the left of these shutters there was a concrete platform above a set of stairs and a ramp, and a metal door where there was another body guard standing before it. Diana noticed a security camera pointed down at the door.

The security guard in the black suit led Diana towards this door where they stopped before it. A lock then turned from the door and it opened on its own. Diana was led inside and she entered a dark corridor with half-paneled cardinal red walls and old cherrywood floors. A long old rug was stretched out across either point of the long corridor. There was a mildew smell of the old structure and the lights were dim. It had an atmosphere like a haunted house. Her steps on the creaky old floor echoed. The guard led Diana down the hallway and then through a set of double doors at the end, which took her to a small lobby where there was an elevator at the end.

Diana waited for the elevator doors to open and then she continued through with her escort. The elevator went up a short distance and then opened again. Diana was then led out along a corridor where there were some paintings on the wall and a continuation of the dimly lit lanterns. The building had a regal atmosphere, but the condition of the walls, floor and sight of some cobwebs around the lamps and corners showed a lack of care in the maintenance of the building. Diana was led right around a corner, down to the end where there were a set of double doors, and then to the end to a junction where she was led left and then to a set of doors at the right.

Two bodyguards at the door opened the set of double doors for Diana and she promptly walked in to enter a large room. The room was mostly empty, but it had the same regal atmosphere as the rest of the house. This room was well-kept unlike the other rooms. The panels of the walls were a similar dark oak wood to the floorboards with a hint of red in them. However, unlike the rest of the house walls which were painted a dark red, the walls in this part of the building were of stone and they were tall. Beams crossed through the middle of the walls and then over the ceiling, and columns every so often to support the size of the room. There were various candelabras around the room and two large gold chandeliers that hung from the ceiling. The room was tall, at least two-stories in height. At the other side of the room, behind a raised platform, there were benches like those in the gym at Lord Phoenix Secondary for people to watch games from. At the center of these stands was a podium. In the space that the stands looked down to, there was nothing more than a table and a chair that faced the podium directly. At the sides of the aisle in front of the stands there were curtained archways that led out and provided access from rooms at the side.

"Please wait here," Diana's escort said.

Diana was then left in the room. She looked around the room again. She then took out her phone and looked to see what Helene's location was now. Helene was still on Cliffe Island, but to the south near Grafton Bridge around a set of properties to the east of Southton. She was near the castle that was private property in that area. In the least, the radius of Tristan (Helene's) approximate location was in this area. Diana put her phone away as the door opened and Cardinal Calavera walked in with open arms.

"Ms. Cambridge," the cardinal said. "What a pleasant surprise."

"I have what you wanted," Diana immediately said back to him. "I spoke with the girl, and she went back to the location of their stronghold just like I thought she would. Before she could escape though, I planted a tracking device on her."

"This is remarkable news!" the cardinal exclaimed. "Yes, you have exceeded my expectations!"

"I also have a gift for you, your eminence," Diana replied, reaching into her jacket.

The cardinal took a single step back as Diana put her hand in her jacket. He looked tense. He then relaxed as she produced the dark pinkish-red rock. His eyes fixated on the rock and widened. The cardinal looked back at her.

"Where did you find that?" the cardinal questioned.

"It was a present," Diana answered. "From the chief of the local people of Isla Paraiso in the Caribbean. It was a present for some humanitarian efforts I helped in last summer, and it came with a story about these vampires – apparently this material is capable of bringing great harm to them. I want to offer it to you as a present…"

Diana extended the rock towards him. The cardinal looked at the rock carefully in Diana's hands. He then brought his hands up, palms to the rock and ushered it back.

"Now, now," the cardinal remarked, rubbing his hands together. "I cannot accept this – you keep it. You're going to need it for the fight that is about to ensue."

"Fight?" Diana questioned.

"Follow me, Ms. Cambridge," the cardinal said, leading Diana out of the room.

Diana followed the cardinal out and then they went right and down the rest of the corridor. The cardinal stopped to speak with one of the guards, whispering into his ear. When he was finished, the man nodded to him and then left. The cardinal then took Diana into a parlor where there was a fireplace, some expensive-looking sofas, a pool table, and various decorations such as a shield, a statue of some knight armor, and a bear skin rug. Diana was taken to a set of double doors at the end and then brought through into a conference room.

The conference room contained a large and thick table that was lit by lamps in the center. There were at least twelve seats in total in the room with a larger chair at the head of the table. Behind the head chair, on the wall, there was a mount of a boar that faced the room. At either lateral side, there were flat screen TVs. At the end of the room there were a set of double doors that went out of the meeting room and back to the corridor. From the ceiling, there was a projector aimed to the boar. Diana noticed a rolled up projector screen near the boar, hanging from the ceiling. In the middle of the table, Diana also noticed another device, similar to the projector above, but facing the chair.

The cardinal sat down in the head chair while Diana stood by the doorway to the parlor. A tablet sat in front of the cardinal and he began to tap at it. He then waved his hand to Diana for her to come over.

"Come," the cardinal said, "stand by my side, dear Ms. Cambridge," he insisted. "I am to announce of our work in a meeting with my colleagues. You are to be commended for your actions…"

Diana stepped over sheepishly. She then stood next to the cardinal on his right-side.

"What is the location of our enemies?" the cardinal questioned Diana.

Diana took her phone and showed him. The cardinal looked.

"Aegis Castle?" the cardinal remarked. "Hm, this is a surprise, but a welcomed one."

Dian put her phone away. The cardinal looked forward and brought his hands together and onto the table. Diana straightened up and looked towards the camera. A ringing could be heard from some speakers in the corner as a video call was being placed through.

Cardinal Calavera spoke as soon as the ringing stopped and said, "My dear brothers, ever since I was placed in charge of my archdiocese seven years ago, I have worked tirelessly to uncover and eliminate the threat within this region that is the remnants of the experimentation orchestrated by our great enemies, the Order of St. Athanasius, and the remnants of that horrid cult we attempted to rid from this world sixty years ago. As you know, many cells loyal to the message of this secret society remain in the world, but the monsters that they have created are the worse kind of threat against our survival. Today, we are on the cusp of a pivotal turn in the fight against these monsters as we have now learned the location from where they operate from, and it is no less than Aegis Castle."

Cardinal Calavera paused for a moment.

"Within these walls, the last remaining survivors of the experimentations conducted by the Order have made their home and most likely in the process of rebuilding. This castle, right under our noses, has become a breeding ground for the type of bigotry, intolerance and hatred that cannot be allowed to point its nose out from the underground they hide from, and which results in the deaths of many lives. Many lives have been irreparably lost and damaged by this foul race of people. Today, no more. With this new information that I have been given to me by our agent in the field, the lovely Ms. Cambridge, I will organize a team to have this castle torn apart and the last of these monsters physically eradicated. Today is a great day for us, my brothers, since the revolution sixty years ago."

The cardinal then said something in an unrecognizable language. The camera then turned off and the priest stood up to turn to Diana.

"Come," the cardinal said. "It is time."

Cardinal Calavera led Diana through the structure and downstairs where they came to the garage at the rear of the building. The two shutters were open and there were two armored black vans parked with their rears. Diana saw there to be many people below, dressed in dark blue tactical uniforms and with the insignia of the Harlech Police Department on their shoulders, and the words 'Police' at the back of their vests. On the left shoulder, a patch said 'ETF,' which was the abbreviation for the Emergency Task Force, or SWAT unit of the Harlech P.D. Some of these supposed tactical police officers were speaking with some private security guards in black suits. The cardinal led Diana down a platform and then looked at the men around him. He then clapped his hands together and began to speak a language that Diana did not understand. Cardinal Calavera gave a lengthy speech before the men went to the vehicles.

"Ms. Cambridge, for your efforts in this pursuit, you will ride with us and pay witness to the fall of evil," Cardinal Calavera stated, leading Diana to the back of a van. "The endeavor that we are about to take on is all on you, pay witness to it and I'll see you at the castle."

Diana looked to the cardinal as he waved to her. She was rushed into the back of the van by some of the policemen as the van's engine started. The van then set off as she sat down, and two policemen closed the door behind her. Diana sat down in the middle of the many men she was with and placed her hands on her lap as she waited to arrive at Aegis Castle for the assault that was about to unfold because of her.

Act 6, Scene 4

Diana continued to sit in the back of the armored van with her hands on her lap as they drove along. There were no windows in the back of the van, but it was lit by a bright LED light above. The tactical police officers, which Diana looked to suspiciously, were armed with assault rifles and various other gear. All of them wore helmets and gas masks that covered their faces and heads. She looked at all of them and saw that they sat with discipline, looking across from each other like robots. The van drove for several minutes on smooth road until suddenly they made a sharp turn and began to drive over a rougher surface. Diana struggled to hold on as there was only a bar above that one could grab onto.

The van continued to drive and then they made a sudden brief stop as if they had hit something before continuing on. Diana noticed the slope in the car change as if they were climbing a hill. Within a few more seconds, the van finally stopped and the room became flooded with a greenlight.

The mercenaries dressed as policemen rushed out from the back of the van, yelling at each other in the same unknown language that the cardinal had been speaking to them. Diana was left behind in the rear of the van as they cleared out. She then stood up, bending over at the tall ceiling, and then hopping down. Diana looked around and saw the other van as well as some other cars, including two large trucks that had searchlights on a platform. The searchlights were being moved to point towards the castle they were in front of. Another vehicle had a cannon on it, which blew smoking shells that fell into the inner grounds of the castle. There was even a helicopter flying around. Diana saw that they were at the second gate of the castle, past the initial gate by Norwich Street and up the hill to the inner walls of the castle. The mercenaries moved in groups and took position at the side of the road as a battering ram was brought towards the wooden gate doors into the inner castle grounds.

A final vehicle arrived behind all of the others and it was an armored SUV driven by more mercenaries dressed as ERT officers. They went around to the rear passenger door and opened it. The cardinal stepped out and looked around. He then began to shout towards the men in the alien language that Diana was unfamiliar with. She watched as the battering ram began to hit the wooden gate. A loud thud could be heard and the gates sort of moved inwards, but did not budge. A second impact did the same, but the third caused the gates to finally open. Some mercenaries shot canisters from handheld launchers, creating a cloud of smoke, which they ran into as they opened fire. The cardinal met up with Diana as they watched.

"I want to confront her," Diana said. "Iustina has to pay for what she has done."

"You will have plenty of time, my dearest," Cardinal Calavera responded. "I will make sure of it. However, first we must call her out... with the blood of her minions, no doubt."

The cardinal was handed a lit torch by one of the mercenaries.

"Today, is the end of these monsters," the cardinal stated, walking forward. "Come, we must not get left behind."

Diana followed as the smoke began to clear. They passed through the gates under escort by up to six mercenaries who followed them with assault rifles. They met up with the others who had taken position at the large arched doors of the castle. Diana looked around the yard and saw that it consisted mostly of stone with little to no life around. Some mercenaries had begun to take apart some wooden benches and throw them into the middle. The cardinal shouted something to them, waving his hand around the sort of bonfire that they were creating. Diana watched as the men with the battering ram hit the doors to enter into the castle.

Meanwhile, once all of the benches had been added, about four in total, the cardinal dropped his torch and created a small bonfire.

"Tear this place apart," the cardinal remarked in a loud voice. "Take every one of them from this insidious place and have it razed to the ground. And when that is done, I want the earth salted so that none may know of this place and what once was here, and no life may spring from this retched ground."

A mercenary came with a megaphone for the cardinal. He took it in his hand and then looked up to the castle façade.

"Countess!" the cardinal shouted. "Come out from the shadows that you hide from! We have you surrounded! There is nowhere else for you to hide!"

The doors bashed open and the mercenaries poured in, opening fire. Diana could hear screams from within. She stood back to wait for the smoke to clear, and once it had dissipated slightly, she moved in to step into the castle. The doors had been smashed down, so she stood onto them and then looked around the castle entrance hall.

The interior was not that different from the exterior, where the exterior of the castle was constructed out of a smooth greyish-beige stone and the roofs of an orange-red shingle tile. The inside consisted of smooth stone walls and lit not by lamps, but by candle light. The floor consisted of smoothened cobblestone. A statue at the rear of the foyer, atop of a landing between two sets of stairs that branched left and right and then went down to the ground floor at a single wide set, was of the Virgin Mary with her hands extended outwards and head tilted, looking down. Behind her, there was a beautiful circular stained glass window above, and two more arched stained-glass windows. Two white banners at the side walls, above sets of doors that went left and right had an upright black cross with the points from edge to edge. Below the left and right staircases there were archways that went down into corridors that branched off left and right respectively.

Diana waved her hand so that some of the smoke before could dissipate. She then jumped back at the sight of a dead body before her. Diana looked at the corpse that lay at her feet of a young woman with similar very light fair skin to Helene, but this woman had brown hair. She was dressed in modest clothing, but bloodied with a streak of blood across her face. Her eyes and mouth were open, but she was clearly dead. Her arms were at her side, palms facing up. A leg was twisted to the side and bent. Diana looked away from this body as a mercenary pulled the corpse away, and then her eyes shot over to one of the archways underneath the left stairs as she saw a shadow for a brief moment.

The mercenaries continued up the stairs and into the halls at the side on both the ground floor and second floor, guns blazing, and a small team set up a perimeter at the entrance, while others began to do as the cardinal had asked, and rip apart the furniture, bringing some of the wooden parts out to add to the fire. Diana looked at where the shadow she had seen was with intent and began to go off on her own, entering through the archway and stepping down into a corridor whose floor consisted of old wooden floorboards. Mercenaries had followed her into the corridor, but not to join her, but instead rip portraits from off the walls and spread gasoline around in preparation for a fire.

Diana saw a floor lamp fall over and the bulb crack. She went over and picked it up. The pole of the lamp was made of a firm steel with engravings around the entire cylinder. She took off the bulb, which was held in place not just by the screw, but two thick oval wires. She also removed the lampshade and threw it onto the ground, and kicked off the feet to create a spear-like pole. Diana took the sharp stone from out of her pocket and began to place it where the bulb was, fastening it by the clamps that kept the lightbulb in place. Diana tightened it so that it fit snuggly and then she tested her weapon with a couple of jabs into the air, seeing that the stone held. With this weapon in hand, Diana ventured forth into the west-side of the castle, going through a set of double doors that went into another, but longer hallway.

The corridor that she had entered had many doors at the side, about three on each side, with a final one at the end towards the left-side. The doors were shut, but she was not interested in them. The walls in this portion of the castle were lined with wallpaper and consisted of wooden panels at the bottom half. At the end of the corridor there was a painting next to this final door that was open and led into a small room. The painting depicted a scene from Dante's *Inferno*, with the many layers of hell.

Diana entered the room next to the painting and saw that it had another painting and an ottoman before it. To the right of the room was a large set of wooden doors that had been left slightly open. Diana pushed through and entered a circular room with many windows around the side. Above the center of the room was a domed ceiling. On the floor below was a depiction of the black sun. A mural above was painted and showed a romantic depiction of Heaven. Diana continued through a door on the side, which took her to a courtyard surrounded by stonewalls and triangle-like in shape. There were two alcoves around the courtyard with wooden doors on the other side. A third alcove on the left had an open door. Diana crossed and entered through, coming into a narrow corridor, which took her into a small room. The room then led into a stairwell that went down. Over the stairs there was a large painting that embellished the top of the stairs. Diana continued down and reached a corridor, which she went down to finally reach a set of large wooden doors.

Diana pushed against the wooden doors and entered into another, larger circular room. She looked around and saw that it was like a parliament with stone benches plotted around like wide crenellations, all looking to the center where there was another depiction of the black sun set in stone. The walls contained a pattern of arched windows. Above there was another domed ceiling with another depiction of art, but this time of a beautiful and rich garden, the Garden of Eden, with Adam and Eve in the center. A narrow arched door could be seen at the side. Diana continued through and found herself in an adjacent circular room. This room was messier and contained rubble around. Diana looked up and saw that the room went up for a couple of stories upwards. At the top of the tower, light could be seen pouring in from an opening above. A set of iron bars blocked off a room at the side, which looked to contain the stairs that went up and around the side of the tower. Diana went over to a crank at the side of the gate and began to raise it up. Her hand slipped as she raised the gates, and she saw that the gate immediately fell and smashed into the ground. Diana looked at the spikes at the end of the gate and began to raise it up again, slowly but surely reaching the top. She gently let go of the gate and saw it slip down again, but she then cranked it up again and then took her spear and shot it through the chains, ensnaring the mechanism and preventing the gate from collapsing down. Diana took a deep breath and then went through to look up the stairs.

Diana's attention then shifted as she heard a noise from the other chamber. She looked out and saw a shadow in that direction before she could climb up. Diana went on and through, re-entering the parliament room and then returning back to the courtyard. Diana stepped outside and looked around, seeing smoke from the other side of the castle. She walked across to the corridor she had come from, seeing that the circular room had caught on fire and it was impossible to walk through. Diana returned outside and then stopped right where she was to look across to a balcony at the other side of the courtyard where the countess, Iustina Vaduva, could be seen looking down to her with a serious glance. She wore a black dress, a black cloak with a hood not raised up, and had black lipstick over her lips and eyeliner under her eyes. Diana's attention focused onto her as she walked forward and raised her hands up.

"Diana," Iustina called out, "what are you doing here?"

Diana looked at her with hatred in her eyes. She refused to respond. Instead, she clenched a fist at each of her sides.

"You're here with these rogues, aren't you?" Iustina remarked. "I should have known you were with them…"

"There she is!" a voice shouted out.

Diana looked to the side as a couple of mercenaries appeared atop of the wall to the right. They raised their weapons up. A fourth mercenary appeared with a grenade launcher and readied it. The helicopter nearby flew in and shined a light at her. All of them, but the one with the grenade launcher, opened fire at her. The countess jumped down and with a great, but not supernatural speed, she ran across and threw knives that she produced from the side of her dress at each of the mercenaries, hitting each of them with precision. The mercenary with the grenade launcher even fell over and landed on the ground below. Diana looked aside and covered her face as Iustina stopped before her.

The helicopter began to malfunction and crashed atop of the building to the left, causing the archway through to collapse. Diana maintained her arm as a dust cloud roared over them. She then saw Iustina step towards her. Diana took a step back.

"You have been misled, child," Iustina remarked.

"Yes," Diana responded, looking at her through the dust, "I've been seriously misled. It's no wonder you came into my life at the same time as that other woman. Since the beginning of the month, I've been misled to believe that you were my friend…"

Iustina stopped before her. Diana sprinted towards the right wall and grabbed the grenade launcher. She then took it and aimed at Iustina. Iustina moved in and before Diana could fire, she grabbed Diana by the neck and raised her up as if she weighed nothing. Diana squirmed as she was raised up.

"If you are with those that threaten my children and home," Iustina said, "then I will treat you all the same…"

Iustina threw Diana around with great force, tossing her onto the embattlements above the left-side and hitting a wall behind the wall-walk. The impact against the wall made a minor dent. Diana fell over and struggled to recover. The countess moved quickly as she ran up and picked her up again, throwing her back into the courtyard like a ragdoll. She was then taken again, and thrown up to where the dead mercenaries were, where the knives had hit them dead-center into their skulls. Iustina moved in towards Diana again, but she scrambled away and took a grenade from the body of one of the mercenaries, pulling the pin and causing a cloud of smoke to form.

Diana jumped down and went around to where she had dropped the grenade launcher, picking it up, and then going to the other side of the courtyard with the grenade launcher ready. Iustina could be seen through the smoke as soon as it dissipated slightly. She saw Diana too and jumped down, but before she could reach her, Diana fired a cartridge, and it hit her dead in the stomach. The effects of the cartridge were not what Diana had expected. The cartridge erupted as it his Iustina and created a cloud of thick brown smoke. Diana watched as the countess fell to her knees and began to choke. She then walked towards her with caution. Diana raised a sadistic smile.

"How does that feel?" Diana questioned, bringing the grenade launcher around her back on a strap and then squatting before her. "For the past half of this day, I've had to choke on my tears because of what you and that other woman did to me."

Diana grabbed the countess by her neck. She then threw her onto the ground. The countess attempted to intercept Diana's punch, but the gas had made her weak and slow. Diana punched at her face and then picked her up by the neck, dragging her and then forcing her onto her feet. Diana raised her hands up and proceeded to continue punching her like a punching bag. The countess was powerless to stop her. She backed up towards against a window, and Diana pushed her inside. Diana hopped in and then went to her, proceeding to kick her in the side.

"After all the pain I've faced..." Diana remarked. "All the memories I had thought I lost... Tristan's life that now hangs on by a thread...! So tell me, how do I fix him?! How do I reverse what Helene has done?!"

Iustina glared at Diana. Diana grabbed her by her hair and began to pull her down the room towards a fireplace. She picked up a fireplace poker and raised it up to beat her with it. However, before the first strike could hit, Iustina countered and grabbed it. She then hit Diana in the ankle with it. Diana fell over. Iustina stood up and picked Diana up, throwing her through a window as the two went back into the courtyard.

Diana scrambled to escape the countess as she came for her. She stood up and brought the grenade launcher around, but she caught up with her and picked her up. Diana was thrown back to the other wall-walk, and then again through a larger window where she landed on the other side. She quickly recovered and prepped the grenade launcher, aiming it out the window as the countess jumped in. Diana fired it and it hit her in the chest, igniting and bringing them both into the cloud of brown gas. Diana breathed slowly and saw that she was unaffected by the gas. She then stood up and walked over to the countess, picking her up and knocking her into a wall. Diana then faced her.

Iustina looked as if she was choking. Her hair was amess and she was shaking. Diana clenched her teeth as hard as her fists and proceeded to hit her in the stomach. She then threw her onto the ground.

"How do I save Tristan?!" Diana yelled. "Tell me, what is the cure?!"

Diana began to hit the countess with her fists, beating into her as she was silent and coughing out loud.

"Tell me!" Diana yelled out.

"There is no cure…" Iustina murmured in a choked voice.

Iustina caught Diana's wrist with full strength. Diana trembled as she sat up and squeezed at her wrist. The countess' hair had fallen over the front of her face, masking her serious green eyes. Before she could break Diana's wrist, she stood up and threw Diana into a dry wall with such a force that Diana came to the room on the other side. Diana cried out in pain as she landed. Iustina walked through the other side calmly, patting dust off her clothes.

Diana scrambled up with anger and charged at her. She tackled her through back onto the other side and their impact caused the floor to collapse and for them to land in the room below. Diana was knocked back while the countess stood up. Iustina then grabbed Diana and threw her into a bookcase in the room, causing some books to fall over. She was then thrown through a doorway and taken into the small room before the staircase that went down to the parliamentary chamber and the east tower. Diana scrambled to stand and then ran off, down the stairs, and into the corridor before the chamber.

Iustina followed and when Diana saw her behind her, she ran down the corridor, readying the grenade launcher and then turning around to drop on one knee and fire it at her. The cartridge hit just as Iustina was about to pounce onto Diana, causing her to fall before her. Diana looked back at her and then threw the grenade launcher aside. Iustina was paralyzed and gasping for breath.

Diana grabbed the countess by her cloak and pulled her into the parliamentary chamber where she lay her down in the center. She then left and went into the other room to retrieve the spear, returning to walk over to where the countess was still gasping for breath, but attempting to crawl away. Diana went up to her and placed her foot on her back, stopping her.

"Good will always triumph over evil," Diana remarked, panting. "People like you, will always be crushed by people like us."

Diana looked down at the countess as she struggled to breath.

"What are you really…? You're nothing but a freak…"

Diana raised her foot up and went around to bring her foot down onto Iustina's neck to steady her head. She lowered the spear down and brought the tip to Iustina's cheek. She squirmed. Diana then raised the spear up again to deliver the final strike, and then brought it down to the countess' head.

However, before she could pierce through, Diana's focus was broken by the sudden whisper of voices from within the room. She looked around and began to see various children, as young as one-years old in the arms of older children, and others as old as old as eight or nine years-old standing on their own, appear from behind the castellations around the outer rim of the chamber. Diana saw the various children, all with the same fair skin, but all of them with different features from dark brown hair to light blonde hair, some with a reddish hue, and others without. There was also variety in the colors of their eyes, as these were people of light. Diana looked at one of the children, a five or six-year old who stepped forward towards Diana. The boy had blackish-brown hair and blue eyes. He timidly approached Diana and looked up to her.

"Please don't kill my mommy," the child requested in the most innocent voice.

"G-go away, children…" Iustina remarked. "R-run…!"

"Children?" Diana questioned, looking back at Iustina. "What are you talking about?"

Diana looked back at the countess collapsed on the ground. The light in the room lit her hair up in a different shade. Diana flinched. She looked back at the boy as a tear fell from his eye. Diana noticed some of the other children to be crying as they watched.

"Please don't kill our mommy…" another said.

"Please don't kill our mother…"

Diana heard other voices in a similar tune.

"Mother…" Diana muttered, stepping away from the countess and looking at her.

Tears fell from Diana's eyes. She looked at the countess with her arms stretched outwards before her.

"Oh my God…" Diana remarked, dropping the spear and falling to her knees. "God forgive me!"

Act 6, Scene 5

Diana jumped as she felt a hand on her shoulder. She fell backwards and attempted to crawl away from Iustina.

"Easy, Diana," Iustina remarked.

Diana stood up and turned her back to her. She then attempted to leave.

"I have to go," Diana said, going towards the exit.

"And go where?" Iustina questioned. "Has your mind cleared? Have you realized who your true enemy is?"

Diana stopped and did not respond.

"Neither I nor my Helene took your love from you. The fact that we all had met each other at the same time is nothing more than a coincidence."

"I've led these people to your home and they're killing innocent lives... blood is on my hands..."

"And you intend to run away from that..."

"What is this place?"

"This is my home," Iustina replied, "or what remains of it. Aegis Castle once belonged to my husband, and together we have raised the children here who have no one like them, but each other."

Diana turned around and looked to Iustina.

"Perhaps I should explain in further detail..." Iustina said. "All of us are the products of an experimentation in which man went too far... The idea was that of a man named Tristan Williamson, the final leader of the Order of St. Athanasius, a secret society of priests whose aim was the protection of the Catholic Church from infiltration and the preservation of Roman Catholic traditions. In the 1960s, all priests who had an association with this sect were excommunicated, exiled, and some even assassinated in this decade of assassinations. A spirit of revolution had fallen over Western Civilization during this time period, and no institution was safe from the wind that came out of the Second World War. However, despite this fallout, there remains very few that are devoted to the cause, and they were led by this man, Williamson, whose final project took the form of advancing human capabilities beyond their current condition. He desired to have humans evolve... as they had already reached the peak of their natural progress, but could achieve so much more... He put together a team of scientists, took specimens from throughout the world, and through surrogate mothers, raised us, the world's first superhumans... However, the people that you have brought to the castle who work for our opponents, a satanic society known as the Children of Moloch, have sought us out and attempted to rid us, seeing us in specific as being the largest threat to come against them since the Second World War. Williamson was killed, as were the many scientists when the laboratories were attacked by a raid co-opted by federal law enforcement in the United States. Those of us that survived have lived in fear of being hunted and killed, and in an effort to preserve and safeguard many alike, this castle was meant to serve as a place of refuge. My children here... many of them are orphans..."

Iustina walked to one of them and squatted down. She placed a hand at the boy with dark hair's cheek.

"I love every one of them... As I said, the Children have sanctioned bounties against people like us, and as a result, many of us have died over the last thirty years even though we've attempted to live out normal lives. I am one of the few from the original experimentations, most likely the last, and these children are the children of parents, either one of or both, of the people that I spent my days with in that convent where we were born."

"Why does the 'Children," refer to you as vampires? Aren't you similar?"

"We are not vampires though..." Iustina remarked. "We were meant to be as beautiful and wise as angels, but in the end, we were nothing more than test subjects because any further trials were stopped before they could take place."

"Wh-when Tristan was bleeding out, Helene bit into Tristan's side and it caused him to become infected with a virus though..."

"What happened there, most likely, is that Helene had seen that your Tristan was bleeding out and offered him a gift that we hold in which venom pours from our teeth. This venom offers healing powers, but it is a potent substance."

"Tristan is dying because the artificial immune system, given to him by his mother (himself an experiment), and his mother a member of the sister organization of the Order, is clashing with some sort of virus that is destroying these nanomachines. If I don't find a cure for it, Tristan could die very soon...!"

Iustina looked at Diana with concern.

"I had no idea the situation was like that..." Iustina remarked. "I also had no idea that Helene had done so much harm to you, or that she was the one that had been with your beloved Tristan. To that, I must express sorry twice. Helene is a girl that my love and I adopted, and who was especially loved by my own beloved. The loss of my husband, her father, hit her hard, especially since she's been under the influence of that witch who was under his sphere. Alas, there is no cure."

"So, Tristan is doomed to die then..."

Iustina looked apologetically to Diana. She then raised her sights up.

"Wait," Iustina said, "perhaps there is one more hope..."

Iustina began to walk towards the door that went to the east tower. Diana followed.

"My husband was an intricate man," Iustina expressed. "He was a man of science and ingenuity, and he studied all sorts of very strange things in his time. His personal room is at the top of the east tower. I will take you there, and maybe there is something you may use…"

Iustina pushed against the door to the east tower and allowed Diana to pass. She then faced her children.

"Children, barricade the doorway and do not let anyone through! If you hear trouble, remember to hide!"

Diana and Iustina then went to the base of the east tower. Iustina went to the crank and began to raise the gate. She brought it to the absolute top where it clicked and stayed. She then went and began to climb up the stairs.

"Tell me, who are these people that I've brought here? This isn't the first time I've met with these people… the people who call themselves the 'Children of Moloch,' because last summer, as part of a bizarre incident, I ran into them several times…"

Iustina nodded and then said, "What I know about these children of Satan is what has been told to me by my husband and his own research, and that is many years ago (thousands of years ago), there were several meteorites that landed in the Antarctic and from these meteorites, there came a horrible creature with the sinister power to change shape and mimic other life forms in their outer appearance."

"A shapeshifter?" Diana questioned.

"Yes, exactly," Iustina confirmed. "However, these were not merely nor simply bloodthirsty ravenous creatures. These were rational creatures, but they are also Fallen creatures. Somehow, they had escaped the Antarctic where they came to meet with human civilization and become one with it. There, they found their place and they have walked among us ever since. Within the Order, they have received a name that describes all of these entities and not only the ones within the Children of Moloch, many of members of which, are not even shapeshifters. We refer to them as the 'Chosen,' because they believe themselves to have been Chosen by God when in reality, they have been chosen by Satan who is their father. It was believed by my husband that these people were literal fallen angelic beings, although he lacked the proof to prove that theory. Over the years, the possession of the ability to shapeshift has become lost on a majority of the Chosen and only a very few exist, who my husband say possess extraordinary abilities, and are at the top of the hierarchy of the Children of Moloch."

"What exactly is the danger in these 'Chosen?'" Diana questioned.

"The danger in the Chosen is that they subvert and destroy societies which they infiltrate," Iustina explained. "By no means, as far as I know, are they dangerous creatures face-to-face, but over the years, they have developed a tendency to enslave the people that allow them to live amongst them. However, in their own greed, they eventually bring about their own fates as people learn to rise up against them. The skill of which that the Chosen fear most in us, is the ability to 'sniff' out these shapeshifters, and it is for this reason that they wish us gone most of all."

"So, the story I heard was right then..." Diana replied.

Diana proceeded to tell Iustina about the tale from Isla Paraiso so that she understood.

"How many of these Chosen are there in the world?" Diana questioned.

"By today's standard, it is estimated to be two percent of the world's population," Iustina answered. "The number of which that possess the ability to shapeshift, and in other words, contain the original structure of their ancestors with no mutations, is unknown to me but likely significantly low; as many of us as there are them."

Diana and Iustina reached the top of the stairs, which took them to an open wooden platform with a space in the center, protected by wooden railings that looked down to the bottom. At the side there was a wooden staircase that went up above. Diana followed Iustina to the stairs.

"How do you defeat a shapeshifter?" Diana questioned. "In the story, it said that they have tough outer bodies."

"I am not sure exactly, but people like me were made with strength thought to be enough to stop a shapeshifter if we ever got into a fight with one. However, we were also taught to never fight a shapeshifter alone, and in truth… I've never met a shapeshifter in my life. So I cannot say for certain, but if the story that you told me is true, then that rock you have should work well against them."

Iustina pushed against the trapdoor above them and then climbed out into the room above. Diana followed and stepped out.

"I have never been allowed up here, and ever since he disappeared, I have respected that decision," Iustina remarked. "As time goes on, I will eventually have to accept the fact that my love is gone… Please, see if you can find something of use out of all these things that he's collected."

Diana looked around the immediate area. There were lots of shelves. The room was also very cluttered. On the shelves there were lots of plastic boxes, cardboard boxes, and various random tools scattered in an unorganized fashion. Diana stepped forward and came to a workbench at the outer side of the tower with a view from a window of the city. Atop of the workbench there were vials, empty and full, and some jars that had brains submerged in murky liquids. Diana looked at these strange objects with skepticism and slight disgust.

"Jeez…" Diana muttered, "this place is worse than Charles' old lab.

Diana flinched as lightning flashed. Her eyes then jerked towards the wall before her as she saw the shadow of a figure behind. She immediately turned around and yelped out. Iustina looked as Diana had let out a scream and clenched her breast. Diana's eyes widened with shock.

"What…?" Diana whispered.

Behind the shelf that formed the aisle by the trapdoor, there was a messy twin bed in the corner next to a mannequin that wore the full outfit of the Mysterious Stranger. The mannequin wore the torn trench coat with the hole from when Diana had pierced him with the harpoon, the gas mask, the helmet – everything. Behind the mannequin, there was a wall with various weapons hung against it. Below there were cases of munitions.

Diana stepped forward and picked up a picture frame on the end table next to the bed. She looked at the picture and saw that the picture was an old picture of her as a child. Diana quickly sat it down and then turned to the bed, looking at the wall which was covered with various pictures that made Diana even more uncomfortable. Against the wall, there was a map of the province of Alberta and British Columbia, side-by-side, with a string going from Harlech and to a picture of Diana taken in secret, and another string going from St. Nazaire going to a picture of Tristan. Both of the pictures depicted the former couple when they were at least thirteen years old. Near the picture of Tristan, there was a newspaper clipping of a road-side accident that claimed the lives of two people, Elisabeth and Zachariah Merrick, and by the picture of Diana, there was a newspaper clipping of the murder of William Cambridge with a picture below of Diana taken in secret and her mother. Next to this display, there was a satellite image of a facility from above. Diana recognized it as Cabernet Laboratories. Around the map there were strings going from some of the entrances and towards pictures of these areas. There were also pictures above, one of which was a clear shot of the fusion reactor. Below this display, there was a map of the Ural Mountains, specifically Wicked Mountain and the Tsarina resort. Next to this, there were some newspaper clippings of Diana's successes in the Nattau Derby as well as some photographs taken from afar and in secret of Diana and Tristan together, holding hands and another of them kissing. Above and next to this display, there was then a map of Egypt with various markings on top of it, going to photographs of various monuments and dig sites, and then there was a map of France with various markings that showed the path Diana and the family had taken on their tour of the country. Below, there were news clippings from the United Kingdom, one of Finn and Tristan from the security footage that was taken of them at the plant, another from the shooting that occurred at the Cunningham Lodge, and others of the forest fire that ravaged Northumbria-Berwick. Below this, there were photographs taken from a distance of Tristan's father, the psychic, Maxim Bauer, and next to this were four profiles of each of the four psychics with an 'X' marked through each of their photos in red marker. Next to this, there were photos taken from afar of Diana and Tristan, most likely in St. Nazaire, and then a news clipping of the shooting at the RCMP detachment in the same city, the fire that engulfed the church, and the shooting at the border. Lastly, there was a map of Asia with markings in China that had an 'X' at certain points. Diana then looked down at the end table where she saw a postcard like the one that had been sent to

Everest and Vienna, inviting the mysterious stranger to the ball at Villa Paraiso, or at least half of it. The other half of the invitation was missing, ripped in half by whomever the mysterious stranger was. Diana quickly looked over to Iustina who stood by the workbench.

"Who was your husband?" Diana questioned. "What was his name?"

Iustina closed her eyes and took a deep breath. She then opened them and looked to Diana peacefully.

"Damian," Iustina answered. "I knew him only by that name, the name given to him at his birth. He told me only to refer to him by that name…. My sweet, dear Damian…."

The two of them then looked to the trapdoor as they felt a seismic vibration followed by some gunfire.

"My God… no!" Iustina remarked. "Find what you need and deliver Tristan back into life. I must go and save my children!"

"Wait…!" Diana remarked.

It was too late. Iustina had left.

"Let me help…" Diana muttered.

Diana went to the work bench and looked around. She quickly noted the plant in the corner of the room. It looked just like the plant that Charlemagne had. Diana looked around and then found a dirty needle. She pulled the plant out from its pot and extracted the venom from the roots as Charlemagne had told her to. She then squirted it into an empty vial she had found, closing it with a lid and twisting it to make sure it was nice and tight. Diana then put the vial into her jacket inner pocket, but stopped as she saw some other vials with a transparent blue liquid inside. She picked one up and read the label stretched across which said, "Water from the Fountain of Youth." Diana looked at the label unconvincingly, but took a couple of them into hand and stuffed them into her pocket. She also took a couple of empty vials and placed them into her other pocket, but before she could leave, she stopped to pick up a vial with some dark red liquid inside. The label read, "O- Blood – Tristan M." Diana stuffed the vial with the vial of venom from the plant in her inner jacket pocket before she went downstairs to join Iustina.

Act 6, Scene 6

Diana met with Iustina where she was crying in the center of the parliamentary chamber with the corpse of a child in her arms. Diana stopped just at the entrance into the room as she saw all the massacred children with a look of horror. Diana's hands and legs shook. She grabbed the frame of the door to steady herself and brought a hand to her mouth. She took deep breaths and then carefully made her way over to Iustina, looking around the entire room. Near the entrance going back into the courtyard, there were two dead mercenaries with knives through their masks. Diana touched Iustina on her shoulder.

"These demons have gone too far..." Iustina remarked. "All of my children... dead..."

"I'm... I'm to blame for this," Diana muttered. "I brought them here... I caused all of their deaths."

"Now is not the time for self-loathing," Iustina replied in a cold voice, laying down her child. "Now is the time for vengeance of all these innocent lives... Helene is in the West Tower where she is healing in the fountain of youth. She won't be able to fend for herself on her own. We have to hurry..."

"Fountain of Youth?" Diana questioned.

"It is a small fountain connected to a spring whose waters have a rejuvenating effect for us, and those like us..." Iustina replied. "This is why my husband bought this castle to house us, because it is one of the few places where such a spring exists. We must hurry..."

Iustina went across the room and towards a cabinet against the wall. She opened the doors and took out a sword that was displayed inside. She attached a belt around her waist and carried the sword at her side. Meanwhile, Diana collected the grenade launcher with some smoke grenade pellets and the spear. Iustina and Diana then left the chamber and returned to the courtyard.

The blaze that had been set on the castle had grown worse and lit the dark sky that was covered above in clouds of smoke. A helicopter could be seen flying nearby with a searchlight below. There was no more shooting that could be heard in the distance. It was slightly quiet. The exit into the other circular chamber had caved in. Next to it, Diana could see a short arched tunnel that went into one of the side gardens within the walls of the castle, but it was blocked by a portcullis.

Diana followed Iustina up a section of the wall ahead that had collapsed so that they could climb up to the wall-walk, and then enter through the center of second floor of the castle. They went down a corridor and entered into the foyer. They took cover by the balustrades as there were mercenaries below. Diana eyed them through the slots in the rail guard.

"We'll have to pass them quietly," Iustina remarked. "We don't have time to engage them."

Iustina kept down and then swiftly went around and towards the other side. Diana followed. They entered another large corridor with a red carpet down the middle. Iustina turned at the junction and went down to a set of double doors at the end. She pushed through them and then continued down a similar corridor, stopping at the corner to the right where they took cover. Iustina peaked around the corner then faced Diana behind her.

"There are two of them posted just outside the doors to the west tower," Iustina reported.

"I'll lay down some cover," Diana said, bringing around the grenade launcher.

The two of them switched sides and Diana then popped out to launch a smoke grenade towards the mercenaries. Iustina then went in and rushed over with the sword drawn. Diana followed and they met up with three more mercenaries around the sides that they could not see. She went in and engaged one, taking him down and then moving to the other. Diana pounced on him and brought her leg down on his neck. Iustina then brought the sword down and finished him off by stabbing him through the heart. The two then went towards the door.

Iustina pushed against the door and they entered into the base of the west tower. The chamber in the ground floor was larger than the other chambers with six columns connected to each other and the walls by rib vaults. At the end of the room there was a tympanum with water flowing down and into a shallow pool of a bluish-green liquid. In the middle of the fountain pool there was a smooth stone rectangular pedestal where Helene was placed within the water without being submerged or made to float. She wore a simple white dress and nothing more. There were some monitors and other equipment to the side. Some wires were attached to Helene, particularly underneath her dress at the breast and an oximeter on her finger. In front of her, Diana saw the back of a man in black clothing, kneeling down to her with his hands hovering over her body. Iustina rushed forward.

"Get away from her!" Iustina shouted.

Cardinal Calavera quickly grabbed Helene and raised her up even though she was unconscious. All of the wires that were connected to her fell off. He held a dagger in his hand and brought it to her neck as he held her as if she was a ragdoll. The cardinal looked over to them with a serious face.

"Not another step," the cardinal warned, looking to Diana. "So, you failed to slay this woman and instead have allowed her to deceive you once again?"

"I haven't been deceived," Diana remarked. "At least not from her! You're the one who's killed innocent children. You're the one who's holding a knife to the neck of that innocent girl!"

"Innocent is not an appropriate term for this kind," the cardinal replied, groping Helene with his other hand, bringing it around the front of her body and towards her breast. "They are monsters – abominations whose evolution have no place in the world we have envisioned. At last, they are no more, however…"

The cardinal brought his nose towards Helene's cheeks and neck as he sniffed her.

"… it would such a shame to kill one who is so beautiful, yet so deadly… aren't you, Ms. Köhlen."

Diana's ear twitched as she sensed people move in behind her. Three mercenaries moved in and pointed their assault rifles to them from behind. Diana froze.

"I'm afraid that this is where we must part," the cardinal remarked. "Thank you again for your help, Ms. Cambridge, and to you, Ms. Vaduva, farewell. I hope that hell is kind to you!"

The cardinal began to shuffle to the side and made his way to an archway that went into a set of stairs. He then disappeared.

"Diana," Iustina said, "get down!"

Diana looked to her. She ducked down. Iustina span around and produced three more knives from within her cloak, using them to kill off the three mercenaries before they could even fire a bullet. She then went off and sprinted after the cardinal. Diana followed.

Iustina moved faster than Diana, running forward as the stairs at the side came to a stone base of the tower where the open shaft extended upwards with wooden stairs that went up to a platform above. They eventually separated as Iustina led the way and a distance grew between them. By the time that Diana reached the top of the staircase, Iustina was already above on the roof. The staircase led to the wooden platform similar to the east tower, but with an opening in the ceiling where a large bell could be seen hanging. Diana went up the staircase and went through the trapdoor. There, Diana saw Iustina with the cardinal, dagger to her knife now and Helene passed out on the floor at the edge. Iustina's sword was on the floor at her feet. Diana froze as she saw the cardinal with her taken hostage. A helicopter flew nearby. Iustina struggled with the cardinal's grip around her neck.

"Don't you move another few centimeters," the cardinal threatened.

Diana stayed where she was. She looked around the roof. The roof contained a half-wall around the side and in the middle there was covered space where there were various bells hanging from the open ceiling of the pointed roof. In the open space in the middle, there was a wooden railing around. The trapdoor that Diana had come out of came out near the edge of this center space. The top of the tower was similar to the top of the tower at Medici Manor where Arturo's bedroom was. However, there was no beautiful view of all of Nattau County from here, nor was there the sunshine and blue skies of the region, but instead the crack of lightning and dim grey clouds, and the lights of the bright city as it stormed down. Diana stared towards the cardinal as Iustina continued to squirm.

"Let her go," Diana muttered.

The cardinal gave a diabolical laugh.

"What kind of impact do you think a beast like this would make from a fall from here?" the cardinal questioned. "I doubt she'd survive."

"We can talk about this…" Diana reasoned.

Iustina broke free from the cardinal grip. She then disarmed the cardinal as she jabbed him with her elbow and then kicked up the sword into her hand. Iustina took the sword to the back of the cardinal and then stabbed him, piercing through the back and out the other side. The cardinal let out a sudden yelp and then fell over. Iustina patted her hands and then walked over to Helene casually.

"And that is that…" Iustina remarked.

Diana looked over in shock. She shook her head and took a deep breath. Diana turned around.

"Relax, my child," Iustina said. "It is over…"

Diana breathed slowly and closed her eyes. Iustina knelt over and brought a hand to Helene's cheek.

"At least one survives…" Iustina remarked in a quiet voice. "My poor child…"

Diana turned around and looked over to the cardinal. His body was motionless on the floor. The sword poked out. Diana looked at the sight closely. Her eyes then widened.

"Shapeshifter," Diana muttered.

"Hm?" Iustina questioned.

"He's a shapeshifter!" Diana shouted. "Look!"

Diana pointed to the bloodless corpse of the cardinal. The body began to shake. In an instant, the arms stretched out and extended, losing their human form as they took on a sort of strange, elongated stem or vine-like form. Iustina shouted out as the arm ripped through her stomach and pierced out the other side. A terrible moan came from the corpse of the cardinal as it erupted and was replaced with the strange formless shape of a terrible beast, one that caused Diana to cringe in horror and anxiety. Diana rushed out of the way as another arm attempted to come around to grab her. She took cover behind a bell and the arm hit the side of it, causing the bell to chime. The moan grew louder. Diana stayed in cover as the shapeshifter pulled off the corpse of Iustina, causing her to collapse next to Helene.

The beast then came towards Diana, but was left to the perimeter as it was too large to enter under the cover where the bells were. Its vine-like bluish-black arms were kept back by the array of bells that protected Diana. Diana stayed in cover as she attempted to maneuver around. The beast yelled out to her.

Diana observed that Iustina's sword was still stuck in the back of the beast. She got a better look at it and saw that it had great horns and terrible yellow eyes. Its composition was a mixture of animals. Its arms were like the tentacles of an octopus at one side and the large claw of a crab at the other, its torso like that of a lion and its head between that of a wolf and a bull. At the side of its body it had legs like a large spider, and at its hind it had legs of a lizard and a hairy tail like a rat. Its outer surface was pink and veiny as one could see the veins within the delicate slimy outer layer. Diana readied the spear in her hand.

The creature attempted to grab Diana as she maneuvered around the bells to get in close to stab at the beast with her short spear. The shapeshifter took Diana by the ankle, causing her to immediately stab at the tentacle with her spear and cause it pain. Diana hit the bell by accident as she retrieved her spear, hitting it and causing some noise. The creature cried out in pain as it heard the sound of the bell.

Diana paused for a moment and then hit the bell again. The creature shouted out. She hit it again and then ran off to the next, hitting it and then getting in close. Diana charged the beast with the spear and hit it in the chest. She retracted the spear and then hit a bell with the back of it before going in for another jab. Diana pulled the spear out and then felt the tentacles of the beast grab her and squeeze her.

The bells continued to echo around as the beast whipped Diana around and then threw her back. Diana landed safely inside and then proceeded to go around again. She hit some of the bells and came out, readying the spear and throwing it towards the head, but hitting the neck. Diana ran in and jumped up, grabbing the spear and then jumping over onto the back of the creature. The creature raised itself up, causing Diana to tumble backwards as she grabbed the handle of the sword. She held on and looked below at the drop that awaited her if she let go. Once the bells had stopped, the creature began to spin around at its place, smashing the half-wall around the top of the tower with its tail.

Diana quickly pulled the sword out and then grabbed the spear. She held on and was grabbed by the shapeshifter. Diana cut off the root of the tentacles that had nabbed her and she fell onto the side of the roof. She then scrambled away, hitting some of the bells as she went to rest behind the biggest bell. The creature moved around to attempt to get to Diana, moving in its tentacles with caution as it attempted to find her (the creature was too tall to even look into the alcove). Diana moved around with both the spear and the sword in hand.

The shapeshifter moved in the opposite direction from her. She began to go in through the middle and then faced the shapeshifter head on as it cried out in pain from the many bells that played. Diana proceeded to slash it at the front with the sword. She then took the spear and prepared to jab it through the head, but was grabbed before she could. Instead, Diana stabbed the spear into the neck again and cut off the vines that had grabbed her. She pivoted herself around onto the back and stabbed the creature into the back. The creature yelled out. A flash of lightning hit nearby. Diana left the sword where it was and retrieved the spear. She then hopped off and returned to cover. The shapeshifter calmed down as the bells settled.

The helicopter flew in and shined its light down. The shapeshifter cried out a loud yell and then began to climb up onto the roof above where Diana was. Diana moved towards the edge, but also eyed the helicopter as it prepped its guns, spinning them up. Diana took grenade launcher and aimed for the cockpit with it, shooting and piercing the glass. The cockpit windscreen cracked. The helicopter opened fire, but began to fly around with less stability.

The shapeshifter grunted as bullets began to pepper it at the side. Diana then moved out to the perimeter to get a view of the beast above. It had climbed up to the top spire where it held a vine around. The other arm came down to hammer Diana. She jumped out of the way as she was attempting to steady the spear to javelin throw it. Diana then ducked down and dropped the spear, causing it fall over as a bolt of lightning came down and hit the beast through the sword. The shapeshifter cried out and was set aflame.

Diana looked to the side as the helicopter returned and began to spin up its miniguns to open fire at her again. She ran into cover, leaving the spear behind, and took out her final weapon, the grenade launcher, and began to prepare another shot as she evaded the bullets. The bullets hit the bell and began to hit the beast again, causing it to cry out. Diana saw the ceiling catch on fire and stayed near the edges to escape the pending collapse of the roof.

Suddenly, the shapeshifter took its arm and transformed it into another series of vines that grabbed the side of the helicopter. It took the copter and threw it towards Diana, causing her to jump down and out of the way as it crashed into the side of the tower and caused some of the bells to collapse. A fire engulfed the west-side of the west tower. Diana looked over to where Helene still was, but before she could stand up, the floorboards collapsed and she came tumbling down each of the stairs before hitting the bottom of the tower.

Diana saw Helene's body land near her as she made a rough landing, but survived the fall due to the many flights of stairs. Before she could move, the largest bell came down between them followed by the debris and then the beast, which caused the floor to collapse again as they landed and fell into the chamber with the fountain of youth. Diana rolled her landing and struggled to stand up.

The shapeshifter broke out from the debris and shouted out in pain. Diana saw that part of its tail had touched the fountain, causing it to sizzle as if the water were acidic or corrosive. The sword was still in its back. Diana rummaged through her pocket and retrieved a vial of the water. She then threw it at the creature, hitting it at the side and causing it to drench the creature with a small, but effective splash of the holiest of water. The shapeshifter cried out.

Diana moved in, with less cover to use, she took cover by the column. The shapeshifter brought its crab-like arm towards her and hit each side, entrapped her behind the column. It then took its tentacle-like arm and cut through the stone column, forcing Diana to run off to the other side. She stayed in cover and took out her second vial of water, preparing to throw it and then launching it and hitting the side of the head. Diana then ran forward and climbed onto the side, grabbing the sword and take it out.

Diana attempted to run up the back and stab the beast in the head, but she was thrown off and taken to the other side. She hit the door as she landed and was separated between the sword. Diana quickly recovered and took the spear which was nearby instead. She then ran around the opposite-side, hiding behind a column and staying put as the shapeshifter attempted to attack her. Diana moved to the next column and then the next as the creature attempted to destroy each of them, and she took the spear and threw it at the side of the creature, piercing it.

However, before Diana could go in and grab the spear, the creature took ahold of her and raised her up. Diana squirmed. The creature enforced its grip with its other arm and then began to bring Diana towards it. The shapeshifter looked down at her, raising itself as a mouth opened at its chest. The mouth had a horrible snake-like tongue and many teeth at the sides. The creature brought Diana towards this mouth, but before it could assimilate with her, there was a chink of metal. Diana looked up and saw the chandelier above come down and hit the creature in the back. Iustina's sword landed nearby and Diana was dropped.

Diana looked to the right and saw Helene there, awake and on one knee. The shapeshifter shifted its attention to Helene, allowing Diana to go and retrieve the spear. She pushed the spear in, causing the beast to lower its body down so that she could climb up and then pull the spear out. Diana took the spear and laid it down into the vertebrae of the creature.

The shapeshifter yelled out. Helene, with Iustina's sword in her hand, climbed up the other side and began to go up the neck. She stabbed the sword into the side of the creature, causing it to tip up and for Diana to fall. Diana grabbed the spear nearby and then went around.

"Now!" Helene shouted to Diana. "Push it in now!"

Diana nodded to her and took out her last vial of water. She threw it towards the chest of the beast where the lips of the mouth was. She then went in and stabbed it below the mouth and started to push it forward with all of the force she could muster. The creature fell backwards and became caught in the wires of the medical equipment by the fountain. Some explosions began to detonate from the machines as they fell in the water. Diana was blown back before she could look to Helene who continued to hold on at the neck, maintaining the sword.

Diana looked over to where the creature was shouting out in pain as it sort of drowned in the shallow pool, thrashing around. Diana couldn't see where Helene was, however, before she could stand up and look over, she collapsed and blacked out.

Act 7, Scene 1

Diana slowly opened her eyes. She looked forward and saw a mess ahead at where the creature lay dead. The chamber was dark. Diana walked over with cautious steps and went to the corpse of the beast. She pulled out the spear and held it in her hands. She then began to look around the debris for Helene, or even Iustina, but was unsuccessful. Diana stopped and looked back at the creature. She put a hand in her jacket and felt the vials secured within. She then went over and began to fill the empty vials with water, but saw that the pool was empty. Diana hopped down and began to go around the back of the creature. She then jumped as the corpse of Helene fell as Diana placed a hand on the shapeshifter to maneuver around.

Helene was lifeless and her eyes were wide open. Diana placed a hand at her head to check her airway, but she was not breathing. Her heart had stopped for who knew how long. Diana picked her up and then began to carry the body out from the chamber. She took her all the way to the front of the castle where it was deserted. The fires had settled down, but the interior was amess. Diana went outside and then took the body over to the bonfire where the charred corpses of her brothers and sisters were. Helene was set down before them, and with a limp, Diana began to walk away from the grounds as she heard police sirens close by.

• • • •

Diana returned to the University of Harlech and made her way carefully back to the operating theater where Charlemagne was with Tristan. She entered and he looked over to her.

"Where have you been?" Charlemagne questioned. "I've been attempting to contact you?"

"I've been... busy," Diana stated, retrieving the vial from her jacket. "Here..."

"What? Where did you get this?" Charlemagne remarked.

"Please, cure him," Diana said. "What Helene did to him... She tried to save his life, but in the process, infected him with this virus that wasn't supposed to do what it did. She had no idea of Tristan's immune system. It was only supposed to heal his wound, not make him into one of them..."

"How do you know of this?" Charlemagne questioned. "Did you find the others? Are there others?"

Diana did not respond.

"I was wrong to blame Helene for what happened between me and Tristan. Maybe I was even wrong to blame and be mad at Tristan... He hasn't been the same since last year, and a part of me believes that the boy I loved once may never return. I was a fool to fall in love with a boy and expect that to last..."

Charlemagne began to set off in creating a cure.

"You did what you could, and the fact that you've come to save him even though he hurt you was the right choice," Charlemagne simply said. "We'll have to celebrate... although it would be wrong to make plans to celebrate so soon..."

"I won't be seeing you again, Charles," Diana stated.

"What?" Charlemagne questioned.

"I'm emancipating myself from the family," Diana remarked. "What Tristan did to me... it was not his whole fault, but it was also not my fault entirely. He hurt me. We can never be together again, but at the same time, we're still your two adopted children. I'm sorry, but because of that, I can't be a part of that connection to him. I have to move on, because if I stay, I might never move on..."

Charlemagne was silent.

"Thank you for all the adventures and wisdom, Charles," Diana said in a soft voice, hugging her cousin, "because of the care and love that you gave me, adopting me and opening your home to me, I've become a different, better woman. I will always love you, Charles…"

Charlemagne was astonished. He struggled for words. Diana looked to Tristan.

"I don't need Tristan in my life so that I can live," Diana stated. "I hope that he can be the same… Tell him… tell him nothing… Goodbye, Charles."

With her final words, Diana left the room. Charlemagne watched her leave and then sat down at his stool. He brought a hand to his forehead and then looked over to Tristan scornfully. He continued to work so that he could produce the cure.

• • • •

Diana left Cliffe Island and took a taxi to retrieve her bike left at the cathedral. Afterwards, she went to her old neighborhood of Keswick and drove down to a dive bar accessible from an alleyway off Pulteney Street and Trutch Street. Diana parked her bike and then hopped off. Before she entered the bar, she looked at her phone to see that the time was slightly past two o'clock.

The interior of the bar was rugged and simple. It was a standard sport and dive bar with sport banners, flags, and jerseys, TVs nearby, booths, tables, and a counter at the side where the bartender served drinks. The bar was quiet and there were a few patrons, most of them passed out. There was a pool table towards the back of the bar and almost no windows aside from those that looked out to the alleyway. Even then, these windows were translucent and made of stained glass in a diamond pattern of red-green-yellow.

Diana looked around the bar and then went towards the counter as she saw someone with a leather jacket, head down with a hand around a drink. The man had dark hair. Diana went over to him and sat down next to him. The man was listening to the music and in his own thought. He looked casually to his side as he saw Diana sit down next to him. Diana sat down next to him almost as if she knew him, been with him the whole time, and just returned from the washroom.

The man looked at Diana through his faint light blue, almost grey eyes, and dropped a look of surprise. The man was slightly unshaven and had thin dark hair that was a pepper-black. He also had thickish eyebrows. He raised a smile as he saw Diana and then spoke in Scottish accent.

"Good God," Scot remarked. "Look at what the bloody cats dragged back in…"

"Did you miss me?" Diana questioned.

"Missed you?" Scot repeated. "Of course, I've bloody missed you. How've you been my little angel?"

Scot put his arm around her and then embraced her by the side and kissed her atop of the head. He then looked over to the bartender.

"Oy!" Scot yelled. "Get a drink for my prodigal daughter here!"

"She doesn't look nineteen, Scot," the bartender responded.

"She's not a narc, you buffoon," Scot argued. "Just give her a pint of beer, eh? We've got to celebrate! I vouch for her… put it on my tab."

The bartender poured Diana out a glass of beer and then pushed it towards her. Diana looked at it and then gave a timid smile to Scot.

"So, what bring you to Harlech? How old are you now... I think you've got to be at least eighteen, right?"

"Yeah, that's right," Diana replied. "I've actually been here for a while, but to be honest, I've been avoiding Keswick."

"Oh, how come?"

"I'm in university," Diana said. "I'm at Declan Walham University, studying science, but I don't want to stay. I think I might drop out..."

"What? Why?"

Diana shook her head and answered, "It's just not for me. I got in because I needed an excuse to come back to Harlech and be with my (now) ex-boyfriend, but we recently broke up and now I'm re-evaluating my life."

"What? Wait, who was your boyfriend? It wasn't that kid, was it? What did he do to you?"

"It was, but relax, please," Diana insisted. "What's done is done, and I don't want anything more to do with him, or any of that," she said, sighing. "That's why I haven't been near Keswick though... because I've become absorbed into this new life that I had where I was happier, safe, and in good protection, but now that it's over, and I've left the family, it's time for me to return to my roots – to where I belong."

"I'll tell you where you belong," Scot said. "You belong with the Syndicate, working with me, that's where. I've had dreams of this moment, so please tell me that you'll join."

"As a matter of fact, that was my intention in finding you," Diana replied. "I want to join the Syndicate, just like we were supposed. I want my life to return back onto the course it was previously on."

"Well said," Scot remarked, downing the rest of his scotch. "It's getting late, so how about we go and see the old

Montgomery now before it gets any later, huh? I'll drive – do you drive?"

"I have a motorcycle," Diana said, "but I also know how to drive a car. Let's go and see Montgomery."

. . . .

Charlemagne watched Tristan with crossed arms as he slowly woke up. His heartbeat had returned to a steady, relaxed rate. Tristan began to squirm in his bed as he opened his eyes. He looked up to the bright lights above him and then around the immediate area. He turned onto his side and saw Charlemagne. Charlemagne continued to look at him, unimpressed.

"Where am I?" Tristan questioned. "What happened?"

"What do you remember?" Charlemagne questioned, standing up and going over to Tristan.

Charlemagne began to examine Tristan. He checked his eyes and then looked at him.

"Hm?"

"I..." Tristan hesitated to speak. "I remember the car crash, and... I remember phoning you. Where's Helene?"

"She's gone," Charlemagne replied. "I don't know where she's gone to though. I suppose that's the same of what I can say about Diana..."

"Diana..." Tristan muttered, bringing a hand to his head. "No... No...!"

Tristan sat up and leaned over. Tears fell from his eye.

"Why did you have to wake me up? Why couldn't you have let me die?!"

Charlemagne looked at Tristan with contempt.

"Get ahold of yourself," Charlemagne remarked. "I don't pity you, Tristan. What you did to Diana does not give you the luxury of pity... no matter what you've been through or are feeling. Instead, all I can give you is my sense of shame... shame that this is what you have decided to let yourself become."

Tristan didn't respond.

"Honestly, have I taught you nothing? What were you thinking? What gave you the right idea that you could go ahead and go off with this woman when Diana had melded your souls together? What you've done, Tristan... it's nothing short than adultery."

Tristan didn't respond.

"Hmph," Charlemagne said, "while my lessons may have been lost on you, it wasn't lost on Diana, particularly, the vital lesson of self-sacrifice. The only reason that you are alive, is because Helene had given you a chance to heal and me time to find you, and because Diana (despite what you did to her) went out of her way to somehow secure the enzyme I needed to create the cure that rid you of the virus that nearly took your life. Instead, you've placed yourself thirty years ahead of where I was – ungrateful for the blessed life that you have and instead lingering in what could and should."

Charlemagne shook his head. He then went into further detail about what had happened with his immune system and, details about the virus that he had from Helene, and the cure he had to construct. He then told Tristan about the flower from Isla Paraiso and how despite that the one at the penthouse had withered, Diana had found another and sought out other metahumans like Helene. He also told him about the metahumans, what he knew about them, and the fact that Helene was one of them. Charlemagne then returned to his computer as he sat down at his stool.

Tristan stayed sat up, hands around his legs and together before his knees. He stared in front of him. Charlemagne stood up and came back to administer some drugs into Tristan's arm. He looked away as he injected him.

"Unfortunately, because of your... irregular immune system, you're going to have to be careful until I can start treatment to restore your nanomachine levels back to what they were. Currently, they're ten percent of what they were..."

"Yeah, that's me... bubble boy..." Tristan muttered.

Charlemagne inserted the used needle into a sharps container and then prepared to remove the intravenous needle from Tristan's arm.

"We won't be able to do this therapy here... you'll have to come to Cabernet Tower for that. We can't stay here..."

"Where the hell are we even?"

"We're at the university, in a construction site Cabernet Construction is responsible for," Charlemagne replied. "When I heard what happened, I spoke with Heavner and he was able to gain access of this place for us."

Tristan put on his shirt and then climbed out of the bed. He remained seated as Charlemagne went to put away some materials.

"Am I staying with you until I get some nanomachines, or can I return to my dorm and move on with my life?"

"If you think I'm going to let you be alone after all that's happened, and the apparent suicidality you've gained, then you have another thing coming..."

"I didn't ask for this, you know," Tristan said. "I didn't ask for you to come into my life. I didn't ask for all these experiences... I had a normal life before all this, you know."

"You could have still had a normal life had you acted normal," Charlemagne remarked. "Of course, no normal person does what you did, no less to do what you did to Diana..."

"Isn't that the explicit point?" Tristan questioned. "That I'm not normal...?" he said, breathing sharply as he adopted a saddened look. "No, a normal kid can be stressed about school and his girlfriend, but I didn't just have that for the last two months. No, instead... I had to stare death in the face as I thought my best friend had died when he fell... an inch away from being able to take my hand so that we could escape together. Then, I had to process the fact that the people I thought to be my parents, weren't my parents, and then see my real father had died... with me oblivious to the fact that he was my father, and then soon after meeting my actual mother, I had to see her die as well. And then there's the everlasting trauma of being abducted, tortured, and brainwashed to serve a neo-communist's personal, private army. And as if that wasn't it, there's all that crap with the pedophiles and the cult, and the realization that we live in a desolate, evil world. There is no such thing as justice. There is no such thing as good. It's all a fantasy... And in the last two months..."

Tristan went silent.

"I've lost her. Diana loved me, and I'll never experience another moment with her again..."

"Did you love her?" Charlemagne asked.

"I don't even know..." Tristan replied. "Does someone who loves another person do what I did to Diana?"

"My thoughts remain the same," Charlemagne remarked. "I feel sorry for Diana, not you."

"I'm sorry," Tristan apologized.

"Don't apologize to me," Charlemagne responded. "Apologize to her."

"But I'll never see her again..." Tristan remarked. "Ever."

Act 7, Scene 2

Diana rode in the front of Scot's sports car as they drove from a secured parking garage near the dive bar, over Penultimate Bridge, and then up from Westford to a neighborhood known as Foxwood Vale. There, they drove through the small village and then reached the large mountainside property known as the Mayfair, which was where Oswald Montgomery took his residence overlooking the rest of Harlech. Diana looked to the side at the evergreen trees as they drove in the thickness of night down a dark road.

"Montgomery hasn't been doing too good," Scot noted. "I'm afraid he might be in his last years, in which case, we could be heading into some turbulent times in terms of succession of his role... His daughter has an interest and she's been active with us ever since his memory has started to fade a little, but some people within the ranks of the tactical division aren't very keen about her stepping in if he were to die."

At the end of the road, there was a gate where private security welcomed the sport car belonging to Montgomery's commander of his private army, and then drove onto the front of the property around a fountain in the center. The Mayfair was a traditional English-style mansion with white-framed windows, stone walls, and grey stone balustrades along the perimeter of a tall hip roof. The mansion consisted of three-stories, not including the attic. The courtyard in front of the gate consisted of stone where there were some vehicles parked in front. The driveway drifted off to the side where there was a garage.

Scot parked his car in front of the mansion and then went up to the front door with Diana. He knocked on the door and a butler opened to the door and welcomed them inside.

"Master Oswald was not expecting you in this evening, Master Damian," the butler stated in an eloquent English accent.

"Is he awake?"

"I believe he is in the parlor upstairs," the butler replied. "I will let him know of your arrival."

"Thank you."

Diana walked forward with Scot as they entered the large foyer or entrance hall of the mansion. The space was grand, significantly larger than the mansion back in Allabrese. The foyer at Mayfair consisted of a wide space where there were stairs at the end that went to a second level above, and at the sides from the front doors. Behind these sides, one could immediately go left and right to enter the aisle that wrapped around the entire foyer below the second level, which wrapped around the second floor. From the ceiling, there were roof windows that looked down from the deck above. In the middle, there was a grand chandelier over a fountain at the very center of the open space below. The floors of this central space consisted of a pristine white marble tile. The walls of the manor consisted of a carved wooden panel with wallpaper within a rectangular frame on the upper half. The mansion was heavily decorated in portraits, paintings, and pictures frames, some of which with antique photos that extend the Montgomery legacy. Diana and Scot went to the fountain where they waited for the butler to return from above.

"Master Oswald would be happy to see you," the butler announced.

Scot led Diana upstairs around the right-most staircase by the entrance to go directly up and then to the left where they followed a corridor to the left. At the end of the corridor, the butler opened a set of doors that came to a parlor. Diana saw Montgomery sitting in a wheelchair with a glass of scotch in his hand, looking into the flames. His head was tilted down as he had dozed off. He was dressed in a smoking jacket with black trousers at his legs and dress shoes at his feet. He had retained most of his physical features since the last time that Diana had seen him, except for the use of a wheelchair. Scot went over to him and tapped him on the shoulder.

"Huh? What?" Montgomery questioned in a weak voice. "Oh, it's you... What do you want?"

"I have a surprise for you," Scot said.

"Hm?" Montgomery questioned, placing a hand at his ear.

"I said," Scot repeated, louder, "I have a surprise for you."

"What's that then?" Montgomery asked, looking over to Diana.

Montgomery squinted.

"Is that...? It is!" Montgomery remarked, giving a hearted laugh.

Mr. Montgomery wheeled his chair around so that he could face Diana.

"Well, if it isn't Ms. Cambridge, back from her retreat in the countryside... How are you doing...?"

"It's nice to see you again," Diana replied with a smile.

"What have you been up to?" Montgomery questioned. "Come, sit down... We have much to catch up on..."

Diana sat down in an armchair nearby, while Scot sat down on a sofa.

"Diana's told me that she's interested in joining the ranks," Scot remarked. "She's also told me that she's had some interesting experiences over the last two years since we saw her, and thinks she can join the tactical division with ease."

"Oh, is that so? What kind of experience?"

"I've been trained in close-quarter combat by one of the finest institutions in Japan," Diana stated. "I have also received brief, but extensive guerilla warfare and basic modern combat training from one of the world's most elite fighters."

"Well, we'll have to see then, won't we?" Montgomery remarked. "Scot has wanted you on the team since he knew you existed all these years ago... In fact, he's expected you to eventually come to where you belong."

Mr. Montgomery took a handkerchief from his breast pocket and began to cough into it. It was a thick cough.

"When can you start?" Montgomery then came to ask.

"Whenever you need me to," Diana replied. "I'm in school at the moment, but in January that won't be an issue because I'll be dropping out. I just have to finish this semester though, but it won't be a problem."

"Good," Montgomery responded, looking up. "This is very good... Yes, times have changed in recent years, but the necessity of our forces have never been more needed than ever. My dream, however, is far gone... Even I'm unsure of the fate that this city will face in years to come, what with talks about this virus all about, possible mandatory vaccinations, the implementation of microchips, and all that sort of thing.... We are in anxious times, and if you are to join my elite ranks, then you must know of this important role that my elite forces play. The Harlech Syndicate is mandated to keep order in Harlech where those that prefer chaos lurk. That is why, when I lost the election campaign all these years ago, I vowed to achieve my dreams by alternative means. I founded my security business, and now we are one of the leading businesses in that sector of the province. I never gave up on the people of the town even if they were being led astray, and that is something that you should keep on your mind, young Diana. Remember to defend the people of this town who are in need of assistance... Do you understand that?"

"I do," Diana affirmed.

"Good," Montgomery replied. "Now, where are you staying? You are welcome to stay with me in my home until we can get you a better home, or would you rather stay with Damian?"

Diana looked over to Scot. Scot looked back to her.

"I have a penthouse in Stoneridge with a view of the sea," Scot said. "I also have a spare bedroom that I'd be happy to offer you."

"Wow, that's nice of you, but I have my own place… my old apartment. It's technically on hold by the government until I turn nineteen, but it is my place."

"Alright then, I'll drive you back into Keswick then, and we'll talk in the morning."

"Yes, we can all talk more in the morning… it is rather late, especially for a Sunday morning…"

Diana and Scot stood up and said goodbye to Oswald Montgomery. The two then returned to the car so that Scot could drive Diana back to the bar, to her motorcycle.

• • • •

Tristan returned to his dorm later that same day and sat at his desk, writing into a book as he looked out the window. Finn sat in his bunk bed atop and hit a ball against the ceiling, bouncing it back to him and throwing it again repetitively. Tristan gave a sad sigh as he looked out the window.

Finn looked over to him. He then continued to bounce the ball.

"You're a real twat, you know that, right?" Finn said to him.

"Thank you," Tristan sarcastically replied. "Thank for the criticism, which is really making me feel better about myself…"

"You know, before we walked in, Diana and I had a little chat… She said she was worried about you, and that she wanted me to keep an eye on you for her. She also told me some other stuff, about how my death traumatized you, and how you met your actual folks last year, and such… We're supposed to be best friend, Tristan, and I didn't even know these things about you?"

"It's my personal life…"

"Isn't a personal life meant to be shared with, say, the people in your personal sphere? Like me?"

Tristan didn't respond.

"If you're going to be like this, then please, just leave me alone so that I can have some peace…" Tristan insisted. "I'm sick and tired of people left and right telling me that I'm being dramatic, or that I should chin up… because nobody seems to understand that my situation is not normal."

"It's not about the intensity of it," Finn remarked. "All our problems suck ass, and we all like to get off on that our sufferings are more relevant than yours, but that's all crap. It's all the same in the end… the impact that is… but what's pitiful is when that suffering is for nothing. I'm not discouraging you, Tristan. You've had it rough. I wish I had known how rough it was, but you have only yourself to blame for that because you never told anyone. It wasn't an excuse to go and break her heart (Diana, I mean). You're eighteen now. You're responsible for your own actions, and with that you should have known that your actions have consequences and to have known of these greater consequences that impact the entire world. That's all in the essence of it, you know. You may have praised me for my ideas, but it's not enough to share in them. You have to act in them as well, and it has never been an idea of mine that infidelity is based, because it isn't. I hope that in the least, you could have learned from this… you massive twat."

"Please just leave…" Tristan groaned.

"Fat chance," Finn replied. "Your… I mean, my dad, told me to keep an eye on you because you want to kill yourself. Like I'm going to leave you alone even for a moment…"

Tristan frowned and brought a hand to his forehead, supported by his elbow on the table.

"If I were to kill myself, I'd be disrespecting the effort Diana and Helene went to save my life… I don't even know what Diana had to sacrifice so that I could be alive…"

"I'm still not leaving you alone…"

"I wasn't arguing against it," Tristan muttered. "All I want to do is die…"

"No, all you want to do is run away like a sissy, but I'm here to make sure you stay," Finn replied, pivoting his legs over. "You can't get rid of me – I'm your guardian's son, remember?"

Tristan groaned.

"Chin up," Finn remarked. "You may have lost your bird, but you've still got old Finn, and I won't go away… even if you cheat on me… maybe…"

Tristan shook his head. He closed his journal and then placed it aside. Finn dropped down and placed his hands on Tristan's shoulders.

"Come on, we'll go for a walk and then we can cuddle and chill," Finn remarked, patting him. "You need some fresh air."

Tristan sighed. He stood up and grabbed his coat. He then followed Finn towards the door.

"You know I was kidding about the cuddling part, right?" Finn remarked to him before they left.

Tristan gave a light smile and shook his head.

"Yes," Tristan replied, laughing.

"Good," Finn responded, smiling at him.

The boys left out the door and shut it behind them. They then went outside and went for a walk around campus, chatting together as Finn smiled and shared his time with his best friend, who only had him to rely on from now on.

Epilogue

Diana drove her motorcycle to the front of the four-story apartment structure at 15868 Bennett Street where she was raised. She wore a backpack around her back and had changed clothes since Halloween night. She took the bike around to the alleyway and then came around to park it near a dumpster. She took off her helmet and locked in in place, and then she removed her backpack to place it on the dumpster ahead of her. Diana raised herself up onto the dumpster and then threw her backpack onto the fire escape above before jumping up to pull herself up the ladder.

Once Diana was up, she picked up her backpack and began to climb up the ladder to the fourth floor where she was able to open a window and enter into the darkened bedroom of her parent's former bedroom. Diana saw a mattress in the corner of the room, which she used to sleep on, and a door on the right that led into the small bathroom. A graffiti mural had been sprayed on the wall to the left. Diana stepped through and entered into the main space of the apartment, which included an open kitchen.

The kitchen was just as Diana remembered it with the white-black tiles, birch cabinets, and laminate countertops. Some of the cabinets were missing their doors. The stove had been smashed in at the front by a brick and the light inside had burnt out. In front of the kitchen, the white dining table still sat, although with a leg on its side. The chairs were missing. In the living room, the old sofa had been torn apart, possibly by a wild animal. Like the wall in the bedroom, the wall at the opposite-end of the living room had been spray painted.

Diana went around to the front door where there was a closet at the side. The closet doors had been torn off their hinges though. Diana opened the front door and looked at the #12 on the front and then closed the door. She pushed the door closed as it was left ajar, causing a loud slam to echo through the apartment building. Diana returned to her bedroom and took off her backpack. She then began to take out some small items, including her laptop, a Bible, and some clothes. She set everything aside and then opened her laptop, but not before lowering the lid and looking at the floorboard below her feet as they creaked. Diana put her laptop to the side and leaned over. She then stood up and knelt down at the floorboard.

Diana knocked at the floorboard and saw that it was hollow. She began to attempt to tear the wooden floorboard panel, but struggled to do so. She stood up and kicked at the wood, breaking off some of the floorboard so that she could dig her hands in and raise it. Inside, Diana found a small trove of goodies. She knelt down again and looked at them.

Inside the floorboard, Diana picked up a small plastic sandwich bag that contained a few wads of cash, mostly of small bills, and in another one, she found two semi-automatic pistols with two magazines. Diana looked at the guns and blew the dust that had settled onto them. She then began to examine them carefully. She held a serious face as she did so.

Diana placed the magazine into the handgun as well and then cocked it. She pointed the pistol forward as if she was about to fire, but refrained from doing so. She placed the gun down and looked at the other, which was in the same design. She picked it up, cleaned it, and then loaded it. Once that was done, she placed both of them underneath the floor again, concealing them as she put the floorboard back where it was. Diana sat at the mattress and took a deep breath. She looked around the dark room and then over to the window to look out into the night. With another deep breath, Diana gave a solemn look as she sat where she was, on her own, as she was three and a half years ago.

"Among the priests, there may, of course, be some who use their sacred calling to further their political ambitions. There are clergy who, unfortunately, forget that in the political struggle they ought to be the champions of sublime truth and not abettors of falsehood and slander, but for each one of these unworthy specimens we can find a thousand more, who fulfil their mission nobly as trustworthy guardians of souls and who tower above in these depraved times, as little islands above the universal swamp."

– Adolf Hitler

www.ingramcontent.com/pod-product-compliance
Lightning Source LLC
Chambersburg PA
CBHW051941220626
47052CB00004B/741